Young and Hungry

Young and Hungry

Ms. Michel Moore

and

Marlon P.S. White

www.urbanbooks.net

Urban Books, LLC
97 N18th Street
Wyandanch, NY 11798

Young and Hungry

ISBN 13: 978-1-62286-728-8
ISBN 10: 1-62286-728-9

First Trade Paperback Printing November 2016
Printed in the United States of America

10 9 8 7 6 5 4 3 2 1

Distributed by Kensington Publishing Corp.
Submit orders to:
Customer Service
400 Hahn Road
Westminster, MD 21157-4627
Phone: 1-800-733-3000
Fax: 1-800-659-2436

Young and Hungry

Ms. Michel Moore

and

Marlon P.S. White

CHAPTER ONE

"I can't breathe! I can't fucking breathe! Get your damn hands off me, you crazy, big son of a bitch! I ain't bullshitting with you!"

"Naw, dawg. I ain't gonna be able to do it!"

"You dead-ass wrong this time around, blood! I ain't one of these average lames you used to playing the tough role with! I gets money!"

"Look, youngin', you might just wanna shut your damn mouth and miss me with all that. I gets money routine. You ain't making no real noise in the city, only whispering in these streets, just like the next man," Black Tone insisted, not letting up one bit.

Li'l Ronnie's breath reeked of stale cigarette smoke and liquor as his words rang out as he tried to negotiate a reprieve. "You tripping, nigga! Get your hands off me. You out of order!"

"Naw, playboy. I'm afraid thangs done went too far for all that. See, now we done crossed over into the 'zero fucks given' zone. Ain't no come back!"

The shoulder-to-shoulder crowd inside the packed club was annoyed. Yet it was an unneeded and unwanted commotion that had to be dealt with. Never mind he was dismissing all of them, as if he was better than the next. They ignored that, some still sipping from their drinks. Amid the crowd's idle chatter, they fought to understand the man's muffled words. They could care less about his hate-filled pleas for mercy as their party had been abruptly interrupted. The houselights had come on. The music had ceased to play. And the cameraman was packing up for the evening. It was working on close to midnight, and this was the second "Adios, amigo" occurrence so far. People were starting to ask for their money back, and the owners and staff, including Black Tone, had finally had enough. Someone had to be made an example of if the establishment had any hope of maintaining order the rest of the evening and during the many nights soon to follow.

Bullshit. Bitches. Bottles. It was just another wild, off-the-chain night at Detroit Live. No question that it was one of the hottest nightclubs in town, if not the hottest of them all. It always went down. Thursday thru Sunday was nonstop partying. That was an absolute given. Known for having a constant lineup of guests, ranging from local high-profile rappers and city councilmen to females who worked as cashiers at Wal-Mart and men who were janitors at the local elementary school, Detroit Live had somehow managed to avoid getting shut down. The nightclub had dodged various tickets and violations from the city officials, and it appeared that the powers that be worked in the owners' favor. Until the city police, the FEDS, and the ATF raids and padlock notices showed up, if you wanted to turn up and be seen, the riverfront hot box was the place to do it, the place to get your gangsta reputation stripes.

Of course, the usual suspects were in the house, further adding to the semi-controlled chaos at Detroit Live. Cases of champagne were being popped. Chicken wing bones were disrespectfully tossed underneath some tables. Gators ruled the floor, and packs of extra-long weave controlled the VIP booths. As always, when things were going too good, you could look forward to one, maybe two, simpleminded assholes showing up and showing out. Right here, right now was no different. Li'l Ronnie had got out of hand. Smacking random females on the ass and spitting at a couple of waitresses, he was gone. The nephew of Ethan, the most notorious heroin dealer on the east side of the Motor City, had blacked out. He'd let the top-shelf Hennessy VSOP and Seagram's Gin double shots convince him that he was bigger than the game. Unfortunately for him and his pride, mixing dark and light liquors was the wrong answer. At least for tonight.

"I told you, I can't breathe! Get your hands off me, nigga!"

"So damn what? You think I give a shit you can't breathe? Do you?" Black Tone yelled.

Li'l Ronnie had been snatched up out the booth by his thin-material designer T-shirt. The soles of his shoes failed to touch the floor as he was air dragged out of the red velvet roped-off area. Roughly escorted to the middle of the dance floor by his neck, Li'l Ronnie was on display as the elaborate lights continued to flash despite the houselights being up. As the young wannabe hooligan tried to maintain his swag, he was called out, no holds barred.

"You all up in here like you running things here at the club. You was a boss back there in VIP, so, I'm begging you, by all means, be a boss out here!"

"What?" he replied, acting as he had not heard the challenge.

"You heard me. We all wanna see you show us how good you is with them hands you keep putting on my female customers' asses. Step to me! That's the only thing I want you to do. Try me!"

Li'l Ronnie knew he was on Front Street. Through his intoxicated eyes, he saw several hood rats whispering, while a few others giggled. Friends and foes alike knew he had this coming. He'd been showing his natural black ass for the past twenty-five minutes or so; now it was time to pay the piper, aka Black Tone. Li'l Ronnie's so-called crew had bailed on him no sooner than he'd initially started clowning. It wasn't that they were soft, by any means. It was just that they knew this club, out of all spots in the coldhearted city they called home, was not the one to act a damn fool in. It was like signing up to get an automatic ass kicking.

"I swear on everything I love, you li'l pussy, you better kill my black ass," Li'l Ronnie bravely vowed as a few people yelled, "Worldstar!" with their cell phones held high. "'Cause if you don't, that's ya ass! I swear, you better kill me! I mean that shit!"

Black Tone always stood tall. Not because he was six feet four and solid muscle, but because he had the heart of a warrior. He had unselfish intentions when it came to doing what he felt was right. The steadfast giant had the same demeanor every night he was at work. Whether there was trouble or not, he was completely unbothered and committed to making things go smoothly. Some patrons needed a little extra attention in the "how to behave in public" department. And this was one of those circumstances.

"So you gonna kill me, huh, big shot? Is that right, boy?" Black Tone showed no signs of leniency or remorse. He tightened his grip around the man's throat and command marched him to the club's front door. The second part of Li'l Ronnie's night was about to begin. There would be no more second chances given. No more warnings. Fed up, Black Tone made it be known he was clean out of fucks to be issued. Therefore, it was easy to conclude, there was no hope of this situation having a happy ending for the ill-bred patron of the club that had a burning desire to pop off.

"You better send me on my way, because I'm telling your big, goofy ass you don't know who you dealing with. If you don't let me go, that's your life. You done," Li'l Ronnie warned with conviction. Feeling that his bloodline with Ethan would garner him a free pass, he had tried this approach.

It didn't work. Li'l Ronnie had wanted to appear to be a superstar and to have all the attention on him that night. Well, his wish had been granted. Ironically, his uncle's current girlfriend and a few of her friends were also in VIP. They were shaking their heads over what was taking place. Sable used to kick it with Li'l Ronnie when they were younger, before he went to juvenile and knew he didn't have good sense. The part-time stripper and full-time female hustler knew how her teenage love would get when he was drunk. At this moment she chose to turn her head, so as not to see firsthand what was surely coming next.

With a stunned audience in awe, Black Tone proceeded to skull drag Li'l Ronnie out the front entrance of the club. "Well, then, that's just gonna be my ass! See, don't nobody come up in this club, acting out like they ain't got no type of home training. That ain't what we do here. Matter of fact, while I'm thinking about it, why don't you slap the fire outta my mouth? You know, like you said you was gonna do to the waitress if she didn't hurry her ugly ass back with your drinks. Talk that bullshit to me, youngin'. Spit at me!" Without so much as breaking a sweat, Black Tone tossed Li'l Ronnie near the valet shed that housed all the keys, causing it to shake. "That Hennessey courage you rocking with gonna have you on an all-liquid diet if you keep messing around with me. Now, go somewhere and get on, before shit really gets real!"

Reaching both hands around his own sore neck, Li'l Ronnie stared up from the concrete pavement. His pride had been damaged. Known for being a beast in his small circle, he'd shamefully been outnumbered by one person. The immature man-child now understood the true meaning of being up shit creek without a paddle. Promptly, Li'l Ronnie took several deep breaths. Relieved to be free from the beating he'd ultimately caused from his reckless mouth, he secretly thanked God. Not wanting to appear openly straight pussy, he dumbly continued to act as if he could go another couple of rounds with Black Tone. "Dude, you should've killed me. I swear on everything I love, you should've! Now, that's gonna be your ass!"

"Look, get the hell on before I really get pissed! This ain't what you really want. Not now, not never." Black Tone glared down at the intoxicated idiot, knowing he was talking out the side of his neck. He'd been in enough altercations with enough guys throughout the years to know when a buster really wanted that bloodthirsty rhythm and was prepared to dance or not. This was a no-brainer. He knew Li'l Ronnie wasn't about that life or nothing that came with it. Black Tone was ready to bet big money on the fact that even if this dude was related to Ethan, as he claimed to be, his DNA must be tainted. Black Tone and Ethan had had a mutual understanding for the past year or so. Trying to remain as low key as possible, he would never condone or tolerate anyone set claiming his name on no bullshit drunk tirade at the club, especially one that Black Tone was presiding over.

"You done messed up, big man, Watch!" Still out of sorts, Li'l Ronnie leaned on the side of the wooden valet shed and got back up on his feet. It was apparent to all he had revenge on his mind and the thought of murder in his heart. Humiliated, he wobbled toward the parking lot, trying to dust the dirt off his clothes. "On my life, nigga, that's gonna be your ass," he proclaimed over his shoulder before climbing in his car and finally driving off into the darkness of the night.

"Okay, lame. Let it be known. I don't give two shits about ya' life! Matter of fact, fuck your life!" Black Tone shouted loudly at Li'l Ronnie's taillights before turning his full attention back to the growing crowd. "Okay, listen up. I'm talking to you wannabe gangsters and you broads too. Move all that cheap weave out y'all ears. Pay y'all asses careful attention. See that dude that just came flying out the front door headfirst? He was an asshole. He likes to talk shit to waitresses and spit at them. He likes to order bottles, then not pay. He was an idiot. If you hope to not end up like his stupid ass, then you might not wanna try any of that bullshit." Black Tone's voice was beyond stern. His facial expression matched his pitch. He had just about enough ruckus for the night and was not willing to put up with any more. "So to ensure y'all don't, I'ma need y'all to pump y'all's brakes and slow this shit all the way down!"

The boisterous crowd huddled together. They were all ears, anticipating gaining entry to the already packed establishment. But not before getting a clear understanding about how things were going to go down from this point moving forward.

"It ain't gonna be no more people getting through these front doors if you good folks don't wanna play the game right. Let's make this shit flow easy, and we all gonna have a good night." The menacing bouncer's heartfelt words echoed off the nightclub's paint-chipped concrete wall as a slight chill from the river filled the damp air.

"What about if you just have your paper ID?" some smart-ass interjected, much to the disgust of others waiting on line.

"Look, nigga! My house, my damn rules! Y'all under-stand? So have your IDs, not any Photoshop paper, out in your hand. And please don't try no 'I ain't got it with me' scam. I ain't in the mood for it. I'm warning you. Not tonight!"

"Yeah. Y'all heard him. Not tonight with that slick bull-shit!" A girl in the rear cosigned, hoping to gain brownie points and possibly jump the long line.

"Now, the bad news is my dog got hit by a damn car this morning and was killed. That toy poodle was my best friend in the world. Now he's gone! He died in my goddamned arms, and I'm sick about it!" Black Tone was talking his regular shit, but with him, people could never really tell, so no one wanted to risk laughing. He was overly intimidating with his words, but far better with his handwork. So for the anxious partygoers, why take a chance of getting choked out on the humble? They, like most people he'd encountered, let him do what he did and say what he said. As long as they got into the club, that was all that mattered, to most.

"Wow. That's so sad," the same female replied while tugging down her tight-fitting skirt.

Stretching out his arms, Black Tone appeared even bigger than life than he normally did. "But guess what? Lucky for me, the good news is, for all the hell my black ass know, it was one of y'all suspicious-looking bastards driving that Honda." He slowly eye fucked the crowd with a devilish grin. He managed to make each one feel guilty for some bullshit they know they had nothing to do with, and nervous too. "So I gotsa check all y'all one by one so I can try to get justice for my baby!"

Often wearing black Timberland boots, a gray hoodie, and steel-lined leather gloves, Black Tone was known throughout Detroit. He was legendary in the local club scene as a bouncer who could ruin anybody's night at any given time. Weighing in at a little bit more than 312 pounds, he stood taller than the average forty-ounce fed dude in the crime-ridden city. His short-fuse temper was infamous, to say the least. If it cost twenty dollars to get inside the venue he and his crew—known as ZFG, short for Zero Fucks Given—were doing security at, then flat out Negroes had better have their cash in hand. It didn't matter it they were blind, crippled, or crazy. Male or female. Black Tone didn't discriminate or miss a beat. He made no exceptions to the house rules. No sneakers meant no sneakers. No blue jeans meant no blue jeans. And when he said no bullshit on his watch, or risk getting your shit possibly split to the white meat, he meant that as well.

"Dang. Wow, big man. Why you gotta be so disrespectful and what not?" A random guy spoke out, obviously feeling offended. "Is all that name-calling necessary? I mean damn!"

"Oh, okay. I see we got another brazen one tonight, caught all up in his special emotions." Black Tone's size fourteen special-order boots paused, then turned completely around. Still appearing solemn, he mean mugged the guy, coldly staring him directly in his eyes. "Matter of fact, you look like a damn dog killer! Where was you at about nine this morning huh? Was you anywhere near the West Side . . . Joy Road?"

"Come on, man, with all that. Just let us inside already. It's almost midnight, and the price gonna jump! Or is that the bag you working out of?"

"Whoa! Everybody stop and look at this funny-style poodle killer with all the mouth that want his dental rearranged! Bro, you must be on a serious mission tonight, huh?" With sinister intentions, Black Tone grinned, showing the gap in his perfectly white teeth, as he slow walked down the otherwise quiet line of people toward his verbal opponent.

The guy, determined not to look like a straight pussy in front of the crowd, which was anxious to gain entry, tried his best to stand his ground. "A mission? Dude, what the hell is you talking about? Mission? We just wanna go inside the club and party. That's it!" With his chest stuck out, he took a deep breath, bossing up even further. "All that other shit you talking is over the top. Don't you think?"

"Over the top here at Detroit Live, huh? Imagine that. Is that how you think we get down? Boy, what you on? What kinda pill you done took?" Black Tone loudly laughed, rubbing his right hand slowly over his unshaven beard. "Okay, bro. I tell you what. I ain't gonna hold you up no more. Who all with you? How many in your group?"

Feeling somewhat relieved things were going to go in his favor, the mouthy guy replied, "Five," as he proudly pointed them all out. "We all together. All of us!"

"Okay, y'all five can step out the line and come up here toward the front door." Black Tone signaled to his right-hand man and cousin, Wild Out. "Anybody else rolling with them?"

The crowd was both silent and confused, not knowing what to think of Black Tone's seemingly docile attitude.

"Okay, then cool. It's just these five," Black Tone announced.

"See, that's what in the fuck I'm talking about. All you lames in line, acting all scary and carrying on. This nigga just big as hell, that's all. He bleed blood just like me and you!" Overjoyed that his assertive behavior had gotten him and his friends special treatment, the man was feeling himself.

Sensing something wasn't right, one female out of the "lucky five," who had been to Detroit Live more than once or twice, fell back. Showing her money and ID, she informed Black Tone and Wild Out, who was now posted by his cousin's side, that she'd rather wait in line with everyone else. She blurted out that she didn't want any trouble, let alone the same treatment the guy had been getting when they first drove up.

"You sure, baby girl?" Black Tone winked his eye at the tan-skinned beauty. "'Cause ain't gonna be no more trouble popping off tonight—at least not on my end."

"Naw, I'm good! I ain't into confrontation." She waved her hand to the side, further distancing herself from the other four.

"Me either, Ma." Black Tone cracked his knuckles and spit a stream of saliva threw his gap and onto the curb, barely missing the boy's two-toned Pradas. "I'm into problem solving!"

Seconds after nodding she was 100 percent certain of her decision, the entire ZFG crew, led by their fearless leader, showed her she'd made a wise choice. After the two guys and the other female who had chosen to stand tall helped their unfortunate friend to his vehicle, undoubtedly driving him to the nearest hospital to get his surely broken ribs tended to, it was back to business as usual at the popular Detroit hot spot.

"Okay, two clowns down tonight! Who else wanna join the circus?" Black Tone sarcastically joked.

To Black Tone, it was nothing; it was all part of the job he had signed up for. For him it was business and never personal! The new club owner, Amir, had gladly made his trusted head bouncer the police, the jury, the judge, and the executioner. At Detroit Live Black Tone was the law!

It'd been an extremely long twenty-four hours full of crime in the city. Everything from selling drugs, rape, a few dozen assaults, a couple armed robberies, home invasions, and a high-profile quadruple homicide on the far east side of town. But if you had what some would call the misfortune of being birthed and raised within the twenty-five-square- mile radius of Motown, the number one ranked worst city to reside in, in America, you were no stranger to murder or mayhem. And definitely not to the consequences that came with it. To some, it was all they knew—a lifestyle. Cut from a much different cloth, people in the D were born in, not sworn in, to struggle in general. The city was strapped for cash and was trying all sorts of incentives that had never been heard of or thought of to stay above water. Day by day, week to week, the city's officials were making and breaking government laws and statutes as they went along.

The majority of below-poverty residents were immune to "the unfortunate chain of events" that would make many, if not all, of suburbia's elite cringe and hold town meetings packed full of concerned home owners. Some ill-bred residents of Detroit were hood warriors of the night and day. They wanted to have a good time, no matter what the cost or occasion: drink a li'l, smoke a li'l, dance a li'l, and hopefully get back home to the comfort of their bed without getting killed, shot, or robbed.

It was nearing a little after three in the morning. The last of the overly intoxicated customers had gotten their keys from the valet and would hopefully make it home without catching a DUI. To the staff at Detroit Live, whether their patrons went to the casino, the after-hours clubs, or even a motel with some random person they'd met that night meant little or nothing. As the cash was counted, the houselights went up on high. Amir, a hypocrite to his deen, thanked Allah for financially blessing him with another night.

Thankfully, the club's zip code was not included in the already in place monthlong experiment Detroit residents were subjected to. That meant that for now, he and his staff wouldn't have to camp out and personally protect their livelihood. Fortunately, his elderly father and his younger brothers, who owned a party store in 48238, had also dodged the bullet up until now. Sadly, for hundreds of other home owners and business owners alike caught up in the zip code sweep, posting up and bearing arms to protect what they'd worked so hard for had tragically become a way of life.

"We had a pretty decent night, excluding a few assholes," Black Tone said as he helped collect some of the bottles that had been tossed onto the floor.

Amir smiled, nodding his head. "Yeah, all and all, it was good. Your cousins didn't act that much of a damn fool."

"All right, now, sand nigga," Black Tone replied, giving his boss a smirk and returning the nod.

After doing the payout for his men, he watched the waitresses continue to clean. Close to an hour later, after closing the doors, they were ready to call it a night. After making sure the female staff was escorted to their cars, Black Tone waited for the owners to lock up and set the alarms. He knew that his behavior at the club was sometimes over the top. He knew he definitely ran the risk of some half-crazed Negro, caught in his emotions about being tossed out, wanting to seek revenge. Black Tone had grown up in an extremely rough neighborhood. He was no stranger to having to look over his shoulder for the unexpected to pop off.

As he climbed up in his truck, he put the key in the ignition and turned the high-powered engine over. Seconds later he was pulling out into the late night, early morning traffic. He lived a good twelve or thirteen minutes from the club, and on his way home Black Tone stopped at the gas station. He knew most folk knew better than to attempt even to slow down that time of night at that intersection. It was known for robberies, but he could care less. He was known for handing niggas they asses, armed or not.

Adjusting his gun on his hip, he got out, ready for whatever. The one random guy who was standing by the side of the doorway decided not even to ask Black Tone if he wanted to buy some weed. Knowing that tangling with a man of Black Tone's size could potentially not go his way, he wisely stepped over to the right. After purchasing his grandmother the small bag of peppermint candy he'd promised her before leaving the house they shared, the guy finally headed into the darkness of his block.

CHAPTER TWO

"Here comes this bitch nigga from down the way." Dre leaned back on the concrete steps, watching his longtime neighbor drive up.

"Who? Where?" His running buddy jumped, paranoid and buzzing from the weed they'd been blowing all night.

"Down there." Dre nodded his head over toward the side. "That wannabe tough, big, goofy-ass nigga Tone. You know, ole boy who think he the damn block police or some bullshit like that! Like he can't get got."

Now twenty-seven, Dre had been living in the same house since he was born. He'd never been outside of Michigan, not even on a short stay. In and out of trouble since he was a youth, he and his little sister, Alexis, had seen their fair share of people come and go off the block. The once close-knit community had changed for the worse over the years, thanks to the forever growing crime rate.

Of course, Dre and his dim-minded cohorts were much to blame for the recent spikes in 48238, as well as the other experimental zip code power outages nearby. They had no conscience or regard when it came to the atrocities they perpetrated on their own. They would rip and run the streets all times of the day and night, terrorizing others residing in close proximity with their break-ins, loud music, public fights, intoxication, and car theft. Nothing was off-limits to Dre if it meant having a good time or hitting a quick lick at the expense of others.

***

Black Tone, however, was nothing like his constantly victimized neighbors, and Dre knew it. Little fat-ass Anthony, the kid Dre grew up with and bullied, was no more. He was now known as Black Tone, and things were different, extremely different. Their families used to go to church together way back in the day, before times changed. Dre and Alexis's mother had died suddenly of breast cancer, leaving them basically to fend for themselves. Although Alexis fought to do the right thing and stay on point, her older sibling was the complete opposite. In and out of juvenile, then the county jail, he had done what he felt he needed to do to survive for both himself and her.

Black Tone didn't care about their plight or how close they used to be years ago. This was here and now, and he wasn't going to tolerate Dre disrespecting him or his ailing granny. He knew it would be impossible for him to run the households of others and set the bar for what they would or would not bow down to, especially when it came to Dre, yet he had his home under control. After a few brief run-ins with his old church pew buddy, Black Tone had made it perfectly clear that Dre or any of his people were not to sit on the stairs of the vacant houses on either side of his house. They were not to cut through his and his granny's backyard or even slow down as they went by in one of the various stolen cars that they joyrode in. Bottom line was, just like he ran things at the club, he ran them on the block. Black Tone had zero fucks given when it came to making sure his granny felt safe and secure in the house she'd raised him in. His mother had died in childbirth, so his granny was all he had ever had. She would forever be A1, even if it killed him.

Dre kept his eyes focused on Black Tone as he parked his truck. Wishing he could steal the triple midnight-black

SUV and sell the rims and the sound system, Dre reached in his pocket. After pulling out his pack of Newports, he lit one. Taking two, then three pulls, he blew the smoke up into the night air. Studying every movement his neighbor made, he caught a glimpse of Black Tone's forever present firearm posted on his side as he got out of the vehicle. As the moonlight served as the only light on the scarcely populated block, Dre could tell Black Tone was cautious of his surroundings and on high alert as he walked up toward his porch.

With nothing but petty schemes polluting his mind and soul, Dre skeeted a small stream of spit through his front broken-off tooth. *One day his ass is mine. I'ma get that nigga together just for old times' sake.* Dre wanted nothing more than to run up and sucker punch Black Tone in the jaw, take his truck keys, and skirt off like there wasn't nothing to it. Yet he weighed his options and knew that as much as he daydreamed about how that scenario could play out in his favor, the reality was it never could. At least not tonight.

"Dawg, I'm telling you, I swear before God and the devil, I'm gonna get that ho-ass nigga one day," Dre told his running buddy. "On everything I love, he gonna get right, or get the fuck on. Him and his good snitching grandmother always calling the police! They be worried about all the wrong shit around here."

Convinced that one day soon the tables would change and his block and the entire city would turn around for the better, Black Tone and his granny had agreed to stay put and fight the good fight. Black Tone loved his neighborhood. Despite the dilapidation. Despite the reduction in residents. Despite Dre and his band of idiots bringing havoc to everyone.

Not wanting to get caught slipping, Black Tone looked over his shoulder. He kept a careful eye on Dre from the moment he pulled up until he walked inside his house and turned the several dead-bolt locks, as he knew the man he had once considered a friend was no more. Black Tone and Alexis, however, were still on the same page. After sending her a text message asking her to let him know when she made it back home safely from her shift at the strip club, Black Tone checked on his granny. Then he climbed in bed and quickly fell asleep. While asleep, he started to dream about Alexis and the pact he made with her years ago.

"Your granny made these cookies just for me?" Alexis asked, her eyes swollen with tears, which were still streaming down her cheeks. It had been days since her mother had woken up in excruciating pain and had been rushed to the hospital. There less than thirty-six hours, she had been hit with the terrible life-altering news. The mother of two young children had been diagnosed with breast cancer. The doctors, family members, and friends were all amazed that she was in the late stages of the disease and had not suffered pain prior to this.

"Yeah, she knows oatmeal is your favorite." Anthony sat on the porch, next to his little neighbor from down the street. She was heartbroken. They'd just been at the door, listening to his granny and other ladies from the church form a prayer circle. Each holding hands, heads lowered, they asked God to show mercy and favor on Alexis and her older, mischievous brother. They cried out for the Almighty to spare her mother, hoping He would do just that.

Anthony and Alexis also prayed for that same miracle. While caught up in their emotions, they saw a small kitten walking around one of two abandoned houses on the street. With nothing else to do, the always stuck-to-gether pair went to investigate the feline's whereabouts. Anthony was what old folks back in the day called big boned and big for his age. He struggled to breathe as his asthma kicked in. After reaching in his pocket for his inhaler, the overweight youth took two short puffs and continued. They peered in through the broken basement windows of the abandoned house. There was no sign of the brown furry animal. Anthony wanted to be a hero for a still sad-faced Alexis and find the kitten no matter what. The pair stood motionless at the rear of the house. The doors had long since been stolen, and the wood siding had been snatched off as well. The grass and weeds were overgrown and filled with debris.

Anthony took Alexis by the hand. Cautiously, they entered the musty-smelling dwelling. Huge sections of paint and plaster covered the filthy floors, and there were holes in the walls where the copper pipes had been removed. Thinking they heard the soft sounds of the kitten's meows, the two followed their ears and headed up the staircase. Upstairs, each step they took was a definite hazard as the weather-warped floorboards crackled. Just as they were seconds away from opening one of the closets, they heard voices from outside.

"Who is that?" Alexis looked to Anthony for answers.

Slowly, he crept over toward the window. "It's your brother, Dre, and some other guys."

Alexis knew what that meant. They both did. She and Anthony needed to get out of the house and back across the street as soon as possible. Dre was a bully. The whole little crew he ran with always followed his lead, and they were all bullies as well. They had no filter on who would be their victims: they went after young and old, big or small. Despite Dre and Anthony basically being in the same age group, Alexis's evil-spirited sibling showed Anthony no mercy. Despite the fact that Dre's mother and Anthony's granny were so close, Dre seemed to go harder on his neighbor.

Making their way back down the stairs as quickly as possible, they noticed Dre's voice getting closer in the backyard area. Realizing they couldn't leave the same way they'd come in, Anthony motioned for her to keep quiet and head toward the front. Unfortunately, some of Dre's crew was posted on the front walkway, passing a blunt from person to person. Anthony and Alexis were trapped. They fled into the kitchen, then dipped off into a side room, what was once the pantry. As their hearts beat rapidly, Anthony fought not to have a full-blown asthma attack. He was wheezing, trying desperately to get air. Slipping his hand back in his front pocket, he realized he must have dropped his inhaler as he and Alexis were trying to escape Dre's certain wrath. Still trying to remain still, he glanced over to the middle of the kitchen floor and saw the lifesaving instrument lying near the spot where a stove once was.

Alexis knew she had to do something to help her friend. She knew there was no need for Anthony to be rushed to the hospital on the humble because her brother and his crew always wanted trouble. With the quickness, she darted out of hiding and snatched up Anthony's inhaler. She rushed to give it to him, and he happily took it out of her small hands, then raised it to his lips and took two long puffs, closing his eyes. Anthony's only hope now was that Dre and his crew would vacate the premises without causing any trouble.

"Drag that dumb motherfucker in here. His ass gonna pay up with blood for fucking up my damn bag," Dre ordered one of his followers, who did as he was told.

Alexis's eyes grew twice their size as she listened to her brother stomp out some guy who supposedly owed him money. With his friends rooting him on, Dre ruthlessly increased the intensity of his tirade, and the boy's ear-splitting pleas for mercy grew louder. After what seemed like an eternity, Alexis's older brother finally stopped. She and Anthony heard Dre and his homeboys talking about how his victim couldn't take a beating like a real G and what a bitch-ass nigga he was. A few moments later Alexis heard the small kitten meow once more from the other room. Then a sound she'd never forget followed: a squealing, agonizing moan. In its last moments the innocent animal saw the sole of Dre's sneaker come crashing down on its tiny body. Showing no compassion, the hooligans, led by Dre, left the abandoned house. Seemingly with no remorse, they could be heard laughing while walking along the side windows.

Making sure it was safe to come out of hiding, Anthony promised Alexis that no matter what, he'd always look out for her. The two then peeked around the corner and saw the poor kitten's lifeless body over in the far corner. Then they saw the rear of the boy's head. When his body and arms started to shake, Anthony realized the teen, who was barely older than he was, was having a seizure. Immediately, he stepped in and helped him the best he could. After making sure the boy was somewhat calm, Anthony and Alexis rushed out the rear doorway. After jumping through the grass and running down the driveway, scared and confused, they darted across the street to Anthony's house.

Alexis sat down on Anthony's porch, staring at the abandoned house like a hawk watching its prey. She was terrified for the boy they'd left stretched out on the dirty floor. He had stopped shaking before they fled, but had still been bleeding from several huge gashes that graced his cheek, forehead, and right arm, which he'd more than likely used in an attempt to shield himself from Dre's callous blows.

Anthony slipped inside his house, still struggling to breathe normally. Barreling through the living room almost unnoticed, he saw that his granny and her bible-toting brigade were still going at it, verse after verse. He wanted to tell his granny and Dre's mother what he'd just seen, or at least heard, take place. Anthony wanted to let the prayer circle warriors know that the woman they were asking God's help for had raised no more than a heinous monster who preyed on those weaker than himself. That Dre had smacked him around on more than several occasions, and that the permanent mark on his left upper arm had been made by Dre when he slammed the bathroom door at church on him. Yet Anthony chose not to bring even more chaos and sadness to the day. Instead, he lowered his head and kept quiet. Thank God his normally observant granny hadn't paid attention to his watery eyes and the blatant paleness of his skin. If she had, that would have been all she'd wrote in the way of calling an ambulance for Dre's victim, and the medical rig would have been loading him up instead. After inconspicuously taking the cordless phone off the dining-room table, Anthony took a few more puffs of his inhaler, then called 911.

Anthony went back out the front door and joined Alexis. Neither one said a word. Their focus was on the abandoned house as they waited to see if the injured teen could finally shake off the beating and walk out on his own. Five minutes went by, then ten, before the mentally drained children heard the sirens in the near distance. Turning their heads, they each made eye contact with Dre, who was headed back up the block, solo, calling out for his mother. By the time Dre reached the front of

Anthony's house, the ambulance was pulling up across the street.

With the noise of the sirens having interrupted the women, they spilled out onto the porch to see what was taking place. Knowing that he'd double-checked his worker now turned victim for any cash and taken his cell phone, Dre couldn't understand how the boy was getting medical attention so fast. There was no way he could have called the ambulance on his own. Dre had just walked with the rest of his crew down the block before realizing that his mother had locked him out of the house. The ambulance issue was becoming a momentary mystery until he glanced up at his little sister and his neighbor.

"Yo, how long y'all two been sitting up there?" he quizzed, giving them both the evil eye.

Alexis didn't respond as she got up and practically ran behind her mother's skirt. That was all Dre needed to see to figure out the rest. Mean mugging Anthony, he let it silently be known between the two of them that the beef was definitely on. It didn't matter to him that his mother was knocking on death's door; all that mattered was revenge.

CHAPTER THREE

"Damn. I must be bugging. What in the fuck did that pale-faced bitch on television just say on breaking news?" Dre closed the empty refrigerator door, in total disbelief. Raising an eyebrow as the pit of his stomach growled, the troubled thug couldn't believe his ears. "Did she say what I think she just said? Oh hell, naw! It couldn't be," he said out loud while grunting. "These white bastards must think it's April's Fools Day around here. Yo, did you hear that shit!"

"Come on, dude. Fall back with all that. I'm high as fuck," one of the guys camped out on the living-room floor complained, smoking the tail end of what was once a nice-size blunt. "I don't know what that crazy-looking female just said. I told you I'm high as hell and hungrier than a fat kid in the lunch line! Matter of fact, where the food at? Wake your fine-ass sister up to cook some grub. Maybe some of them scrambled eggs she be hooking up!"

"Man, fuck all that eating bullshit you talking 'bout! Yo, real spit." Dre turned the struggle-size flat-screen's volume up as he smiled with contentment. "It's 'bout to be live all day and night around these parts! That lady just said by noon today Detroit Negroes gonna be living like we in some third world country or some bullshit like that!"

"Say word, oh yeah? A third world country? So what that mean, Dre?" He inhaled while wishing he had money for a hamburger deluxe or at least some chili and cheese fries. "What's gonna jump?"

"Damn idiot! It means you should've stayed your dumb ass in school!" Dre laughed at his homeboy's stupidity, knowing it would end him up in jail or dead sometime soon.

"Man, fuck school and all that. Just tell me what that shit mean. Obama about to pass out some more free phones or something up on the corner? Or is my baby mama about to get an increase on her stamps?"

"Naw, asshole! It means desperate-ass, grimy throwaways on the come up, like you and the rest of these broke fools knocked out on the floor, about to run wild in these streets! Tonight it's about to be better than Christmas, income tax time, and any FEMA scam we could run on the government. You best wipe that sleep out your eyes and strap up!"

"For real?" The young goon instantly perked all the way up, almost forgetting he was hungry. "But why they letting that shit go down?"

"Because the white man got a master plan brewing down the line for all of Detroit and the rest of these mostly black populated cities—an ulterior motive in store for our sleepwalking asses!"

"Huh? Damn, Dre. I'm confused."

"Of course you are, my dude! Just the way they want you to stay." Dre knew his words of wisdom were lost on his elementary school dropout homeboy and just shook his head. "Yo, just consider it a gift from the great Caucasian powers that be and get ready for a huge come up, fool."

"July 30, 2016, will undoubtedly be marked as a day that goes down in history, not only in the financially bankrupt city of Detroit, but across the nation as well. By no later than twelve noon today, a town that has been long known to be forever resilient and tough will systematically go dark. The city officials have already been trying random rolling zip code power outages to save money, but sadly, it has not been enough. The unprecedented action was not viable. Matter of fact, some critics think the brazen "Lights Out" plan caused more harm than good," said the news reporter.

She went on. "Nevertheless, one by one, the city's failing infrastructure will shut down, leaving the declining population at odds. With the federal and state governments at a complete stalemate over the crime-ridden town's general finances, by strict laws put in place over thirty years ago, Detroit will be forced to endure a sure to be grueling and dangerous twenty-four-hour span without the basic necessities a city needs to survive. Shockingly there will be no electricity, no running water, no ambulance service, and no municipal buildings operating for the duration of that time. Most tragic of all is the fate the downtrodden citizens will face given the terrifying fact that no firemen or police will be on duty to patrol."

The world was hours away from seeing the tragic outcome of a major city in the United States of America becoming financially bankrupt thanks to countless crooked elected politicians at the helm, misappropriated funds, a declining population, and the fact that the remaining residents live below the poverty line. The city could easily be compared to the war torn country of Somalia. Tensions had rightfully grown.

The cameraman nervously panned the already alarmed residents who were starting to gather at the front door of the tenth precinct building as the news reporter delivered her grave commentary on what was bound to transpire in the hours to come. The pair had already been verbally threatened by a rowdy crowd at their last location and been told to go back to the other side of Eight Mile before, as one teen shouted out, "Shit gets real!"

"The newly elected mayor and the chief of police, who was appointed just days ago, are urging residents to bear arms and protect themselves by any means necessary. They also have made a statement for all the criminals, arsonists, and anyone else that takes advantage of this horrible glitch in the system on this unseasonably scorching hot July day, and I quote. 'From dusk to dawn, while you are out victimizing the next person, someone may very well be at your home, stealing from you!' We here at the Channel Seven broadcasting house wish the city of Detroit good day and good luck. The eyes of the world are watching and the heartfelt prayers of many are with you!"

CHAPTER FOUR

"Please, Allah, be with us! It doesn't make sense. How can the regime walk away from an entire city like that? How? They just give up and walk away? Just like that? No police? No fire department?"

"Regime," Hassan teased, repeating his elderly father's choice of words. "It's America, Pop. They do what they want over here. You've been here enough years to know that. Now, if you want me to book you a first-class flight back to your beloved motherland, I will. You can join the war. Maybe be a foot soldier or something like that!" Full of sarcasm, the also Iraqi-born youngest son mocked his father's outrage and confusion at the barrage of news reports about the officially bankrupted government and the abandoned city they owned and operated a business in. "And please, Pop, speak English. You know it's hard for me to understand you and Mom sometimes."

"Hassan, stop playing around with that foolish talk. This is serious. And in the name of Allah, please hurry up!" He grabbed his red- and cream-colored head wrap and wooden prayer beads after finishing his hot herbal tea. "You should be ashamed of yourself, having so little respect for our native language. We are not a part of America, no matter how long we have been on this devil-tainted soil. I keep telling you and your brothers that! Now, you heard what the news just said, and I know them savage-minded coons have heard too! We don't have long before that area turns into a madhouse. It will grow very bad very, very soon!"

"Yeah, I heard what they said. And I'm coming, Pop. Just let me finish ironing my shirt."

"Your shirt?"

"Yeah, my shirt! Just because you don't care how you look doesn't mean I don't care about my appearance." Hassan continued spraying light starch on the thin designer fabric. "And, Pop, stop with all the name-calling in English or Arabic."

"Hassan, you are being foolish! This is an emergency, I tell you! Very, very serious! There will be no power or running water in all of Detroit. This is a tragedy! The abeeds will try to do anything today. We have to be ready for the animals at all times. I keep telling you and your brother that! They can't be trusted. Blacks are not your friend. They don't even like themselves. No race on Allah's earth is like that."

"Yo, Pop, stop it! You tripping. Everybody black ain't all bad! It's people in all races that trip out. Hell, your own brother and his sons are not perfect."

"Don't 'Yo, Pop me' with they nigga talk. This situation is serious, Hassan, and can't no black person be trusted, not even the ones that follow Islam, and not even Obama! Now hurry up, son. This is serious, I tell you. Time is running out. We must rush."

"I know it is, Pop. I know. But what? I'm supposed to look crazy out in them streets because Detroit gone broke? They ain't got that bread, but I still do!" He primped, still talking in slang, despite his father's blatant objections.

"You don't have any money, Hassan. The money is mine until the day I pass over to paradise . . . old money I brought from the old country. And I don't know what you call yourself getting all pretty for. Those people over there don't care how you look." He lowered his head at his third-born son's ignorance. "My misguided son, when will you learn those fools care only about you letting them go five or ten cents short on a bottle of liquor? They're a bunch of wild animals, and by noon today they will all be uncaged, with no one to answer to!"

"Listen." Hassan, the younger of three brothers who helped their father run a Linwood and Glendale liquor, laughed proudly, sticking out his chest. "Me and Mikey got a reputation to uphold on the block. They love us over there."

"Love? Did you say that?"

"Yeah, Pops. *Love*. We like gods! We got love in the hood! Now, what's it gonna look like if we show up to work looking like you? Well, at least me."

"Gods? Please, son, don't talk stupid to me. Those people don't love you, Mikey or Amir at that house of sin nightclub he owns." The arrogant father took pride in what he said next. "And what's wrong with the way I look? I dress appropriately. I'm Muslim. The Koran says . . ."

"Look, Pop, before you go around talking about what the Koran says, look in the mirror. People buying liquor from us and Amir is just as haram as you selling it to them, so chill on all that judging. It's twenty-sixteen. Everybody just trying to do them!"

"Twenty-sixteen? Do them? The next thing you're gonna condone is all that wicked homosexual behavior running rampant in the world! *Stafallah!* That's what is really haram. They're all going straight to hellfire!"

"What?" Hassan paused, brushing his thick, black, low-cut curls. "You tripping, Pop. Chill!"

"No I'm not! The world is going mad! And if you don't be careful while running around, going against my word, and socializing with them black, Ebola disease–carrying animals at that store, you gonna feel the hot flames of hell just like them!"

"And all of them over there in that hood ain't wild animals, especially my girl Alexis," Hassan announced with certainty while continuing to get himself together for the day. "She good people. I keep telling you that time and time again! My girl is official."

"Your girl . . . your girl?" Pops angrily stroked his long graying beard. "So now that bony, pole-swinging porch monkey running around in a tiny skirt is your girl, huh? The one that has that bastard baby? The one you sneak in the rear of the beer coolers when you think I'm not looking? That young girl? Stafallah. Stafallah. Your poor mother would grow sicker to hear such things come out of your mouth. You need to ask Allah for forgiveness for even saying such a thing."

"Pop! What's wrong with you?" He stared his father directly in the eye. "You gotta stop talking about her like that. She's a good girl. Alexis is in school, getting a trade. She's different. She has a plan. We have a plan."

"No, Hassan. Plan or not, she's not different from her people. It's impossible." The elder of the two stood his ground in his lifelong, generationally taught beliefs. "That girl is gutter filth, like her entire begging family, especially that no-good, thieving brother of hers, Dre, who you insist on thinking is your friend. I keep telling you time and time again to stop having her behind the store counter like she belongs there. She doesn't. That young girl is hungry. She knows we have money in this family, old money, and she wants to get her greedy, non-deserving black paws on some of it."

"Look, Pop, fall back on all that! That's my girl you keep talking bad about," Hassan argued while still showing respect for his elder, as he'd been taught since birth. "I don't hear you saying all that stuff about Mikey's wife, and the entire family knows she cheats on him and treats him like garbage. Her you worship, while Alexis, who treats me like a king, you hate."

"Well, Mikey's wife is at least Muslim."

"Alexis can convert to Islam tomorrow. Then what?"

"Well, Mikey's wife is still our own kind. Her bloodline is not tainted."

"So what?" Hassan got in his emotions as he tried to prove his point. "When is the last time you seen her pray, or even drive past a mosque, for that matter? And at Ramadan, she didn't fast one day!"

"Hassan!" The racist, set-in-his-ways old man raised his voice, hoping to end the discussion so that they could be on their way to the store. "When will you learn, male or female, blacks can't be trusted? I keep trying to tell Amir that much, as well, when he insists on bringing that big black slave that works for him around me." He once again spoke in Arabic. "I'm telling you like I told Amir and Mickey. Don't be a fool living in a fool's world. You can never relax when they are around. The moment you do, you will one day regret it. Now let's leave."

Ignoring his father's constant insults in both languages about the people who spent their money and bridge cards every day to enable them to all live as large as they were was working his last nerves. He knew the hood respected him, despite what his father believed. And the way he was regularly putting it down on Alexis, he would bet his life she was in his corner. Time and time again, she'd proven her loyalty.

Taking into account that the clock was ticking, Hassan made sure his ailing mother was without needs and was resting comfortably. After double-checking his overall appearance in the gaudy gold-trimmed, floor-length mirror, he grabbed his cell off the charger before shoving his wallet in his rear pocket. With his licensed gun on his hip, Hassan finally was ready to make the short-distance drive from Dearborn, the city he called home, to Detroit.

As he and his father climbed into the white cargo van with the dented passenger door, Pops got a call from his middle son, Mikey, asking if he'd seen the early morning newscast.

"Pop, I'm already here at the store. People in the neighborhood are running up to my car, asking if we're gonna be closed for the day or what." Mikey glanced over at his vehicle door to make sure it was locked. "I finally drove off from their needy asses so I could call you in peace."

"Don't you tell them thirsty abeeds nothing. You hear me, Mikey! Not nothing! Not even Tommy." The father's heavy Middle Eastern accent filled the van.

"All right, Pop. I got you. But what are we gonna do? If what the news says is true, in a few hours Detroit gonna be worse than back home, people in the family say. The random outages was one thing, but know it's gonna be nuts."

"I know, son. I already talked to your uncles. And it's true it's going to be terrible. That's why I was trying to get this knucklehead brother of yours to hurry up." He rubbed his ever-present prayer beads once more as they drove. "When people find out there will be absolutely no electricity or running water inside that entire city they call home, they will panic. It's already the end of the month, and they will come with their hard luck stories. They will beg and not want to take no for an answer."

"Yeah, Pops. It's all on the radio too." Mikey solemnly peered out his car window at what seemed like hundreds of people rushing into corner grocery stores, gas stations, and CVS, trying to get prepared for what could prove to be the longest day in Detroit's troublesome history. The fact that they could easily drive across Eight Mile Road or simply step ten yards over into Highland Park was lost to most of the Linwood-Dexter area residents, as they were poverty stricken. Not to mention it'd be crazy of them to vacate their homes temporarily and leave the few valuables they had unattended, knowing what could possibly take place.

Leaving Hassan to do what he did best, which was deal with the multitudes of what were, for the most part, unruly, ungrateful customers, Pops had his other son, Mikey, pull the van around to the rear of the party store and open the sliding door. Once the door was wide open, it was somewhat hidden by the huge metal Dumpster and a few discarded boxes. With the aid of Tommy, their neighborhood do boy, Mikey quickly stacked by the door boxes that were filled to the rim. The boxes contained refrigerated items, and once they'd loaded all the boxes they could in the van, Pops hastily made his third trip to his brother's grocery store, located in the city of Hamtramck, which was only a few miles from Detroit. If they were going to lose cash revenue in sales for God knows how long during this government-allowed blackout, there was definitely no need to suffer the loss of product as well.

"Look, y'all. My old man ain't really trying to open right now. He trying to see what's going on with that blackout bullshit they say gonna jump," Hassan told the people who had gathered in front of the store.

"Well, damn, Hassan, man. Let me at least grab a few beers before y'all close up. And I need a pack of Newports and a Black & Mild. Ain't nobody feel like walking down to the gas station, trying to get credit," Dre said, taking advantage of their common bond as others from the neighborhood attempted to do the same. "Alexis told me to tell you she got you as soon as she wake up!"

"For real, fam, if it was up to me, we'd open this mother-fucker and do what we do. Ya feel me? We'd bang out." Hassan adjusted his shirt so his Gucci belt buckle and gun would show as he tried to talk and act black. "That citywide lights-out mess probably ain't gonna jump off anyhow. They just trying to scare people, that's all. Watch us all scramble around like little ants."

"Man, damn all that 'fam' bullshit you talking about! Your 'sand-nigga ass from Dearborn or where the fuck ever' opinion on the way of the world don't mean jack to us!"

"What?" Hassan halted his one-on-one conversation with Alexis's brother to focus on the man talking.

"You heard me, wannabe black asshole. Now, y'all open for business or fucking not? I need to play my numbers!"

Hassan was suddenly forced to be on Front Street. Like a tropical fish out of water, he started to feel some sort of way in front of his own family business. As much as he, inspired by rap music, tried to imitate the folk his Iraqi-born father and uncles loved to hate so much, there was always a "power to the people," Black Panther–type brother wearing dreadlocks who was calling him out. Today was no different. "Whoa. What's with all the hostility? You must've got up on the wrong side of the bed or something. I'm on your side, fam!"

"My side of the bed? You on my side? Fool, I ain't like the rest of these sleepwalking folk around here. I know what you and your people really say about us behind our back and to our face in your own damn language, while taking our money and dogging our women. Matter of fact, kick rocks with all that yackity yak 'You on my side' bullshit before I have your heart beating real fast!" Deciding to go to another store to get his numbers in before the widely reported power outage, the man rode off on his bike, mumbling something derogatory under his breath.

Dre, Hassan's supposed boy and the brother of the neighborhood girl everyone knew he was fucking with on the regular, just stood there, noticeably mute, not coming to his defense.

"Damn, Dre, dude. Why you ain't say nothing?"

"Me?" Dre shook his head, throwing his hands up. "Hell naw, dawg. That's between you and that other grown-ass man." He smiled devilishly, knowing that guy had rightfully pulled Hassan's ho card for how he always acted. "But, real rap dude, like ole boy was just saying on that mutual respect thang, I bet I can't give one of your sisters this big black dick like you giving mine, now can I? And when you taking my sister and y'all's baby to meet your mom?"

Not really as gangster as he often pretended, Hassan played off his fear of even more confrontation the best he could. Remembering what his father had said earlier, he started to feel like his dad was possibly 100 percent right about some of the things he'd said. Disappearing back inside the store to hook a non-loyal Dre up with the items he was dry begging for, Hassan quickly noticed the glass door coolers were almost completely empty. It was then it kinda hit him; shit was about to get real. There was no more milk, juice, or lunch meat. No more ice cream or freeze pops and no more single sticks of no-name butter waiting to be paid for with Bridge Cards. Besides a dozen or so forty ounces, a few Red Bulls, and several flavors of Faygo soda, the usually well-stocked store looked bare.

Pops hoped and prayed the outage would last only twenty-four hours, so he had made the decision to leave the thousands of dollars of liquor on the shelves and concentrate on the perishable things only. He had taken into consideration what his other family members were saying, and his first mind had told him to just rent a U-Haul and clear everything out. However, Hassan had been in his head. Hassan had convinced him that the people in and around the West Side store they'd been running since the mid-eighties had nothing but love for them. Against his better judgment, Pops had made his sixth and final trip before noon. After giving Tommy a few dollars for helping them, then sending him on his way, Pops gathered both sons together behind the bulletproof counter for a heart-to-heart conversation.

"Look," he said, sternly staring into each son's eyes. "It's almost twelve, and I can tell from the way the streets are filling up and the looks on these animals' faces, things are about to go berserk."

"Come on now, Pops!"

"Naw, Hassan," Mikey interjected, aiming the remote at the small television and increasing the volume while they still had electricity. "Pops ain't lying. It's about to be crazy out there. The mayor just announced he called the president to beg for the National Guard to come in overnight but was denied. He said the damn president said his hands were tied until tomorrow morning."

"Damn." Hassan's adrenaline started to rise as the trio watched video of other shopkeepers, some of whom they knew, complain about the circumstances and vow to close their doors for good if their businesses were vandalized in any shape, form, or fashion.

"I told you these slave mentality people are going to turn into desperate animals. Even the news knows," Pops argued, second-guessing leaving all the liquor in the store. "Maybe we should grab as much of the more expensive bottles as we can and head over to Hamtramck to wait things out. Maybe we can check on the store later, on the way home. I told Amir to do the same thing. We don't want to risk dying over material things."

Hassan knew by the televised reports and the number of people knocking on the front door that things were indeed getting out of control quickly. However, wanting to stand his ground and protect his family's legacy, he reached underneath the counter for the two handguns they kept there. After moving a few small boxes of candy and chewing gum out of the way, he slammed both handguns down on the counter, along with the .40-cal he proudly displayed on his hip daily.

"I'm not leaving, not checking on nothing later. I'm staying!" he vowed as he grabbed the sawed-off shotgun leaning in the far corner. "I know we got that 'hood love' around here and it's gonna be all good, but if it's not, why just let anybody, black, white, green, or blue, take what's ours?"

Mikey, normally tame minded, was starting to take on the same attitude as his brother, raising his shirt and revealing his own pistol, which he, too, was licensed to carry. "You know what, Pops? Hassan is right. I don't know how shit gonna get, but we just can't run away from our own store like cowards or some little kids! I talked to Amir, and he said him and Black Tone and their crew was going to post up down at the club as well."

"Listen, boys. We must be smart." Pops held on to his prayer beads tightly, having lived through several chaotic, lawless blackouts in his motherland before coming to America. "We must be cautious and expect the unexpected of these people. Our lives depend on it. They are animals. You must beware."

"We are, Pops." Mikey glanced at his cell, saw it was ten minutes before noon. "I know how ignorant they can get. That's why you need to take this last box filled with cigarettes and all the Scratch-Offs and go back over to Uncle Mohamed's store and relax. Me and Hassan got this. I'm gonna lock my car behind the fence, and just like everybody else in the city, see what's gonna happen next."

"What are you boys going to do if it gets too rough?" Pops wisely asked. "I'm going to at least send my sister's sons over to sit with you. They been around and know these black people and how sneaky and ruthless they can be. They know how to handle them." With that, Pops headed toward the back door, mumbling in his native tongue.

Hassan focused on the television and wished he were back at home, in the safety of his own bed. Getting worried, he yelled out to his father that sending his twin cousins, who had both spent time in prison for assault, among other crimes, to help stand guard wouldn't be such a bad idea, after all. It might prove to be the longest night ever in the history of Detroit.

CHAPTER FIVE

Black Tone was passed out cold. He was sleeping good. In between putting in long hours down at the club and taking care of his granny the best he could, he stayed exhausted. Disturbed by the constant annoying sound of his cell vibrating, he moved his muscular arm from underneath the sheet. Reaching over toward the other side of the mattress, he blindly searched for his phone. Finally, he grabbed it up and brought it to his face. Not wanting to open his eyes fully, Black Tone squinted at the screen. He pushed the button on the side, and the screen lit up.

Ten missed calls? Seven text messages and voice mails? Damn, what in the entire fuck? By pushing one of the many icons, he brought up the call log. Immediately, Black Tone saw that all the alerts and notifications were from Amir. He dialed him back and said, "Hey, now, my dude. What's the deal?"

"Hey, man. It's not right! It's crazy! It's crazy!" Can you believe this bullshit?" Amir blurted out as soon as he heard Black Tone say hello. "It's not right! It's crazy! It's crazy!"

"Huh? Believe what, man? What's going on? What's the deal?" He yawned, wiped the sleep out of the corner of one of his eyes. "You been trying to get at me all damn morning, I see."

Amir's voice trembled with panic and fear. The one thing he had worried about most since the city of Detroit originally announced the random rolling zip code power outages would finally touch not only his business but his immediate family's as well. "Come on, man. You haven't seen the news this morning? Wake your ass up. Shit is all fucked up."

"Naw. I was sleep until just now. What's popping?" Black Tone sat all the way up in the bed, still just as confused as he was when he first called. "What's all fucked up? What's the deal, Amir? What the fuck I miss? And what damn time is it?"

"Dude, they got us this time. Shit. Matter of fact, the entire city. We need to post up as soon as possible. Tell your crew I'm paying double pay. We need them as soon as possible."

"Double pay? What?"

"Just turn on the damn news, Tone! Not only are these motherfucking bastards turning off the power in different zip codes soon, but they sweeping the entire city for twenty-four hours. Plus, no police or fire. Water gonna be off too! We gotta get ready. It's gonna be crazy, pandemonium. We gotta get down to the club to protect it from your people. The alarm system is gonna be off-line."

Black Tone couldn't believe what he was hearing. Not just the fact that his boss, Amir, had just slipped and used the term "your people" with him, and not as a joke, but what he had claimed was about to occur. After locating the remote, he clicked on the television. Searching through the channels, Black Tone stopped on a breaking news report. Cell phone still in the other hand, with Amir on the line, he turned up the volume. Seconds into listening, he, like millions of others, was speechless. What Amir had said was true. Detroit was going dark at noon. And yeah, *pandemonium* was one of many words that would be used to explain the aftermath.

Black Tone reassured Amir that he'd call a few of his crew who didn't live in Detroit to see if they wanted to earn that double-time pay. He knew for sure it would be a waste of time to call his main homeboys, because if what the news reports claimed was about to pop off was indeed true, they have to post up at their own homes to make sure they went untouched. Before ending their conversation, Black Tone also reminded his boss that he lived in the heart of the city, in the infamous 48238, to top it off, and he would have to make sure his granny and his own household were secure.

"I'ma get off this phone and see what's what. I'll get back with you in about twenty minutes or so," he told Amir.

Amir didn't want to hear that. Selfish minded, all the greedy club owner wanted to hear his head of security say was that he would fuck any and everything he might have had on the table, including his old sickly granny, and that he was on the way. "Look Tone, swing by my people's spot before you head this way. I know it's gonna be super wild up there on Linwood," he warned angrily. "Pops and them moving as much stuff out as possible, just in case motherfuckers try it. He gonna go chill at my uncle's store, but Mikey and Hassan gonna post up all night, until this thing is over, make a stand. Hold shit down for the family and whatnot."

"Oh yeah, they gonna post up, huh?" Black Tone replied sarcastically as both size fourteen feet touched the floor.

Having lived in the hood forever, Black Tone had known Amir's brothers for a few years now, ever since they'd opened the party store. So the statement about them supposedly being on some old protection squad bullshit brought an instant smile to his face. Mikey, the middle son, was as soft as toilet paper. He tried to act as if he was about that life when need be, but Black Tone and most of the world could easily see through his fronting. Mikey let his wife run over him not some of the time, but all the time. That was no major secret to his family or even to the hood niggas she was rumored to mess around with from time to time. And in any culture that was unheard of. If you couldn't at least run your own household, how could you want respect from the next man?

As for Hassan, the youngest brother, he was the most like Amir, in the sense that they both thought they were African American. The way he dressed. The way he spoke. And the way he tried to carry himself in general. Hassan, however, had taken the black experience a few steps further than his older brother. Not seeming to care what his pops, brothers, or the neighborhood they did business in thought, he had been claiming Alexis as his woman for some time. The baby Dre's little sister had had was Hassan's son. There had not been any blood test taken, but the small infant came out of the womb as the spitting image of his alleged pappy, damn near crying in Arabic. Amir was known around the club to have hit off a few of the waitresses and some of the more "eager to get free" VIP treatment females who would breeze through the doors of Detroit Live, but his Iraqi-born arrogance would not allow him to go public with his dark pleasures.

After ending their conversation, Black Tone went to go check on his granny. It was time he made her something to eat and give her her much-needed medications. He had to figure out his next move if he planned on helping Amir down at the club. After ensuring his granny was good, he then tried to contact one of the evening nurses that stayed there while he went to work. After a good thirty minutes or so, the agency finally answered its phone. Considering the majority of their staff resided in Detroit, Black Tone was told they had absolutely no one available to work. That information came as no great shock to him, because he knew that if anyone lived in the city and wasn't smart enough to stay home, that was on them. That he was even considering leaving his own home now had everything to do with the fact that he'd laid down the law to Dre and his boys a long time ago that even dreaming about violating his and Granny's space would end with them suffering a fate worse than the cops being called.

Moments later, Amir called back. Black Tone sent him straight to voice mail, still at a loss about what he was going to do. He then ignored the several 911 texts. Pacing the floor, he wisely came to the conclusion that his granny should go out to his auntie's house in Oak Park, at least until the power came back on. Placing a call to his cousin Wild Child, he killed two birds with one stone. His aunt agreed to stop by and pick up his granny, so he was good. She'd be safe and secure during this mandatory twenty-four-hour power outage. That was his first priority. Black Tone knew that even in his absence, lights out or not, any would-be thief from his way dared not to cross him and disrespect the crib. As far as Detroit Live went, Wild Child said he was good to go on posting up and making that double time.

With that business taken care of, Black Tone called Amir back and reassured him that he'd be covered well before nightfall and certain anarchy ensued. Before he could get his granny's necessities packed and could jump in the shower, his cell rang again.

CHAPTER SIX

Detroit Receiving Hospital, just like all the other medical facilities, was only hours away from shutting its doors. It, too, was going to be affected by the power outage promised by the mayor and signed off on by the governor. Although it had enormous backup generators in place for cases of emergency, the chief operating officer of the medical complex had issued a mandatory order. All non-life-threatening cases were to be immediately expelled from the building. If you could walk on your own, you could leave, was the general mind-set. For Li'l Ronnie, who had stumbled into the emergency room the night before, complaining about his ribs feeling broken, his jaw being swollen, and a bone in his leg aching, that meant him. Lucky enough to have had an X-ray and gotten positive results, meaning he had no severe injuries, he was good to go. The doctor on duty gave him two high-milligram pain pills and advised him to take an over-the-counter aspirin if his discomfort continued.

Li'l Ronnie's body was aching and bruised up pretty bad. Black Tone had kept his word about being brief with him. He had left a lasting impression on the young boy not only physically, but mentally as well. For all the extreme soreness his body was suffering from, his pride hurt more. Nursing a serious hangover to boot, part of him wanted to lie down and sleep for a good week or so. The wannabe tough thug's stomach was roiling. He had the runs, and his throat was dry.

Limping out to his car, Li'l Ronnie was met with the same urgency from everyone in the parking lot as he had been inside the hospital. They all needed to get home or to their businesses before noon. Each person knew that normally, the real crime in the D came after dark, but today even the afternoon would be considered dark. As he roared out of the gated lot and onto the street, Li'l Ronnie powered his cell back on. He'd heard some of the doctors, nurses, and other staff members claim that the city was going dark and that was why the building was practically being evacuated until further notice, but he'd yet to see it posted on the hood bible, Facebook.

Damn. This shit really going down. His head was pounding overtime as the brightness of the sun invaded every window of the vehicle. Tossing his cell over on the passenger seat, Li'l Ronnie jumped down on the freeway and headed toward the East Side. Given that he was nursing his lumps and bruises, every pothole he hit felt like Black Tone was still laying hands on him. By the time he got to his exit, Li'l Ronnie was just as heated from the humiliating beat down he'd suffered as he was when it had just occurred. Pulling up in front of his uncle's house, he saw more street soldiers than usual posted up around the dwelling and on each corner, serving as lookouts. Glancing up in the mirror, he was disgusted with the way his face looked. Seconds after putting one foot out of the truck, Li'l Ronnie started to get clowned about his appearance. Besides his face, his clothes were, of course, dirty. His shirt was torn and out of shape around the collar, and the knee areas of his jeans were ripped.

"Damn, my nigga. What truck you run into?" one of the street soldiers asked.

"Don't worry about all that. I'm good with mines," Li'l Ronnie responded, trying not to limp.

"All right, playboy. Don't get tough toned with me. I ain't the one that got your soft ass all the way together. But if you looking for a round two . . ."

Li'l Ronnie wasn't in the mood to go head up with anyone else, so he just kept it moving. After allowing the black steel security gate to slam closed behind him, he was soon face-to-face with his uncle. Ashamed of his appearance, he lowered his head when he sat down on the couch. "Hey, Unc. What up, doe?"

"Yeah, Ronnie, what's good? Where you been?" He barely looked up from counting his money.

Li'l Ronnie knew his mother's older brother could smell a load of bullshit coming from a mile away and decided to keep things real. "Unc, I been down at the fucking hospital. I was down at the club last night, and this ho-ass buster tried it with me."

"Oh yeah? Is that right?" He momentarily looked up and ignored his nephew's facial lumps, knowing what was about to happen next. *Here comes this slick game he always running when he fuck up.*

Li'l Ronnie started to run down his version of what had taken place. He made sure to include that his supposed homeboys had abandoned him. And excluded the fact that he had been beyond drunk and belligerent. "Yeah, Uncle, they was some weak-ass motherfuckers. You need to straight take them off the ticket. They don't need to get another dollar off any bag you put out there!"

"Is that right? Take them little soldiers you begged me to put on in the first place off the payroll because they ain't stand tall with you on no bullshit! Nigga, it's about to be a full-blown lights out around the city, and you here sounding straight pussy 'cause you got your ass handed to you. You really need to check yourself."

"But, Uncle, that fake police bouncer at Detroit Live was calling you out. Saying your dope wasn't shit and neither was you. On some family loyalty, I had to step to him," Li'l Ronnie lied, hoping to persuade his uncle Ethan to be on his side. "It was that bitch nigga named Black Tone. He needs his ass handed to him East Side style!"

Ethan had had about enough. He, like all his crew, understood the importance of what was going to take place in the hours to follow. He knew this type of shit happened only in movies like *The Purge* or something. He had different spots and stash houses that had to be protected and runners on the streets that had to double tool up just in case a rival crew wanted to make a move on their territory, which they'd fought so hard for.

"Listen up, youngin'. You think I don't know what happened last night? You think I ain't got eyes and ears down at Detroit Live and damn near every other club in the city? I already know you was down there acting a straight-up fool. I got the word from more than a few folks you was up there throwing my name around, like I cosign that 'get drunk, act a fool clown' shit. I done told you to stop using my name like it's a game out here in these streets. Constantly disobeying me ain't what you want!"

"But," Li'l Ronnie protested. He had tried to interrupt and stick to his story, but his uncle had stopped him. He knew exactly who his uncle meant when he'd said "a few folks." That damn Sable. Li'l Ronnie wanted to hate his ex for throwing him to the curb when he got locked up and for then linking up with his uncle, but he couldn't. Deep down inside he still loved her and always would. From time to time he'd go down to the club Sable danced at under the pretense of watching a few of the other dancers, but he always ended up tipping her.

"But!" Ethan was done with his worrisome nephew all together. Despite all the favoritism he had always been shown, he still couldn't do right. If he wasn't fucking up the count, stepping on the product, or just plain drawing too much unwanted attention to the team, he was doing what he had done the night before: trying to use the next man's name to get a pass. "But nothing, dawg. In about an hour these lights about to go dark, and we gotta be ready. So real talk, even though I need all hands on deck tonight, your dumb ass is a liability. So take this here." Ethan peeled off a couple of hundred-dollar bills and tossed them onto the coffee table. "You can take that grip and get out my sight for a week or two. Until further notice, your wild ass unemployed indefinitely, so you might need to just raise up and out."

Li'l Ronnie was heated. He couldn't believe his uncle, his own blood, would turn him out into the street like this. He'd been riding with him ever since he was fourteen, and now because some bitch nigga who wanted to get brownie points had snitched on him, his uncle had turned him out. As far as Li'l Ronnie was concerned, he'd suffered enough. First, he was violated by Black Tone, and now Ethan was turning his back on him. With malice in his heart, Li'l Ronnie stood to his feet. Staring down at the money on the coffee table, he could only shake his head in denial. It had come down to this.

"So you just think you can say, 'Fuck you. You're out the game," just like that? I'm on vacation, or what the hell did you call it? Unemployed until further notice? Come on, Uncle. You know me better than that. You know I'm not just gonna let that shit be. That goofy faggot gonna pay."

Ethan jumped to his feet. Fighting the temptation to have some of the fellas put in a small bit of "Act right" handwork on his kin, he felt this was personal. Rushing up on his sister's son, he startled Li'l Ronnie, as well as his crew, which was posted inside the house as well as out. Using his forearm, the seasoned gangster shoved it underneath the shocked youth's neck. Locking eyes with him, Ethan swore that if he didn't give up the idea of getting revenge on Black Tone and anyone else affiliated with Detroit Live, he would fix it so Li'l Ronnie never rolled in the city again, for him or the next man.

"I hope you understand the words coming out my fucking mouth. You go back down to that club or any other one in a hundred-mile radius, shouting my name, on my dead sister's grave, you gonna join her in the pine box."

Disgusted, Ethan let Li'l Ronnie go. He knew by the expression on his nephew's face that he was hurt and humiliated. Nevertheless, business was business, and the East Side kingpin was fed up with always having to fix things and kiss ass. This time Li'l Ronnie had really overstepped his boundaries at the wrong club. Ethan's tone grew more furious as he signaled for his right-hand man, Bersek, to remove the source of his problem. "Yo, dawg. Get this troublemaking, beige-colored little nigga outta here while I call down to Detroit Live and make shit right."

Feeling he was out in the world alone, Li'l Ronnie hobbled back to his truck. *Fuck family. Family ain't about shit! That nigga took my girl while I was gone. Now he taking my money and hustle!* Not only had he received zero sympathy and zero backup, which he had been hoping for when he pulled up, but the still stomach-bubbling Li'l Ronnie had got blessed with a rude awakening. This made twice in a twenty-four-hour time span that he'd been treated like he was no more than a piece of shit.

Just as he started the engine, his cell vibrated. He looked at the screen and saw a small Instagram icon notification in the top corner. Tapping the icon took him to the page of a thirst-trap female he knew from around the way, one who was with Sable the night

before. *What this sack-chasing tramp want!* Out of
the blue, she'd tagged him in some random video. He
pushed the arrow that had appeared on his screen,
the sound to the video came on. *Son of a bitch! Fuck
the world! Now I know I'm gonna body that nigga!*
Speechless, he replayed the thirty-one-second record-
ing of Black Tone recklessly getting him all the way
together several times.

Li'l Ronnie couldn't believe what he was seeing, what
the entire *world* was now seeing, thanks to social media.
Enraged, he knew he couldn't just go out like that. Li'l
Ronnie knew he couldn't hold his head up in the city anymore if he did. *Motherfuckers gonna feel me tonight for
sure. The streets gonna run red!* Throwing his cell down
onto the passenger-side floor, the bloodthirsty thug was
pissed. After putting the truck in drive, he slammed his
foot down on the gas pedal and skirted off. As he drove,
Li'l Ronnie swallowed a huge lump in his throat, knowing
today was the day he'd have to commit open murder.

Amir was glad Black Tone was going to be on his
way soon. Although he, like his younger brothers, kept
a gun on his hip, one pistol was not going to be enough.
When the city went dark, it would take the National
Guard and police from several jurisdictions to maintain
law and order. Sitting back in his office, he stared at all
fourteen surveillance cameras located both inside the
club and out. He knew that shortly they would go blank
and Black Tone would have to do foot patrols around
the perimeter until daybreak. The one good thing was
that Detroit Live was located in the downtown area of
town, near the river and police headquarters. That didn't
make him exempt from the possible danger that other

high-crime zip codes would surely endure, but it eased his worry some.

Amir's party store was definitely at stake. It was located in the heart of the hood, and so he knew that the chances of it coming away unbroken into, or possibly worse, were low. If he was to bet all his money, legally and illegally made, on the fact that Pops would be happy come morning, he'd be broke. When speaking to him earlier, Amir had urged the elderly patriarch of the family to just lock the doors and secure the building the best they could and to ask Allah to protect their interests. Of course, Pops had thrown up in his son's face that he wasn't tucking tail and hiding like some coward female, so why should he? When Amir had explained to him that he knew the real reason why he and Black Tone had to hold the place down, Pops hadn't liked it one bit but had completely understood. Amir felt that even though he couldn't physically be there at the store, he could at least call and check in before noon.

He dialed Mikey. "Hey. What's good?" he asked after Mikey answered the landline.

"Nothing much, big brother. We over here packing this shit up as much as we can. Pops already took two loads over to Uncle Mohamed's."

Amir was relieved. Apparently, his conversation with Pops had paid off. Leaning back in the huge leather seat, he asked to speak to his father. After a few brief moments, his father was on the line. "Hey, so you took my advice, huh?"

"Yes, only in the way that we have moved the majority of the expensive stuff and most of the other items those animals would want to break in and steal."

"Pops, I know that's how you feel, and I guess I can kinda respect it, but you know better than to call them that. Who around you?"

"Nobody is around me, Amir. And if one of them was, this is my store!"

Amir knew he wasn't going to get his extremely racist father to be politically correct in mixed company or otherwise. Over the years, while either working at a business or running his own business in Detroit, he'd seen and experienced it all when it came to dealing with the black man. Pops had been strong-armed and robbed, had had guns shoved in his face, ribs, and back. He'd been assaulted several times, spit on, talked about, threatened, and accused of financially raping the neighborhood with his prices. All that being said, his oldest son, Amir, understood the animosity.

"Look, Pops. Nobody arguing that fact with you. I'm just saying to chill out a li'l bit, especially tonight. Mikey said you've been moving stuff out the store, so that's good. You go ahead and get over to Uncle Mohamed's and relax. I know Mikey and Hassan will hold us down as a family the best they can."

Pops could discern the uncertainty in his oldest's tone but tried to keep up a brave front concerning the hours to come. "I wish you were here with them, but I know you have your own matters that have nothing to do with me and your brothers."

"Pops, please don't start up again. I already told you the deal on why it's so important for me to be down here at the club. Besides, the twins gonna help them hold things down tonight."

"Yes, that much is true, but it is your responsibility to stand tall with your brothers, not their cousins."

Amir needed to cut off the conversation turned guilt trip. He had to call Black Tone back and see how far along he and some of his crew were. It was only a short time before the unimaginable started to transpire.

"Pops, head over to your brother's store, and I will call you later to check in." With that said, Amir pushed the END TALK icon.

CHAPTER SEVEN

The clock struck noon. As promised, one by one Detroit's neighborhoods, which were already struggling to survive, started to lose power sporadically. First, the Southwest Side, the Delray and Palmer Park areas, and Brightmoor. Then Rosedale Park and clear over to East English Village. Things grew more dire with each passing moment. By twelve thirty, one o'clock the entire city's municipal buildings were dark. It was starting to get painfully clear that what Motown residents and most of the world thought would or could never really take place indeed had. A major city within the United States of America had been deliberately cut off from the rest of the country. With the exception of some loyal police officers whose family resided outside the affected Detroit area and who had volunteered to patrol the streets in their own personal vehicles, the town was completely lawless.

"Okay, y'all. I was just up at the corner store, and Hassan and them already done shut down. They pussy all the way. But the gas stations are still pumping. They cranking, serving people out the front door only. They barely cracking the son of a bitch, but they getting the job done. Still making that money."

"You gotta be bullshittin'. Straight up for real, Dre?"

"Yeah, for real, dawg. On everything I love, I told you shit was about to be on straight bang." Dre clicked the light switch up and down. Then he smiled as he picked up the remote control. He tried unsuccessfully to turn the television on, further proving they had no power. He was elated. "And peep out at this gangster shit popping off. All them sand niggas up there strapped too, like they ready for a fucking war. I mean, they got them real choppers on deck."

"Strapped, strapped?"

They stepped outside, and Dre's hands and arms were flying as he explained what he'd just witnessed firsthand. "Yeah, boy. Strapped all the way live, like a motherfucker. AKs on they shoulders, with extra-long banana clips hanging out they back pockets, like it ain't shit. Plus, they got some of that crazy overseas bullshit a nigga never seen before out in the streets." He glanced around. "I mean, real talk, I can't blame they Ali Baba asses. Fools up there on Linwood going nuts. It's gonna be a long-ass day, not to mention night." Taking a long pull from a Newport, Dre stood on the front porch, filling in his other homeboy, who'd just woken up. "I saw fools running down the street with pillowcases full of stuff they must've broke in somebody crib and stole."

"What in the fuck! Dre, are you serious?"

"Hell, fuck yeah. I'm dead ass. And some young, crazy-ass fool done already stole a damn car and ran a little girl over like it ain't shit!"

"Say word?"

"Yeah, and here the hell his wild ass comes, doing more doughnuts in the intersection, clowning like he ain't did no wrong." Dre shook his head, wanting his piece of the illegal pie before law and order was restored. "Like they said on the news, it ain't no fucking police rolling, so it's time for us to get our shit together so we can get out here and do what we do. Ain't gonna be no flashing-light patrols. And ain't no curfews gonna be enforced. So let's get it!"

After watching several families load their cars with overnight bags, Dre grinned. He figured they would probably be spending the night in a city with electricity and with officers of the law on duty. Sadly for them, Dre put their homes first on the list to get hit. He knew that although they more than likely would take all their laptops, tablets, and expensive jewelry with them, there would still be televisions, DVD players, and video game systems waiting to find a new home.

Dre then gathered together his crew of soon-to-be neighborhood bandits. He told them to take their time as they did their work, because the burglar alarm systems that usually glared at intruders would not working. As he talked, he grinned, knowing he was about to be eating good. After getting a crowbar and more than a few Home Depot heavy-duty garbage bags, the boys went to work. Arrogant, they did not care that it was broad daylight. They didn't give two shits about who saw them and snitched later on down the line that they were hungry and had to be fed by any means necessary.

"We closed! We closed!" Hassan shouted angrily through the bolted doors.

"Come on, dude! We need a bottle of that Hennessy and a few of them Red Bulls! I know they still cold!"

"Dawg, we not open! Not until tomorrow morning, maybe!" Mikey barked, reinforcing his brother's words. He was also tired of the locals banging on an obviously locked door. "Try somewhere else. Damn!"

"It ain't nowhere else to go around here, you ho-ass motherfucker, so why don't y'all just sell that bullshit y'all got in there!"

As time seemed to drag by, three of the four young men found different things to occupy them. However, with nothing much to do in the dimly lit store, Hassan decided to text Alexis. Hopefully, she'd be up by now. The fact that she'd returned to being a stripper only months after giving birth to a baby—who, according to neighborhood rumors, was his—meant nothing to naive Middle Eastern–born Hassan. Whether or not he was the biological father of the fair-skinned, curly-haired, hazel-eyed infant, he still treated Alexis with the utmost respect. Exposing her nude body to a man other than her husband was considered shameful in his culture, as well as his religion. However, Hassan knew everyone went against the grain some time or another. If he judged Alexis for having a child out of wedlock, then he'd have to condemn himself for having premarital sex with her in the store's walk-in cooler and stockroom.

Alexis had claimed on numerous occasions that she was swinging on that brass pole only to get enough money to finish paying for her CNA training and hopefully purchase a house from the new land bank Auction. So the next man seeing her stark naked was only a temporary thing. Alexis was desperate to get away from her nothing-ass brother, Dre. He and his band of no-good cohorts, who were constantly posted at the house their deceased mother had left to them, had turned the home into some sort of Honeycomb Hideout or some bullshit clubhouse like that. Alexis was determined to get her certificate, if nothing else. Sure, Hassan would give her small sums of money on the regular and take her to dinner at some far-out, low-key restaurant, but his overall contribution to the young mother was no great life-changing feat. They lived in two different worlds, two they had yet truly to combine. Yet Hassan was tired of living like that. He wanted to make things with himself and his Nubian queen official. Fuck the world.

"Hey, baby," he said, almost in a whisper. "You up yet or what?"

"Yeah, I guess so. What time is it, anyway?" She peeked from underneath the sheet and saw the sun shining from behind the blanket nailed up to her window.

"It's two thirty, almost three."

"Damn!"

"Yeah, damn is right! What time you get in last night? I texted you at about two and you ain't get back."

Alexis stretched her arms out, then pulled the satin hair cap down farther on her head. "I told you I don't get good reception when I work at that club. So why is you tripping?"

"I'm not." Hassan tried not to raise his voice as he walked to the rear of the dark store. "It's just I be worried about you."

"Bae, I told you not to worry about me. I can take care of myself."

"Well, I can't help it, Alexis. I stay worried about you and the baby. So I'm gonna trip from time to time." Hassan glanced at the rear of the store to see if Mikey and cousins were still preoccupied and not listening to him. He stuffed his hand deep into his front pocket and eased out a gold ring with a small-size diamond center stone. Although he loved Alexis with all his heart, he knew now wasn't the time for them to get married, but later in the evening he would slip the ring on her finger so she'd at least know his intentions were honorable.

"Yeah, okay, Hassan, but stop with all that. I'm good, and the baby good. He's still with my auntie and cousins out in Southfield."

"Well, I know you know the power is out citywide, right? That crap they was talking about all week really happened."

"You bullshitting? I heard people talking about it last night at the club, but shit!" She finally sat up in the bed. "You up at the store? Do y'all have power up there?"

"Naw, girl. We up here in the store, and it's dark as hell. Citywide means citywide, period! Ain't no exceptions because we wasn't born here!"

"Boy, forget all that mess you about to start talking about. You know I don't care about your race or religion, just you! But damn!" Alexis reached for the remote to see if her television would turn on. Of course, it didn't, and this time it wasn't because DTE had cut the wires after catching them stealing electricity again. "You right. Our shit is dead!"

"Okay, so what you gonna do the rest of the day, woman? You cold chilling in the crib or what?"

"Boy, I dunno. I'm just getting my head wrapped around no power. How long this mess gonna last, anyhow? Did they say?"

"At least twenty-four hours. And you know it's no police or fire trucks running. The damn hospitals shut down too!"

"Wow! Man, this is crazy!"

"Who the hell you telling?" Hassan thought about all the money he and his family were missing out on by not being open and shook his head in denial. "Well, boo, on another note, when you get yourself together, why don't you head up here? I got something for you, something special."

"Well, it better be some keys to a plush hotel room out in the burbs somewhere!" Alexis knew staying the night in Detroit was out of the question as she looked around for what to take with her. It was dangerous enough closing your eyes in the city nightly even with the few streetlights that did work.

"Alexis, girl, cut all that out. You know I got you covered. Just come on to the store when you get ready!"

"Yeah, all right, Hassan. Love you, and I'll be up there shortly."

"Well, just knock on the back door by the Dumpster. But call me first, because we ain't opening the doors for just anybody." Hassan stared over at the front entrance as yet another person banged on the door, thinking the CLOSED sign somehow didn't apply to them.

Alexis hung up from Hassan, then called her best friend, Anthony, back. He'd texted her the night before, like he always did when he got in from work. However, like she'd just told Hassan, the reception was poor where she was working, and she was exhausted. She and Anthony had been rocking out for years. And just like he swore to her that day in the abandoned house, he had her back and would always make sure she was good. When the police detectives came and picked up Dre and threw him in juvenile lock up for close to two years for various crimes, Anthony was there, being her substitute big brother. When her mother finally did succumb to her illness, he was there to hold her hand. When her verbally abusive aunt and her many kids stayed in the house her mother had left to her and Dre until she was of legal age, Anthony and his granny were there to help with the transition.

Now both grown, she and Black Tone, as the streets referred to him, were still very close. And he was still looking out for her when need be. He didn't necessarily agree with her relationship with Hassan or her stripping, but it was what it was. As far as Black Tone was concerned, Alexis was always going to be the hood Bonnie to his gangster Clyde.

CHAPTER EIGHT

Li'l Ronnie finally made it home to his suburban apartment. After taking a long shower, he dried off and threw on a pair of shorts. The shirtless, mentally anguished soldier fell back on his bed. After spending the night before drinking, getting into a one-sided battle, and dealing with the various people at the hospital, he was spent. The hot water did absolutely nothing to soothe his aching bones and nothing to ease his attitude. Ethan had put the final nail in Li'l Ronnie's coffin with the black-hearted betrayal and Li'l Ronnie's exile from the illegal family business he felt was his birthright.

Now, cut off and humiliated on social media, he stared up at the ceiling, plotting his next move. Slowly lifting his head, Li'l Ronnie glanced over at the closet. Behind that closed door was everything he needed or wanted to wage his own war. Knowing that he had a small but dangerous high-powered arsenal at his immediate disposal made him feel relieved. He didn't have to beg, borrow, or steal a gun to handle his business. He was good when the time came to put in work. He picked up his cell and tried his best not to look at the video he'd now saved to his phone. However, he couldn't help himself. He pushed PLAY, and his anger intensified with every passing second. Every laugh he heard in the background. Every time he saw a female cover her mouth in shock and each time he watched Black Tone sling him around like some rag doll, Li'l Ronnie got further buried in his emotions.

Standing up on his still very sore leg, he stretched his arms, hoping to shake off his rage and think about how he'd kill Black Tone and not get caught. Definitely not cut out to go to prison, Li'l Ronnie was ready to sit down and do the time given to him if he slipped up. He walked over to the other side of the room and opened the closet door. After stepping inside, he pulled down on the small piece of string that was attached to the overhead light. Moving several of his leather coats over to the side as far as possible, he nodded his head. He reached over a few of the weapons in his cherished pistol collection and picked up one of his favorites. After going back into the bedroom, he took the clip out and emptied all the bullets onto the dresser. Then he opened a drawer and got a T-shirt out. Next, he went into the bathroom and opened up the medicine cabinet. A bottle of alcohol, then peroxide, and he was ready. Ready to use the knowledge Ethan had blessed him and the entire crew with some time ago. He understood he had to do wrong as right as possible.

Li'l Ronnie got out a pair of shooting-range gloves. He was taught they were much better to use than straight-up latex gloves by themselves. He took a pair of the blue-colored surgical safe guards out of the box, then slipped them on. Tugging down at the wrists, he ensured they were snug. He followed up with the shooting gloves, and he was now ready.

First, he took the clip and inspected it. After slightly dampening a small portion of the T-shirt with alcohol, he stuck it down inside the metal confines and twirled it around the best he could. Using the other end of the shirt, he repeated the same exact procedure but substituted peroxide for the alcohol. Li'l Ronnie then sat the clip over to the side to dry the small amount of moisture that was still present. Next on the list was the .40-cal hollow-point bullets he had put on the dresser.

Individually, he picked them up with both sets of protective gloves still on.

Using both chemical-dampened ends of the shirt, the vengeful young man wiped each bullet from top to bottom, then in a circular motion. Looking up from what he was doing, Li'l Ronnie paused, staring off into the mirror. Growing more enraged, he now noticed even more bruising on his left side courtesy of Black Tone. Biting down on his lower lip, he went back to what he was doing—cleaning bullets intended for Black Tone. Convinced that they were all fingerprint and DNA free, he proceeded to reload the hollow points into the clean clip.

Li'l Ronnie loved his peacemaker and brought this one out only on special occasions. He swore he'd never part with it, no matter what, so making sure it was clean was of the utmost importance to him. After a few more minutes, the mandatory task was complete. *Oh yeah. That nigga Black Tone gonna pay before sunrise. That's my word,* he silently vowed, wrapping the fully loaded firearm in a brand-new T-shirt fresh out of the package. After making a few calls, it didn't take Li'l Ronnie long to connect the dots. Detroit was the smallest biggest city ever. Everybody knew somebody who knew someone that always knew everyone. And given the flamboyant, jack-money-off lifestyle Li'l Ronnie liked to live, it wasn't hard for someone to turn him on to some info.

Thirsty to get his plan into motion, Li'l Ronnie cracked his knuckles. He already knew where his soon-to-be victim worked at, but where he laid his head at was what really mattered. He knew for sure that was where the wannabe goon would be the most relaxed. Li'l Ronnie knew that if he wanted to catch Black Tone slipping, at home would be the place to look. Text message after text message in in-box after in-box piled in. Finally, he received the 411 he was in search of. Upon finding out not only the neighborhood Black Tone lived in but also his exact address, Li'l Ronnie took a deep breath. He knew his pride was on the line and shit was about to get real.

Getting dressed, Li'l Ronnie was only moments before stepping out his apartment door. Keys in hand, gun tucked in waistband, he stuffed the paper he'd written Black Tone's address down on in his front pocket. Before he could lock up and head toward his truck, his cell rang. Looking down at the screen, he saw it was his uncle.

"Yeah? Hello," he answered, hoping his kin had changed his mind about cutting him off and was now ready to ride with him against Black Tone.

"Boy, what in the entire fuck is wrong with your retarded ass!"

Li'l Ronnie could almost feel Ethan's angry voice jump through the phone. He stood speechless and confused. He'd already allowed him to yoke him up by the neck and verbally berate him. Just earlier Ethan had announced he was done with him. Now he was calling to curse him out yet some more.

"Yo, Unc, what the hell is the problem now? You told me to get the fuck on, so I'm good."

"Good? You good? Naw, little motherfucker. You ain't good. You dumb as hell. You can't have my blood flowing through your brains." His words were hot as they flew out of his mouth. "You trying to get us all fucked up or what?"

"Huh? What is you talking about, fucked up?" Li'l Ronnie went back into his living room. With the phone still up to his ear, he removed the gun from his waistband and placed it on the coffee table. Waiting to hear Ethan's response and his true reason for calling, he sat on the arm of the couch. "What I do now that got you bugging?"

Ethan was pissed. He hated for the guys in his crew to go against the grain and his word. As far as he was concerned, his word was law. He made sure the entire crew that ran with him was fed, had nice clothes, and if they ever had legal issues, they were taken care of. For that reason, he demanded respect. In or out of the fold, his nephew would be no exception. "Listen, you little piece of shit. I told your bitch ass before you left to leave that bullshit alone. That it was over. You had that ass kicking coming, so just be a man about it. Boss up and take that L."

Li'l Ronnie already knew his uncle's reach was long in the city. But from the way he was going in on him, this was too quick. It was like he had read his mind or had cameras hidden in his apartment. "Man, what in the hell is you talking about now?"

"Look, boy. I told you when you left here to leave that bullshit alone. That guy Black Tone is my guy. Detroit Live is off-limits to you from now on out! And, matter of fact, if I find out you keep getting at motherfuckers on Facebook and texting them, trying to catch up with the dude, I'ma break your back personally. Where the fuck a fool leave a deliberate trail of trying to hunt a nigga down to do some old foul football number shit? You young-style, new-breed motherfuckers kill me. Y'all got the game fucked up!"

Li'l Ronnie shook his head. He knew trying to get up with Black Tone that way was risky, but it didn't matter. If the word was out that he was gonna separate his attacker's head from his body, then so be it. Fuck who knew it, his uncle included. "Look, Unc, you do you, 'cause I'm gonna do me!"

Shrugging his shoulders at that comment, Ethan signaled for one of his loyal goons to come into the house. "All right, Ronnie. This ain't what you want, so consider yourself warned!"

CHAPTER NINE

It was nearing five in the evening. The group of four was starting to get more than bored playing cards and talking among themselves by candlelight. Each ones cell had only a few bars left. They had no way to charge them without opening the rear door and going out to their vehicles. Watching the news on his phone, Hassan knew things were about to get way worse before they got better. He also noticed that they'd need more candles and a few more flashlights to make it through the night. After making several calls to relatives who either were too scared to venture into Detroit, which CNN News had reported was out of control, or were much too busy trying to accommodate the overflow of customers at their own business establishments, the group decided Hassan would risk making the trip to get the much-needed provisions, along with some hot food and fruit.

"All right, y'all greedy assholes," Hassan said as he grabbed his brother's car keys off the counter before knocking potato chip crumbs off his blue jeans. "I'm gonna get three of them big baked chicken and steamed vegetable family-size platters from the restaurant, a lamb chop dinner, a grilled fish sandwich, and two turkey salads." He laughed as he went over the food run list, which was long enough to feed a small-size army, not just four people. "Plus, I'm gonna get some fruit from Uncle Mohamed's store when I check in on Pop and give him a firsthand account of how we holding shit down."

***

Hassan shook his head while holding up his almost dead cell phone in the dim shadows of the store. "Now, besides the food and flashlights, is there any damn thing else y'all want? Because I'm gonna turn this motherfucker all the way off so I can get as much juice as I can from the car charger."

"Naw, fool. Just go get the food," one of his twin cousins demanded from the makeshift bed he'd made out of some cardboard boxes. "If me and my brother gotta come over here and babysit y'all crybaby, scared asses all night, then at least feed us!"

"Yo." Mikey stepped in to defend his manhood. "That's Pop that wanted y'all posted here. Me and Hassan was good." He looked over at Hassan, who was making sure his gun was in his hand before having them unbolt the rear door so he could leave. "Well, I was, anyway!"

Once he was in the car, Hassan powered off his phone, plugged it into the black coiled charger, and started the car's engine. Having unlocked the gate, he slowly backed out of the paved lot. Adjusting the rearview mirror, he eased out of the alleyway, being overly conscious of his surroundings. Under normal circumstances he'd have the music blasting, the windows cracked, and he'd be leaning to the side, styling and profiling, but Hassan knew today definitely wasn't a day to be seen or heard in Detroit, especially if you weren't hood born.

According to the breaking news report videos he watched on his cell, the mostly black residential criminals were attacking any and all Middle Easterners and Chinese shopkeepers they came in contact with, people whose only crime was trying to protect their business from being looted or set on fire. Wanting to avoid becoming a statistic himself, Hassan quickly turned onto Davison Avenue, not once allowing his foot to push all the way down on the brakes until he hit the freeway, which was, thankfully, still being patrolled by the state police.

Dre and his crew had put in some serious work. They'd hit close to ten unattended houses throughout the chaotic neighborhood. The fact that no police were patrolling made them feel untouchable. Feeling like they'd hit the lottery, they stopped back by Dre's house to drop off yet another load of their ill-gotten gains.

Disgusted that Dre was dumb enough to shit where he slept, so to speak, and risk the possibility of bringing unwanted heat to the place that she and her small son called home, Alexis gave her older brother a piece of her mind as she stood behind her car.

"Just what in the hell do you think y'all doing?" She rolled her eyes as she tossed her duffel bag and laptop inside her trunk. "Why you keep bringing all that hot shit in this house? Is you crazy or something? Everybody can see your dumb ass!"

"Girl, chill on all that attitude. It's black Christmas around the city. You best recognize and get your gifts, like me!"

"Gifts? Is that what you said? Are you serious? Boy, you need to get your life!" Alexis grabbed her purse, along with a small bag filled with her books. "You gonna mess around and get killed out here with that stealing mess. Dang, I know how they be feeling. Go get a job or do something productive!"

"And just who is 'they,' Alexis? Who? Tell me that! Your nongreen card–having boyfriend and his prejudice-ass family? You need to stop burning bread on a nigga, okay? That's real fucked up." His rant grew more lethal with each passing word. "And what you want me to do for a job, Miss Think You So Much Better Than Everybody Else? Swing upside down butt asshole naked on a pole, like you do, begging for dollars?" Strangely, Dre found a twisted, wicked pleasure as he clowned his little sister in front of his so-called friends. "Or better yet, Alexis, maybe I should go have some half-breed baby by a rag head motherfucker that can never take your stupid nappy-headed ass home to meet his dying mama! Trust me, li'l sis, you ain't never gonna get no family reunion T-shirt from them wannabe black motherfuckers! At the end of the day it's us versus them. Always was and always will be, no matter how much pale dick you suck!"

Alexis was enraged at her brother's impromptu outburst. It showed all over her face. "Listen, boy, from this point on, you dead to me! Don't ask me for shit when times get tight. Don't think I'm dropping you off at your probation officer no more. I ain't cooking no more food for you and your dirt ball homeboys." She angrily waved her hand in the direction they were standing, giggling like little schoolgirls. "And, oh yeah, since you got so much rotten-ass stuff to say about Hassan and his peoples, stop running up there begging him for shit every damn day, expecting me to pay for it with this pussy!"

"Oh yeah?" Dre dumbly replied.

"Yeah, dummy! All Hassan ever did was try to help ya short bus–riding self, and you out here disrespecting him and me and my son." Giving just as good as she got, Alexis was going straight ham on Dre, and justifiably so. "Now, fuck your 'good being broke' ass twice. Oh, and P.S., all that stolen bullshit you dragging in the house ain't gonna last forever. You and the rest of these 'follow the leader' morons gonna be back on craps by next week. Watch! And when y'all are broke as fuck as usual, don't expect my good pole-swinging ass to help you out! When I finish this semester and get my degree, I'm outta here!"

Dre smiled, acting as if arguing with his blood didn't make him feel some sort of way. Knowing he and his boys had more homes to violate, he wisely ended the argument before he and his sister came to actual blows. "Look, girl, just go where you going and do you. I'm tight on all the rest of that chatter you blowing out your mouth!"

"Fuck you, Dre!"

"I swear, little sis, one day that smart mouth of yours gonna get your ass handed to you, and when it do, don't call me!"

Alexis sucked her teeth before jumping inside her car, then quickly pulled off. As she backed out of the driveway, she just missed running into a triple white Benz truck with the driver slouched over toward his driver's window, trying, apparently, to keep his face low key. Still mad at her brother, Alexis took it out on the driver by flipping him the bird and laying down hard on her horn. After stopping at a stop sign, she waited for a small group of teenagers pushing a shopping cart filled with what looked like miscellaneous items from a beauty supply to cross the intersection. Since she had a look of disgust on her face, the teens decided not to ask her if she was interested in buying what they were selling. Seeing her people run from corner to corner, house to house with this and that made her ashamed to be black.

After dialing Hassan's number three times and getting his voice mail, she finally left a message before turning up into the alley located behind the store. "Hey, babe. I'm here. Where you at?" After parking her candy apple–red Honda Accord inside the open gate, next to a strange vehicle, she slowly strolled to the huge black metal door covered with graffiti. With her phone in one hand, she balled up her other fist, then knocked several times before calling Hassan once more. "Hey, pick up your phone, boy! Where your silly ass at? I'm here!"

"Who the fuck is it?" a voice finally yelled out. "We closed!"

"Hassan? Is that you?"

"Naw. He ain't here," the person on the other side replied, his words seeming muffled.

"Hey, it's me, Alexis." She knocked again, this time with her palm. "Open the door, crazy!"

"Hey, Mikey, some loudmouthed female knocking on this door. She claims she's looking for Hassan."

"Well, who is it?" Mikey asked, coming out of the bathroom, knowing nine out of ten times he already knew the answer.

"How in the fuck he know who the fuck she is?" the other twin crudely answered for his brother.

"Damn. Y'all two getting on my last nerve. I ain't bull-shitting!" Mikey argued, drying his hands with a piece of paper towel from a roll he'd just opened. No sooner than he finished his sentence there was another knock. "That ain't nobody but probably Alexis."

"Alexis?" said the twin at the door.

"Yeah, dude. Alexis," Mikey nonchalantly repeated. "She this female from around the way Hassan hangs out with sometimes."

"A hood chick?" The twin standing at the door looked back over his shoulder.

"You mean to tell me Hassan scary ass banging out some black cat?" His brother cosigned as usual.

Mikey had never dated an African American girl. Sure, most were shapelier than the females that he went out with, but that was beside the point. Black girls, especially those who lived in the neighborhood around the store, were much too wild and over the top for him and his tamed taste. Although, unlike his father, Mikey didn't totally despise African Americans, Negroes, blacks, niggas, or whatever they wanted to call themselves this year, but he damn straight wasn't trying to hang out with them, either. He wasn't all off into that "everybody is the same" crap as his little brother, Hassan, but he still showed Alexis respect on the humble, just in case her baby was ever proven to be his nephew. Of course, he would never allow the boy to play with his own kids, blood kin or not, but he would at least make sure the child didn't go hungry, if need be. "Damn, y'all two idiots. Fall back on all that. I'm about to let her in so she can wait on Hassan. He should be on his way back shortly."

Seconds later Mikey, gun in hand, opened the door cautiously, then peeked out, like his brother had also done before leaving on the food run.

Not more than five minutes had passed in the darkly lit corner of the store before the taller twin cut off into Alexis. "So, you giving our little cousin all that fat ass you got back there, huh? You sucking his dick too?"

"Excuse you? Say what?" Accustomed to being belittled and disrespected nightly in the strip club, Alexis normally didn't take offense to paying customers having their say, but these strangers were out of order and so very random with the attack on her character that she couldn't believe it. "Just who in the fuck you talking to like that!" Alexis fired back, rolling her contact lens–covered eyes. "You got me messed up! Show some damn respect with ya belligerent ass!"

"Respect? Bitch, you better get on with all that!"

"Bitch? Bitch?" Alexis, infuriated, stood to her feet, ready to storm out. "Your sister a damn bitch!"

"Our sister a bitch?" The other twin stepped in, taking his turn at degrading black women, namely Alexis. "Our sister and no other female in our family could ever be considered or called a bitch. See that fucked-up 'nigga state of mind' bullshit you and your people embrace ain't apart of our makeup!"

"Yeah, it ain't in our DNA," the taller twin shouted, jumping back into the tag team verbal assault. "You see, in our culture, we'd kill our women first before we let them run around here in tight-ass skirts, showing off what's meant only for their husbands, talking all crazy to their men, fucking and sucking every dick they see!" He was now also on his feet and towered over Alexis, who was still standing her ground. "Our women have boundaries. They know their place and know better than to go outside of their race and fuck with an abeed! They need to do more than turn off the lights in this tramp-infested city. They need to burn all you blacks or put y'all on a big-ass cruise ship and sail y'all skin-burnt monkeys back to Africa to get retrained in Slavery one-oh-one!"

"Damn. What in the fuck!" Mikey stood in between his brother's girl, possibly the mother of his nephew, and his two blood-bonded cousins. "Y'all need to chill on all this bullshit. Why y'all tripping on this girl like this? Y'all going too far, and for no good reason!"

The twins had the same reply, as if it was rehearsed, and that was that if these little black females with no morals wanted to run around dressing and acting like sluts, then that was exactly how they was gonna treat them, like sluts. That if they called themselves bitches and hoes, and dudes wanted to call themselves niggas, then so the fuck they flat-out were!

Alexis had heard just about enough from the over-the-top, racist twin brothers she'd never laid eyes on before today. *I guess some of what Dre said is true. This is crazy. Where is Hassan?* She was still infuriated from the argument earlier with her brother, and her always present, but seldom seen "thot on a mission" disposition came to the surface. "Look, I ain't feeling y'all or that bullshit y'all talking. I don't know who in the name of sweet baby Jesus you two punk-ass, 'talking out the side of y'all's neck,' stankin' bullies think you fucking with, but you best ask ya peoples Mikey what's really good in this hood. Y'all better fall all the way back, before shit get real hectic for y'all real quick, fast, and in a hurry!"

"Yeah? Is that right, Ebony, Shawntay, Shaniqua, Shakeisha, Mercedes, or whatever dumb ghetto-ass name ya mammy came up with while she was smoking crack?" Things were getting more and more heated as the seconds dragged by. "Well, don't get mad at us because silly little cum Dumpsters like you get off on getting a bag of chips, a pop, and a loosie in return for a king like me getting my dick wet in that huge lip-covered mouth of yours! You black skanks is for entertainment for us, and nothing damn else!"

"Mikey, just let me out and tell Hassan I came by, before your people get some act right on they rude asses and be traveling back to your fucking desert-ass country in a wooden box!" Alexis vowed with certainty, knowing her brother didn't play.

"Hold up, girl. Hassan gonna be back with the food soon," said the more aggressive of the twins as he blocked the door. "You ain't gonna stay and break bread with us? It's like that?"

"Yeah, bitch, it's just like that," she replied loudly, with enough attitude and neck rolling for ten people.

Before Alexis knew what was happening, she felt two pairs of strong hands simultaneously yanking her down onto the filthy concrete floor. After taking one blow across her jawline and another to her ribs, she started to get dizzy. Hearing Mikey's panicked voice demanding the two of them stop, Alexis was short of breath but still managed to yell for assistance. "Help me, Mikey! Help me please!" With one twin's hand wrapped around her throat, the distraught mother felt the reeking moisture from his lips on her ear as he whispered that if she screamed out once more, he'd kill her. Seconds later she was being dragged behind the juice and meat walk-in coolers.

"Guess what, slut bucket? I thought you'd like some dick back here." Antagonizing her with his words, he laughed as he unzipped his pants and then allowed them to drop to his ankles. "I mean, all you cheap fucking black bitches like it back here, don't you?"

Disoriented but relentless in spirit, Alexis tried to fight him off but was cruelly met with a painful combination of three more open-hand slaps to the face. Blood was now dripping from the right corner of her busted lip. The room was spinning. It was almost pitch black, and she couldn't focus. In a final attempt to get him to stop, she called out once more to Mikey. Obviously getting no help or mercy from Hassan's brother, she continued struggling to break free from the twin's strong arm hold. Overpowered and exhausted, she finally gave in when the other twin brutally snatched her panties off, exposing her private area. The last thing Alexis saw before passing out cold was the other twin dropping his pants, as well, and Mikey walking away.

CHAPTER TEN

Li'l Ronnie had driven clear across town, still hell-bent on revenge. What his uncle had said to him mattered not at all. His threats, his promises, and his downplaying of what had taken place at Detroit Live were irrelevant. Ronald James Harvard was his own man and was ready to prove just that. Full of pure hatred, he was done taking losses at the hand of Ethan, as well as others. With his mind made up that the world was truly designed to just fuck him over, Li'l Ronnie was on the hunt.

Deep in thought, he followed the GPS on his cell and turned right, as instructed, then left. Only slowing down for kids darting out in the middle of the street or crack-heads in search of their next rock, Li'l Ronnie quickly realized the west side of town was more out of control than the east. Hearing that he was only three short blocks away from his typed-in destination, Black Tone's crib, the soon-to-be murderer felt his adrenaline at an all-time high. The radio was turned up, and he was blasting his favorite rap song through the custom speakers. He was motivated. He was hyped. He was focused. He was even unbothered as some random female suddenly backed out of a driveway, not paying attention. The fact that she cursed him out and gave him the middle finger meant nothing. Li'l Ronnie thought he recognized one of the guys that she was also going ham on, but he was too far off in his murder-minded zone to even care. He had something to prove, not only to himself, but to his uncle as well.

That ho-ass nigga telling me to play my position before I don't have a position to play, like I'm some half-assed gangsta. Who in the fuck he think he is? First, he take Sable while I'm sitting down in lockup, and then he wanna strip me of all my pride as a man. Fuck him. Matter of fact, after I body Black Tone, he next!

Li'l Ronnie slowly drove down Black Tone's nearly deserted block. After looking over to the left side of the street, followed by the right, he saw the black metal numbers posted on the side of the door. After lifting his gun off the passenger seat, he grabbed the paper with the address written on it. So as not to draw any unwanted attention to himself, he turned the music down. He saw no signs of the truck he'd found out Black Tone drove, but that didn't discourage him. He'd lie in wait for him, if need be.

Total excitement could be seen on his face as he drove around the corner and parked his truck. Popping a few pills and taking a swig from a pint of Hennessy he kept in the glove compartment, he was ready to face the unknown. Somewhat hesitant about leaving his vehicle, with its expensive rims and sound system, parked in a neighborhood he didn't know, Li'l Ronnie eagerly decided to take his chances in the notorious high-crime zip code.

Cautiously, gun tucked in the rear of his jeans, he climbed out of his vehicle and crept through the alley. Despite his sore leg, he then perched down in between two side-by-side abandoned houses. Ten minutes, then twenty went by as he eagle eyed the front of Black Tone's house, searching for any signs of movement.

Smelling the awful stench of dead rodents and maggot-filled bags of old, discarded garbage, Li'l Ronnie felt his patience grow short. In reality, he knew he couldn't wait forever, so he decided to just make things happen.

He knew that the situation in Detroit would prevent anyone from calling the police about a man with a gun, let alone the police responding to the call. He'd seen more than his fair share of pistols holstered on hips and in hand since the clock struck noon. The city was on high alert, and everyone who owned a weapon, legal or not, was brandishing it on this day. Li'l Ronnie was no different.

Stepping out from the makeshift hiding place, he saw that the block was quiet, with the exception of a small group of guys standing in the same driveway the rude female had roared out of. Wasting no time, he darted across the street. Tucking the gun back in the rear of his pants, he felt the barrel rub against his spine as he raised his arm overhead. He approached the house and gripped a concrete window ledge, then lifted himself up. Attempting to look inside, Li'l Ronnie could see absolutely nothing but old furniture through the sheer white curtains.

Out of options, he went around to the front and walked up onto the porch. Brazenly, he rang the bell twice and received no answer. His next move was simple. He'd kick in the side door and wait for Black Tone to return, no matter how long it took. Bottom line, he wanted payback and wasn't willing to wait another day to get it.

It didn't take much for Li'l Ronnie to force himself through the side door. Of course, it was locked and had a chain securing it, but the frame was old. Like most of the houses in that area that were still lived in, its wood was weak and on its last leg. Although Black Tone had bars on most of the windows and on the front door, his granny had advised him back in the day that she never wanted a security gate on the side door, just in case there was a fire and they needed to escape. Black Tone had never had a problem honoring her wishes, because the only fools in the neighborhood known for breaking and entering already knew better.

So this is where this pussy nigga be laying his head at, huh? Li'l Ronnie had his gun drawn. No one had come to the door when he rang the bell, and he hadn't heard anyone at the windows. But that didn't mean no one was at home. For all he knew, Black Tone or someone else that lived there could be watching him from across the street and was waiting to make a move. They could have been chilling, waiting for him to come inside so they could kill him legally. Li'l Ronnie wasn't sure, so he was being extra safe as he made his way up from the basement stairs into the kitchen. Nervous, he took his time as the floorboards made noise. Each step seemed to intensify the noise.

The front living room and dining room were clear, to Li'l Ronnie's relief. As he stood at the edge of the long hallway, he stared down at four doorways. He'd been in enough homes with old-school layouts throughout the years to know they were bedrooms and the bathroom.

Gun still held high in a defensive stance, the now semi-spooked soldier made his way down the hall. The pill and liquid courage he'd had was suddenly gone. Clearing the first doorway, to what appeared to be a bedroom that had been turned into a sewing room, Li'l Ronnie was good. He found no one waiting to crack his head. The second door belonged to the bathroom. After sticking his head inside, he made sure the coast was clear, even moving the shower curtain back with the barrel of his pistol. Easing his body back into the hallway, he continued the task at hand. At the third doorway, he stuck his gun into a bedroom, which had to belong to Black Tone. Letting his guard down, he went all the way inside Black Tone's personal space. Unlike the rest of the house, which seemed like it was caught up in some strange back-in-the-day time capsule, this one room was unbelievable.

The transformation was like night and day, like black and white.

Look at this rat-ass nigga living good in the hood! Expensive laptop, huge mounted flat-screen, king-size bed, a dresser full of cologne and framed pictures of his ho ass with all these rappers, even the damn mayor of Detroit.

Li'l Ronnie had been running behind his uncle for years. He was accustomed to both him and Ethan stuntin' on people when it came to flashy cars, expensive jewelry, and just flaunting dope money all together. No doubt, Li'l Ronnie often took his showboating a little bit further than what was called for. He knew deep down inside that this wild character flaw was the real reason he was in the predicament he was in at the present: having to break into someone's home and kill them.

Li'l Ronnie felt the malice in his heart grow. Here he was, standing in the middle of what he felt was the pit of evil. Everything surrounding him smelled, felt, and was Black Tone, the asshole who in one night had changed the rest of his life forever. If he didn't make shit right and make Black Tone pay for how he had handled him yesterday, he'd never be able to face the world again, or himself, for that matter.

Li'l Ronnie's heart raced. Not bothering to search the last bedroom with the closed door, he sat his gun down on the edge of the dresser. Using his forearm, he swiftly cleared off the contents, sending them flying every which way. In the midst of the sound of the many bottles breaking, he failed to hear a faint voice call out. Enraged, Li'l Ronnie snatched up the closed black- and red-colored laptop off the bed. After raising it high above his head, he brought it crashing down onto the floor. Seeing parts of the electronic device separate on impact, Li'l Ronnie smiled. He was finally getting some sort of satisfaction from the over-the-top ass kicking he'd taken the night before.

Totally out of control, he ran over to the far side of the room and placed both hands on the lower area of the mounted flat-screen, and, using all his strength, he yanked two good times before ripping it down off the wall. After throwing it out into the hallway, Li'l Ronnie paused, thinking he'd heard something.

Wasting no more time, he leaped back over the bed to the other side of the room. Quickly, he retrieved his gun. His arm shook as he listened attentively, and a lump grew in his throat. Li'l Ronnie couldn't swallow and couldn't breathe. As bad as he wanted to send Black Tone to the upper room, the thought of taking another ass whupping if he missed his initial shot was taking an immediate toll. The gun he was holding seemed to grow heavier as the moments dragged by. Small beads of perspiration started to form on his forehead. Soon sweat was leaking from the tiny wrinkles in the wannabe thug's upper brow.

Frozen in fear, Li'l Ronnie heard a tiny cracked voice call out from behind the last bedroom door, the room he had failed to secure.

Damn. What the fuck was I thinking? I dropped the ball, he thought. Not sure of what to do next, he took a deep breath. He wanted to piss on himself but held it the best he could. Li'l Ronnie realized he'd come too far to turn back and not far enough to finish what he'd come to Black Tone's house to do.

Darting his eyes from the closed door to the front of the hallway repeatedly, Li'l Ronnie heard the voice call out once more. Tilting his head to the side, the now petrified small-time criminal thought for sure the voice was saying "Anthony." *Wait a fucking minute. Is that an old damn lady?*

Li'l Ronnie felt a small bit of relief come over him. If his ears were not deceiving him, that wasn't Black Tone hiding behind the closed door to lure him into that room, but his elderly grandmother, the same person who had given him the address and with whom his nemesis lived. Finally finding inner courage, Li'l Ronnie wiped his forehead and took a few steps toward the shut door. Holding the gun steady in one hand, he reached down and placed the other on the glass diamond-shaped doorknob. Not knowing who or what he'd discover on the other side of the dark-stained wood barrier separating him from his fate, Li'l Ronnie braced up. Slowly, he proceeded to turn the knob to the right.

CHAPTER ELEVEN

Black Tone had just arrived down at Detroit Live, much to Amir's relief. The electricity in the city had been out for a few hours, and sheer pandemonium had already set in. News reports were coming in constantly about various small crimes, as well as hardcore felonies, that were being committed. Some houses were burning, while others were being vandalized. There were no police or firemen to come restore order, just residents standing outside on the block, wondering why.

Dedicated to being a devoted grandson, Black Tone stayed around his own house, making sure everything was safe and secure on the home front. He had been living in the neighborhood long enough to trust that even though he and sworn menace Dre had issues dating as far back as when they were kids, Dre and his crew would not violate his dwelling. Black Tone stared out the window, watching Dre come and go repeatedly, carrying bags of stuff inside the house he shared with Alexis and her small son. She and Dre had never seemed to connect throughout the years, even after becoming adults. They both love each other when it came down to it, but that was about it.

After speaking to Alexis earlier, he knew that she planned on packing an overnight bag and getting out of Dodge until this travesty in the city was over. Black Tone had informed her that he'd seen one of her coworkers and hanging buddies the evening before down at the club. He'd reassured Alexis that Sable had been treated VIP well on the strength of her being not only Ethan's woman of the moment, but her homegirl as well. Any of Alexis's people were his people at Detroit Live, whether he agreed with their lifestyles or not. Black Tone would do anything for his friend if she asked. There was no limit to his loyalty, and she knew that.

Having packed Granny's necessary overnight items, he placed the bag near the front door. His aunt called and indicated she'd be by very shortly, so Black Tone left his sleeping grandmother, who was hopefully having pleasant dreams. When he rode by Dre and his crew as they were unpacking yet another load of ill-gotten gains, Black Tone nodded but never cracked a smile. The understanding pertaining to their troubled relationship was extremely mutual: *Don't fuck with me, and I won't fuck with you.*

"Oh my God! Finally! What in the hell took you so damn long? Wild Child and them been down here? Where you been? The light's been out. Folks acting crazy everywhere in town. It's been on the news." Amir held up his cell phone, showing the local breaking news updates.

Black Tone had barely stepped foot out his truck before being bombarded with questions. "Okay. Then, Amir, pump your fucking brakes. They had you covered, so what's the big deal? Besides, the sun ain't even down all the ways yet. You look like you still okay and the building still standing. All the real bullshit jumping off in the inner city, anyhow. Like where I stay at. You know, where your peoples is at!"

Amir momentarily stood silent. He was ashamed of himself. He exhibited selfish intentions in most things that he did, and so the firstborn son had forgotten even to inquire about Pops and his little brothers. He knew his twin cousins, who'd been called in for backup, were no more than two pieces of no-good shit that would slice their own mother's throat if it meant they could get over in the world. Them, Amir didn't worry about. He knew they would be good, by hook or by crook. That sinister bloodline of theirs was tainted years ago. However, Mikey and Hassan were different. Even when he tried to get them to branch off into his side business, they'd been too soft to even attempt to go hard. Pops and his poor sickly mother had spoiled them both, ruined them for the streets. His younger siblings hadn't been forced to run barefoot through the war-torn country he was born in. They were American raised.

"Damn, I got so much on my mind. Fuck. Did you go by there? What's the deal? Is it all good?" Amir responded.

Black Tone smirked as he watched Amir blurt out question after question. Finally, he answered, "Yeah, man. I drove past there, and it looked quiet. It was a few people walking by the front door. I went through the back alley, and the cars were pulled up and locked behind the gate."

"God is good. I'm glad that's one less thing I have to worry about, at least for the time being. As long as Pops and the family is good, I'm good."

After giving Wild Child and the others from Zero Fucks Given that were on post a fist pound, Black Tone and Amir walked inside the empty nightclub. Several battery-charged table candles lit the bar area, making it bright enough to see. Both Amir and his head of security were used to seeing in the always dimly lit establishment, so this was nothing new for them to adapt to.

After making sure the door was closed and they were alone, Amir gave Black Tone an update on what exactly had been happening since the two had parted ways twelve hours earlier. "So, Tone, this morning, as anticipated, I got the package delivered. It was on point, just as promised. Your good friend Brother Rasul came through, as always. It's top quality."

"Cool. That's what's up. A nigga like me aims to please," Black Tone said, nodding his head.

Amir slipped Black Tone his cut of the heroin package. He often played the part of the middleman to cop the drug. Amir and the connect were both Muslim, and he felt that meant something. However, in the drug world, no bona fide plug mattered if you didn't have someone to vouch for your pedigree. Black Tone was Amir's link to his homeboy, so they both made money. After opening up the envelope, Black Tone ran his thumb across the top of the cash, silently counting it. He knew with the money he had in the bank and also hidden in a shoe box at his granny's, he'd be ready to pay for the hip replacement surgery she needed. Her insurance felt she was too old and refused to cover the procedure, but her grandson felt differently. He knew the quality of her life would greatly improve if she could just get out of that hospital bed he was renting.

"Oh yeah. That reminds me. I got a call from Ethan a little while ago," Amir said.

"Ethan, huh? What he wanted?"

"You know he wanted to take a cop and make shit right about that incident last night."

"Yeah, that knucklehead nephew of his. The little idiot with all that mouth. I hope he knows he had that ass kicking coming. We couldn't run the risk of the authorities coming up here last night, because he wanna clown. Especially since my peoples was in town to make that drop-off this morning." Black Tone took his cut of the money out of the envelope and placed it in his front pocket, creating a bulge.

Amir was in total agreement with Black Tone's methods of keeping order at Detroit Live. Although it had been deemed a hot spot with the local cops in the past, since Amir had taken over ownership from his deported third cousin, twice removed, all had been good. The staff and Amir had been forced to call the cops a total of maybe once or twice since he got the keys to the front door and transferred the liquor license. It was Amir's main objective to stay off the radar as much as possible, and if Black Tone made that happen, he was king. No questions asked.

"No, no, no. All was good with him. He knows his nephew all too well, so he said. Ethan said that the boy has been nothing but a headache since he was a small child doing dirt on the block."

"Oh yeah?" For some reason, Black Tone thought about Dre and his longtime shenanigans. He and Li'l Ronnie could have been twins in terms of their demeanor.

"Yeah. He said that sense of entitlement he has because he's his sister's son got him all fucked up, thinking the world owes him something. Ethan told me that his girl was in here watching that boy act a fool and that he needed to be dealt with. So there it is."

Black Tone walked behind the bar and got a bottle of water out of the now nonfunctional refrigerator. Thankfully, it was still cold, and he swallowed the refreshing drink. "Sometimes a good old-fashioned ass kicking is what these lames out here need to act right."

"Well, I told him that what happened last night down here was over with and done, as far as I was concerned. But the boy didn't talk shit and threaten me. He did that to you. I also told him that the package was due in later, and that he'd have to check with you and make sure you was good with it. I mean, the little hood nigga had no respect!" Amir took a seat at the bar and laughed after he referred to Li'l Ronnie as a nigga.

Amir knew Black Tone was going to call him a sand nigga in return, and he did just that. Elated, Black Tone always kept the club and his illegal drug business on target; Amir knew Pops was wrong about him trusting him. Black Tone was more than a bouncer; he was his family. So if he felt Ethan was out of the loop, no matter how much money he spent, then so be it. Point-blank, period, he was out.

"I told him before he cops, you'd holler at him later so y'all could chop it up," Amir added.

CHAPTER TWELVE

Burdened with multiple plastic bags full of food and accessories he, Mikey, and his cousins needed to make it through the night, Hassan kicked twice on the steel door with his Prada loafers. Looking over his shoulder at Alexis's car, he knew she was going to be mad that he hadn't been here to greet her. He knew that she, Mikey, and Pops hadn't always been on the best of terms, but Alexis had never let that stop her from making herself perfectly at home whenever she was up at the store. For Alexis and Hassan, color and religion had never been a major issue between them. Even though they knew any relationship they had would be challenged by both families, they felt their love could be and was "bigger than the game."

"Hey, what took y'all so long to open the door?" Hassan barked when the door was finally opened.

"Slow the fuck down. We ain't hear you, guy. We was at the front of the store, telling some more of them stupid motherfuckers we closed!" one of the twins answered as Mikey, his conscience guilt ridden, stood idly by and mute.

Hassan put the bags on the counter and glanced around the dark store, searching for Alexis. Not seeing her, he immediately turned to his brother and asked him if she was in the bathroom. Receiving no answer, he asked once more. "Yo, Mikey, I said, where ole girl at? I see her car parked out there, so where she at?" Hassan finally powered his cell back on and was blasted with the notifications of several new voice mails.

Mikey, no matter how much he disapproved of his brother and Alexis's relationship, had no desire to be involved in the rape case his lunatic family members would be sure to catch when Alexis woke up from the traumatic beating and sexual assault she had sadly endured. After his trouble-minded cousins reassured him the girl would gladly take a small sum of money and would "get over it," like the many "black whores" they'd done the same sort of thing to in the past, Mikey had prayed that would be the outcome, but he knew deep down in his heart that, tragically, it wouldn't. Family loyalty was above everything else where they came from, and no matter what the circumstances, one member was not to cross another. It was tradition and common law, well, at least in their region of the world. But this was altogether different, and keeping his mouth shut would only slow the inevitable that was going to happen. Lowering his face in shame, Mikey knew he had to confess what had taken place. Even though he hadn't actually touched Alexis himself, he was just as guilty as his crazed cousins, probably even more in his brother's eyes.

"Hassan, look, she came knocking at the door and—"

Seeing that his cousin was the weak link and was not sticking to the game plan, the shorter twin cut Mikey off before he snitched them out. "And I told her we wasn't opening the door for anybody. I told her she wasn't special! I told her to kick rocks."

"What the fuck, dude?" Hassan replied, shocked, as he unpacked the several bags containing the food. "Why you do that dumb shit? She ain't just anybody, fool. That's my girl!"

"Your girl." The twin laughed.

"Yeah, my girl. And if she ain't here, why her car still parked out there?"

Thinking quickly, one twin lied and said he thought that she was with another female and that they must've left in the other girl's car.

Hassan stopped what he was doing to dial Alexis's number, which rang a few times, then went to voice mail. "Well, she ain't answering, but maybe this her that left me a message."

Before Alexis's man could check his voice mail or question them any further, the twins started a false fight with one another as a diversionary tactic. When Hassan and a confused Mikey grabbed the two and separated them, the most boisterous of the pair whispered in Mikey's ear that if they went down, they would drag him down with them. "We already done jailed it, but you haven't!"

Caught up in the commotion, Hassan did just as the twins had hoped: he temporarily forgot about Alexis and her whereabouts. When he finished distributing the food, he told them what crazy and over-the-top type of things was going on all throughout Detroit. He informed them that the National Guard had finally been called out to patrol the perimeter of the entire city to ensure none of the criminal rampage taking place would spill into good, law-abiding communities. They weren't the least bit stunned by this news, even agreeing with the governor's bold last-minute decision. Hassan also told them it was rumored that residents of those other counties and jurisdictions had been strongly encouraged to carry their licensed pistols in full sight, so any wannabe thugs spilling over from Detroit would know not to corrupt the safety of their homes and businesses.

"It's mad crazy out there. It's like some sort of movie or some shit like that," Hassan explained as they ate. "I mean, people in long lines at the gas stations who dumb enough to still be serving out the front door, abandoned cars that have run out of gas being set on fire in the middle of Woodward and on Six Mile and down across John R . . . I mean, damn." He took a huge gulp of cold pop that one of the twins had grabbed from the cooler while double-checking on the sly that Alexis was still passed out. "I ain't never seen so many . . ."

"What? Wild niggas?" One twin remarked judgmentally, his words echoing off the walls of the store.

"I wasn't gonna say that." Hassan frowned.

The other twin anxiously jumped in with his two cents' worth of commentary. "Fuck that, Hassan. Let's keep it real. You know, like I know, them monkey-minded abeeds can't act right on no regular day, so you know damn well they gonna be tripping now!"

"Why y'all always gotta talk shit about African Americans like that?" Hassan calmly questioned as his older brother Mikey remained peculiarly silent. "Everybody ain't like that. It's like saying all of us are terrorists because we Muslims or from the Middle Eastern part of the world."

"Naw. Fuck all that politically correct talk. The way these black people disrespect they damn self is on them. Now, come on, Hassan. You know, like we all do, niggas gonna be niggas to the day they die . . . fried chicken and watermelon eating, pants sagging, forty-ounce drinking . . . hoes not knowing who they baby daddy is," replied the twin who had last spoken.

"Yeah, bro, and don't forget stealing everything that ain't bolted down as they smoking a blunt but can't pay their bills!" the other twin added.

Normally, Hassan was against racism in any shape or form, but as they said, "At one point or another everything in the dark has a way of finding itself to the light." Although he had strong feelings and a deep-rooted love for Alexis, after a few more minutes of coaxing and peer pressure, he joined his two loudmouthed cousins in some of their ridiculing of Blacks, Hispanics, Chinese,

and—not to be left out—the infamous White man. Before
he knew it, Hassan was discussing with them the differ-
ence between getting some bomb-ass head from a black
chick, namely, Alexis, and the Muslim Middle Eastern
girl from the mosque his parents wanted him so badly to
marry. Being young and stupid, he then started bragging
about how good Alexis's pussy was and how she low key
worshipped him. At one point, caught up in showing
out with the fellas, Hassan confessed that even if it was
proven that her baby was his, he couldn't legally claim
it if he hoped to get his financial share of his Pops's
business holdings whenever he died.

"That's my girl. I ain't gonna lie," he asserted, getting
cocky with his comments. "And me and her gonna always
hang out. But you know I can't ever, ever take her home!
That can never happen. It would kill my mother."

Mikey was full of guilt, not knowing what to say or
do next. He still hadn't touched a bite of his food as he
focused on the door of the walk-in cooler, where Alexis
had been left, knocked out cold. His father would be
mortified about the despicable act he'd allowed his cousins to perpetrate as he dumbly stood by. Pops would be
disgraced, not only in the family, but in the community
as well. Mikey wanted to get Alexis help, but even if he
were to stand up to his cousins and call the police, there
weren't any cops to call. After all, Detroit was temporarily
lawless.

CHAPTER THIRTEEN

Li'l Ronnie had his gun shoved in the elderly woman's face. In her lifetime of seventy-six years her weary eyes had definitely seen their fair share of struggle, heartbreak, and turmoil. One might say her cup had been overrun with a dose of each. But this was much different than anything the God-fearing woman had ever had to deal with. This was against everything she'd ever prayed about and everything her grandson had always shielded her from. Since she'd raised Anthony, he had been her constant protector. Come hell or high water, he'd shielded her from the residential dooms most that lived in the city of Detroit had to deal with.

If Black Tone was here, he'd never let this type of thing take place, but unfortunately, he was not. While he was preoccupied tending to the next man's household, his own had been violated. Granny was here alone, by herself. Thanks to his "zero fucks given" behavior and attitude, this pistol-brandishing menace had made himself the king of Black Tone's castle and the immediate overseer of Granny's fate. The bedridden woman was terrified half to death.

"You know why I'm here old woman, don't you?" Li'l Ronnie had suddenly bossed up and become brave. Happily discovering Black Tone was not on the other side of the door, he showed his excitement by towering over the senior citizen and fanatically questioning her. The growing temptation just to take a pillow and cover her head was starting to take over. He could just use his palms and push down, and it would all be over. Black Tone could come in and find his old granny dead and hurt, the same way he was hurt. But Li'l Ronnie felt that him signing her death warrant would be too easy. He wanted his true nemesis to bleed directly.

"When is that faggot-ass Black Tone coming back? Where he at? He wanna be running around like he so fucking tough and his ass can't be got. Like he untouchable. Well, fuck. Look at me now, all up in this nigga shit!" Li'l Ronnie's hate-filled rant worsened as he had not received the evil satisfaction he was looking for.

Granny had yet to mutter a single, solitary word since the ordeal started. Shocked to find out it was not her grandson making all that noise and commotion from the other side of her closed bedroom door, she didn't know what to say or what to think. Silently, she prayed she was having a terrible nightmare and would wake up soon. However, after a few more minutes of getting threatened, she decided to speak. Parting her dry, cracked lips, she started to quote bible verses.

Definitely not in the mood to have church, Li'l Ronnie vindictively pressed one hand roughly over her mouth, demanding she shut up. She didn't. She wouldn't. When her attacker's voice got louder, she prayed. When he grabbed her by both shoulders and shook her until the headboard slammed back and forth against the wall, she prayed. When the devil's servant started to lose his patience altogether, he resentfully slapped her face repeatedly.

The old woman was close to passing out but endured the stinging, excruciating pain of it all and still prayed.

Li'l Ronnie was frustrated. She was strong willed. He was out of breath and quickly came to the realization that he had been beaten by Black Tone the night before and now his granny was winning. Infuriated at the sheer thought of it all, he felt his already explosive anger grow. Locking eyes with the wrinkle-skinned warrior, Li'l Ronnie warned her if she even whispered God's name once more, it would certainly be her last time. Granny was defiant as she spoke out one final time. This time louder and with more conviction than before.

"Yea, though I walk through the valley of the shadow of death, I will fear no evil; for thou art with me; thy rod and—"

Before she could finish the verse, Li'l Ronnie dug deep down inside himself and brought up a huge glob of saliva. Showing the ultimate disrespect he could muster, the deranged monster hawked in her face. "Fuck you, old bitch, and fuck God too," he yelled out as the thick, smelly discharge slid down from her eyes and each of her cheeks.

"And thy staff, they comfort me," She barely got the last strong-willed words out before Li'l Ronnie made good on his threat.

Sinister in his intentions, he reached down and grabbed the lower rails on the hospital rental bed. Using all the strength the devil had blessed him with at that moment, he lifted the bed up to his chest level. "Talk that shit now!" Callously, he then sent the bed crashing clear over to the other side of the room. When it slammed against the wall, Granny's frail body flew from underneath the sheet and the thin blanket. "I warned you, old bitch! Now pray about that," he taunted as she wept, painfully wedged in between the metal frame, the floor, and the wall.

Before the tormentor could turn to retrieve his gun off of his victim's nightstand and leave, Li'l Ronnie noticed something that looked out of place where the bed once was.

What the fuck?

He bent over and picked up an oversize Nike shoe box. After opening it slowly, Li'l Ronnie couldn't believe his eyes. Finally, he would get some of the satisfaction he was looking for when he first kicked in the side door. Li'l Ronnie gazed into the box containing green-, red-, blue-, and tan-colored rubber bands wrapped around nice-size rolled bundles of money. After all he'd been through since the night before, he felt he deserved a come up. Of course, he believed this monetary blessing was definitely it. Li'l Ronnie knew the old woman hadn't accumulated this type of cash, and laughed out loud, knowing he'd found Black Tone's stash on the humble.

Fuck it! That bitch nigga just bought himself some time. He can live a few more days and feel the loss of his hopefully dead-ass granny and his grip.

Li'l Ronnie tucked the shoe box underneath his arm. With his gun once again held high defensively, he ran out into the hallway. Seeing and hearing no one coming to the elderly woman's aid, he then returned to the kitchen, jumped down the four stairs heading toward the side door, and left the same way he'd entered.

Stopping at the edge of the red rosebushes that lined the front of the porch, Li'l Ronnie looked to the left, then right. Overly cautious, he had to make sure there was no extra pair of eyes watching him. If so, he'd have to deal with them, just as he had the stubborn old woman. Once he felt safe, he darted across the street and disappeared between the two abandoned houses he'd perched between earlier.

Back in his truck, Li'l Ronnie placed the show box full of cash and his gun down on the passenger seat. After starting the engine, he put his beloved Benz truck into gear and skirted off. Before making it out of the neighborhood, he crossed paths with the same guy he thought he'd recognized earlier. For a brief second, the two locked eyes. Slamming down on his brakes to avoid an accident, Li'l Ronnie allowed the other guy to have the right of way.

CHAPTER FOURTEEN

Lying in a small pool of blood that had grown between her legs, Alexis felt an excruciating throbbing pain not only in her face but in her vagina as well.

Oh my God. Why?

Battered and bruised, she tried to stand to her feet but couldn't. She wanted to yell out for help, despite the ache in her swollen jaw, but she did not know if her attackers were still close by.

Why did they do this? Why Mikey ain't stop them? she thought.

As her eyes fought to focus in the pitch-black rear walk-in cooler, she heard voices in the near distance. Disoriented, Alexis thought one belonged to her beloved Hassan, but she wasn't sure.

If that's him, why ain't he helping me? Why is he just out there laughing?

Realizing that staying there, waiting to be gang-raped again possibly, wasn't an option, she gathered her strength the best she could. Wanting nothing more than to see her infant son's face once more, the single mother prayed, asking God to help her. As she turned over on her stomach, Alexis reached her arms forward and balled up her fists, and then she crawled, scraping her elbows along the way on the sticky floor. Halfway to the sound of the voice that she now recognized for certain as Hassan's, she saw a faint blinking light over to the side. Getting closer, she saw it was her purse and cell. Fumbling with the phone, Alexis saw Hassan had indeed called her, but for what?

He called but he is not back here helping me? He in there, chopping it up with them animals, laughing and talking shit!

At this point, she didn't know who to trust, especially since the two goons who had assaulted her were obviously friends of her so-called man.

Why in the fuck he tell me to come up here, and he knew he was gonna be gone? He set me up!

Calling the police for assistance was not happening. There weren't any on duty. Requesting an ambulance to treat her wounds was also not an option. Detroit was on shutdown, and like the news reports stated, it was every man for themselves. Feeling totally betrayed and confused about how to get out of the store alive and back to her son, Alexis texted the only two people who, despite the vile things they had said to each other, would have her back—Dre and, of course, her good friend Anthony.

At da store. Nine-one-one.

As far back as beepers and cell phones went, she and her brother had made a pact that no matter what kind of bullshit was going on between the two of them, they would never, ever use the code 911 with each other unless it was a matter of life or death. And other than the night their overly religious mother had died, he and Alexis never had. That was, until now.

Out of breath, she hid behind some cardboard boxes, just in case one of the twins returned, wanting round two of abusing her. Painstakingly listening to Hassan, the love of her life, and the coldhearted attackers joke about her and all other black people, like they were common dogs that roamed the streets, Alexis's hatred for Hassan grew instantly and her belief that her "baby daddy" had truly set her up to be raped increased. Before she knew what was what, she once again lost consciousness. While she was out of it, Alexis's mind drifted back to the day her son was born and she recalled how ecstatic Hassan had claimed to be, even saying he'd denounce his family if they dared to mistreat his firstborn seed for being half African American.

Black Tone and Amir were going back and forth over which person would be stopping by to pick up what package. Not wanting his team to know he was as deep off into the program as he was, Black Tone kept a careful watch on the front doors of the club. He'd told his cousin to come and get him if anything out of the ordinary jumped off. They all understood it would be dark soon and the situation the cash-strapped city was in would soon be plummeting from bad to worse. Well, as most of the mayhem was going down in residential neighborhoods, a few daredevils might be tempted to take a walk on the wild side and try Detroit Live. Black Tone was dedicated to not letting that take place.

Amir took out his cell and started to calculate. Having ordered just enough product to make him a nice hefty sum off the top, he informed Black Tone that possibly leaving Ethan out of the equation this time would maybe not be such a terrible idea.

"That man might need to learn a lesson or two. He can't control his own flesh and blood. The boy shows no respect. He is an animal. And maybe if he can't control his family, he can't control a team. It's pretty much downhill from there." Amir looked up, shaking his head at Ethan's apparent overall weakness as a leader. "If you cannot control those simple things in life, then you cannot control your mouth when need be. A weak man may speak about things he has no reason to speak about if the right amount of pressure is applied."

Black Tone easily agreed. He may have protested about a lot of things that Amir had said about this or that, but this time Amir was speaking the truth. Ethan might need to fall back off the package. The East Side legend maybe did need to get his house in order. After all, Li'l Ronnie did go all the way overboard by claiming his uncle had his back, no matter what. Maybe Ethan did want revenge on Black Tone, Amir, and the club in general. *Who knows?* Black Tone thought as he felt his cell phone vibrate. Maybe he was just playing the game and taking a cop because he still wanted some of that good uncut heroin Amir was getting imported.

"You know what, Amir? For once, you ain't gonna get no argument outta me. True spit, you might be right. Let's freeze that guy out this go-around and see if he still have love for us then. If he still got loyalty to what's right or wrong where his peoples involved. Like motherfuckers say, 'Tell a nigga no. Then you really gonna see how they feel.'" Digging deep into his front pocket, Black Tone removed his still vibrating cell. Glancing at the screen, he saw his aunt's name and number flashing. No doubt he was relieved, because he assumed she was calling him to let him know that his granny was with her, safe and sound.

"Hey, Auntie," he said, changing his demeanor and smiling as he answered.

"Anthony! Anthony! Where are you? Oh my God! Where are you?"

Hearing the panic in her voice, Black Tone leaped to his feet, causing the bar stool he was sitting on to tumble over to the floor. "Auntie, what is it? What's wrong?"

"It's . . . it's your grandmother. Please, Anthony, you have to come home. This bed is too heavy to lift by myself. I tried to call the police and the ambulance, but they said they couldn't come! Please hurry," she begged before abruptly hanging up.

In a rush, Black Tone left Amir standing behind the bar, wondering where his head of security was going on what was sure to be the worst night of the year. Black Tone told Wild Child to give one of the other guys his walkie-talkie and said they had to roll out, and seconds later the two tore out of the fenced-in parking lot. In the midst of Black Tone explaining that something was wrong with Granny back at the house, his cell vibrated once more. Snatching it up from the middle console, he saw that it was a 911 text from Alexis saying that she was up at the store. Jumping down on the freeway, he didn't bother to text his friend back, assuming that she, like his aunt, was getting in touch with him to tell him to come home as soon as possible.

"Nine-one-one? Damn, Alexis. What you done got yourself into?" Dre mumbled, dropping a pillowcase filled with PlayStation games and DVDs they'd just stolen from a house. "Hey, y'all, hold up with what y'all doing, and let's roll up to the corner store real quick."

"For what, dude?" his boy barked as he tried to get two air conditioners to fit in the trunk of the already packed rusted Ford Taurus. "I wanna go back inside and get them pictures off the wall for my mama's living room."

"Man, fuck all that! We can come back later for them bitches. It ain't like no police coming no time soon!"

"But . . ."

"Listen, fool. Alexis just hit me up. She needs me, so let's ride! Now!"

"Dawg, the store ain't even open, so what's so important up there? Besides, wasn't she just going in on your ass and us?"

"And so damn what, guy? That's my sister! Blood thicker than all that other shit you talking about." Dre had had enough of talking to his boy and started the engine. "You rolling or what, motherfucker? 'Cause I'm out!"

Barely able to jump in the front seat as the car skirted off, Dre's homeboy started asking him questions he didn't have the answers to. Driving by several houses with the owners posted on their front porches, guns in hand, the neighborhood menaces made mental notes to avoid breaking into those houses altogether later in the night, or risk wearing body bag suits by morning. Not caring about stop signs or anything else, Dre flew up to a white Benz truck and mean mugged the driver, who waved his hand up for him to go ahead and go first, even though Dre didn't have the right of way.

Where I know that little nigga from? he briefly wondered, swerving by the expensive rimmed vehicle.

Minutes later Dre pulled up to the front of the store and saw no signs of his sister's vehicle. Knowing Hassan, Mikey, and Pops parked in the rear of the normally busy building, he busted a U-turn and flew up the alleyway. Right next to Mikey's Dodge Magnum and another car was Alexis's Honda. Wasting no more time, he headed to the back door of the store while calling his sister's cell. Banging on the rear door as hard as he could, Dre grew angrier the longer it took his sister or Hassan to respond. With her cell phone ringing a few times, then going to voice mail, he started to feel some sort of way.

"Yo, Hassan. Alexis! Open the motherfucking door!"

"We closed, Dre!" Hassan shouted back to make sure Dre heard him through the thick metal material separating the two of them. "And your sister ain't here."

Assuming he was lying and was just trying to stop him from talking to Alexis, who'd just texted 911, indicating something was seriously wrong, Dre went all the way in.

"Look, you rag-wearing son of a bitch! You stopping my money flow out in these streets by playing games. Now tell my sister to come to the damn door."

"Hey, you nigga," one twin recklessly shouted with a tone of entitlement. "He said her black ass ain't here, so get the fuck on! Go eat a banana or some shit!"

Dre didn't recognize the voice, but he knew Hassan and Mikey would have never called him no racial slur, knowing there would definitely be some drama behind it. "Man, whoever the fuck you is running your mouth behind that locked door, fall back and suck my dick! And, Hassan, tell my goddamned sister to come out here before I really get pissed."

"Dre, for real, I ain't messing around. She ain't here, fam! I wouldn't lie to you!"

"Then why her car here, fool?" Dre pointed at the Honda, as if Hassan could magically see through the steel door. "She texted me she was up here and it was a fucking emergency!"

Hassan had witnessed Alexis's brother and his ruthless crew skull drag more than a few guys out in the middle of Linwood and stump they brains out just for fun. And even though he carried a pistol and was far from a punk in his own Dearborn neighborhood, this was Detroit, specifically the Linwood, Dexter, and Davison area, and it was well known throughout the entire city that motherfuckers born and raised around those parts were about that life for real. They weren't just bigger than the game—they were the game.

"Yo, abeed, stop all this questioning and take your bitch ass back to the crack house and check up on your mama!" the same twin yelled as Mikey and Hassan begged him to stop. "Naw, this nigga around here at my uncle store like he running shit! Fuck him and his good pussy-having sister!"

"What! How the hell you know that?" Hassan said, offended. He couldn't believe what had just been said about his girl.

"Hassan, chill out, cuz, and just let my brother handle that escaped slave," the other twin shouted through the door, which, thankfully, was bolted. "You the one that said she had good pussy and the bomb-ass head. You the one that said you be having her on her knees, begging to eat watermelon and get fucked in the ass! You the one that said her baby was a toss-up hood spawn!"

Hassan calmed down, knowing that what his cousin was saying was true. Regretfully, while he was talking shit, like most guys did when they were with their home-boys, he had made those god-awful remarks, and they were just getting repeated, only to the wrong person—Alexis's bloodthirsty brother. The fact that she was in school and was working on her degree, he had failed to say. The reality that she was a good mother to the baby he knew in his heart was truly his son, he hadn't expressed. Hassan had hundreds of positive things that he could've said to show Alexis's true character, but he had kept his mouth closed, showing out for the fellas.

After calling Alexis repeatedly and getting the same response, which was none, Dre felt his heart race with rage. The more racist trash talk the twins engaged in, the more he was determined to get inside the building and see what was really good with his sister and, more importantly, why she was just sitting back, letting these fools go ham. He knew damn well she hadn't text him 911 to listen to this bullshit.

"You piss-smelling, bomb-making terrorists better open this motherfucking door before I deport y'all asses my damn self!" he shouted.

CHAPTER FIFTEEN

"What's going on your way, Amir? I ain't heard from my homeboy yet. What's the deal?" Ethan was both anxious and curious. He had his money already counted and in a thick yellow manila envelope, just the way Amir always requested. Although prejudiced Amir wasn't the only connect in the general area, he damn straight had the strongest product for one's money. "I've been waiting for Black Tone to get back at me so we could squash that situation once and for all, but still no word."

Amir was in his feelings before Ethan called. Knowing that his best two chances of avoiding any unforeseen trouble this evening, namely, Black Tone and his cousin Wild Child, had jumped up and left, no explanation given, he was sick with it. He'd overheard Black Tone address the caller as Auntie, so he assumed whatever was wrong was family related, but so damn what? Like most people in the world, Amir wanted what he wanted when he wanted it. And now he wanted and needed Black Tone's muscle power on deck.

Sitting behind his desk, with a few candles lighting the room, Amir held his gun in one hand and stared at the master walkie-talkie lying on top of a stack of papers. Now was not the time for Ethan, or any other person other than his constantly calling father, to be bothering him. In between Pops pressing him to go by the family store and Black Tone refusing to pick up his calls, the club owner drug plug was heated.

"Look, Ethan, I don't know what to tell you. Black Tone ain't here, so you just gotta hold up."

Ethan didn't like what he was hearing or the manner in which it was being said. He hoped, for business's sake, his main pipeline wasn't slowing down, because if so, his spots and people would suffer immediately. He was already close to out and needed to re-up bad.

"Damn, Amir. I mean, I thought me and you already made peace on that bullshit my sister's son did last night. I thought we was all good with it."

"We is all good with it as far as I'm concerned, but like I said, you need to holler at your boy. I mean, truth be told, he the one that brought you in and cosign for it, so you and him dealing firsthand is only right."

Ethan felt he could read between the lines and felt some sort of way. Not ready to just lie down and play dead about a delay in getting his needy crew back out the gate, he pushed the issue, hoping Amir would give in. "Look, dude, we been doing business for some time now. My money is always straight. I don't complain if the weight is slightly off, and I never, ever keep you waiting. I keeps it official with you from beginning to end."

Amir thought back to the discussion he and Black Tone had had moments before he left. *Tell a person no, then the real them will emerge.* Still upset with Black Tone, Amir threw him underneath the bus to test the theory.

"Okay, Ethan, you right. You have been holding you end down from day one since we linked up. And I told you, I'm good with it. But your nephew clowned here on Black Tone's watch, and he's not as forgiving as I am. I watched the tape a few times, and I can't lie. I don't blame him for being angry. The boy was acting out, hitting my female customers on the ass, spitting at the waitresses, and mistreating the lives of not only Tone but the rest of my staff as well. It went on for a good thirty minutes or so before we finally took action."

Ethan was ashamed of what he was hearing. He was very much old school when it came to the streets and prided himself on being righteous with everyone he dealt with. Now, after years of being a force to be reckoned with not only on the east side of Detroit, but in the entire city, he found that Li'l Ronnie had ruined his reputation. And not only his reputation, but possibly his best plug too.

"Look, Amir, I'm not one to ask another grown man for favors, let alone ask him something twice. Now, my word is my word. Always was, always will be. Now I have handled my nephew and set him down from the game and the streets until further notice. So if I need to speak to Black Tone to tell him that much directly to keep our business relationship intact, then so be it. But I have to know if he's willing to talk soon. If not, I have to take my money elsewhere."

Amir respected that Ethan was trying to keep his cool in light of possibly losing that good uncut product, but only time would tell, since Black Tone was not available to speak directly to him.

"Well, like I said, Ethan, he'll be in touch as soon as possible, so just sit tight. He had a family emergency that just jumped off, I guess."

Ethan ended the conversation on a good note, as he always did when speaking to those outside the fold. He never allowed strangers or otherwise to see him sweat or come out of character. Even though he could read in between the lines and knew he was in the process of being cut off from the bag, Ethan kept his fronts off.

This ho-ass nephew of mine gonna mess around and cost me a whole gang of money and put a lot of my hard-earned spots out of business if I can't secure that work. Fuck that! He done been in my pockets long enough, doing stupid bullshit, and now the damn connect is jeopardized. Blood or not, that boy gotta pay just like the next nigga would that cross me!

"Yo, get me them three fucking idiots that run with my nephew," he demanded to one of his main henchmen who hardly left his side. "I wanna see how loyal they pussy ass is to the family. Yeah, they was smart enough to get the hell outta Dodge when Ronnie was acting a fool last night, claiming my name in vain, but they was also not smart enough to not abandon they manz. Now is about to be the true test of what they made out of."

It was nearing dark when Li'l Ronnie's three running buddies were shoved in the room where Ethan was holding court. While two of them held their heads down in semi-shame over what had taken place, one stood tall. He appeared to have no remorse or second thoughts about his actions the prior night. He was a true man-child and looked directly into Ethan's eyes, showing no signs of fear. Deciding to test the three of them, Ethan started to ask each one their individual version of what took place. He already had what he believed to be the raw and real account from his girl Sable, and the club camera footage, which Amir had supplied, corroborated her account. Just as he thought, the first young guy kinda shrugged his shoulders, torn between ratting his boy out and being honest. However the third one, whom Ethan seemed to take a liking to, did just as he had hoped he would—speak out.

"Look, sir, I don't mean to be disrespectful to you or Li'l Ronnie. I mean, I know he's your blood and all. And I know he was the one that put us onto the bag, but when he drink and take them pills, his ass be on an entire other level," he bravely confessed, not caring how the man who ultimately put money in his pockets felt. "A nigga like me ain't got no real family or no real place to lay my head half the time, so I can't fuck around and get my ass choked out on the humble behind no dumb shit. Where I'm gonna be sick, broke arms or legs, and can't hustle, right? I ain't got no mama to baby me or no girl. I'm solo. Fuck all that! I'm trying to survive and live out in these streets, not be a clown."

Ethan grinned as he sat back on the couch. With ten or eleven long silver flashlights on the coffee table as he awaited nightfall, he was ready to put the three young night warriors to work. The two who were quiet and had no fire in their asses, Ethan had them check in with one of his people in charge of the corners. Passing them each a flashlight, he suggested they tool up and get posted.

"Y'all best stay alert on them corners. Ain't no telling what other crew might wanna take advantage of the power outage and make a play." Seeing them both leave the same way they did when they were ushered in, heads lowered, Ethan knew it wouldn't be long off into the game before their families would be burying them. It was easy to see they didn't have the heart for the streets.

Now left alone with the third boy, Ethan smirked and asked him to have a seat. "Looka here, youngin'. You seem like you about that life. Are you?"

His reply was brief. "I survive. I do what I gotta do."

"Well, tell me this. Just how did you and my nephew hook up? Where you know him from?"

"We was locked up together."

"Locked up, huh?"

"Yeah, we was in two different units, but I worked in the laundry, so I got around."

Ethan knew what that meant. He knew the boy was already accustomed to doing and getting things for a price. Before he cut off into him, Ethan hoped this thing he was about to ask him would be no different. Pay for hire. No questions asked.

"Okay, then, I heard that. Well, I can see in between them other two lames that just left and my nephew that you the one. You the shooter. You the one that makes all the real decisions for all them and probably keeps them from being murdered out here. True or false?"

The young man never blinked an eye when Ethan was describing who he believed him to be. He just sat mute, wondering where all this was going. After listening to his boss make several more assessments, he finally spoke.

"Mr. E, I mean no disrespect at all, but where is all this leading up to? Is there something I can do for you? Because if there is, it ain't no thang. I'll put in work. But I ain't no pussy with shit I do. I ain't into hurting small kids and definitely no old women!"

"Old women and kids? What in the fuck would make you say that rotten bullshit? I ain't never been about that type of garbage and damn showl wouldn't endorse it. I mean, come on, youngin'. I know we out here breaking the white man's law every fucking day. But it gotta be some sort of rules to this here game. Some sort of restrictions. And old women and kids is it."

The young guy wanted to prove himself worthy of moving up the food chain in the organization while somewhat testing Ethan's claims of boundaries. He saw Mr. E's facial expression as he spoke and watched his mannerisms. But he'd learned in his young life what people said and did were two entirely different things.

"Look, sir, like I said earlier, I don't mean any type of disrespect to you at all. And I give Li'l Ronnie props for turning me on to make that money sitting in the spot, but how he roll, that ain't me."

"What the fuck he done did now?" Ethan jumped up, not knowing what he was about to hear. He could tell the youngin' was holding back but at the same time wanted to divulge a few things.

"Hey, I ain't no rat, and I ain't about dry snitching on my homeboy. But what he did was foul, and I can't respect that shit. Fuck that. We all got or had a grandmother at one time or another."

Ethan was confused. He was also exhausted from playing this cat and mouse game. With fury written all over his face, he demanded that this boy who ran with his nephew tell him what was or had jumped off before the tables turned on him.

"Listen, dawg, you better get to talking. I ain't feeling all this extra-slick conversation we having about this or that. Now, what the fuck did that knucklehead do now?"

It didn't take him long to put Ethan up on the latest stunt Li'l Ronnie had done and the fact that Li'l Ronnie had then called him and the others they ran with to brag about it.

Ethan's reaction was heard way down on the corners he'd sent the other two packing to. Pounding his fist against the wall, he made a huge hole in the drywall. He prayed to God it wasn't true. He hoped his sister's son hadn't been so dumb, so stupid, and so reckless to beat up an old woman. And to make matters worse, that old woman was Black Tone's grandmother.

"Fuck, naw. Tell me you making this shit up!" Ethan ran up on the boy and yanked him by his collar the same way he'd done to Li'l Ronnie. "Tell me that ho-ass nigga ain't do that shit!"

"He called us, saying he beat the blood outta her and found some cash. He said he was gonna go ball out tomorrow, after he go to the crib and rest his leg that was still hurting."

Ethan couldn't believe what his ears were hearing. If what was just said was true, then not only had Li'l Ronnie fucked up the connect for sure, but he'd also started what was about to be a full-blown war. He knew Black Tone and Amir were businessmen and tried to avoid the day-to-day hassles that came with the game, but Ethan also knew this was going to be personal. After all, it was the man's grandmother. It had to be on. And cutting him off from the package was just the beginning. Now what Amir had claimed about Black Tone having a family emergency made sense.

Ethan was now madder than before. His nephew had to go if the team was to survive. If it got out in the streets that he condoned bullshit like that, then sooner or later no plug would fuck with him. He was pissed and started to scheme. He released his grip on the youngin' and had him fix his shirt.

"Okay, then, I'm gonna put you onto something. Then I can see how you really move. Now, what did you say your name was again?"

"I didn't," the young guy announced as he stood with chest stuck out, ready to hear what was really good with Mr. E. "But they call me J-Blaze."

Ethan was elated. He wished his own blood was as gangsta and smooth with it as this kid appeared to be. If all worked out, he'd just got him a young dog who knew how to run wild in the mean, cutthroat blocks of Detroit and come back home when he heard his master call.

"All right, then, J-Blaze. Here's what I want you to do." Ethan laid out his murderous plan before calling Amir back to let him know he was apologetic over what his nephew had done to Black Tone's grandmother and to reassure him the boy's days on this earth were numbered, blood or not.

Making their way up to the corners they were assigned to guard, one of Li'l Ronnie's so-called friends decided to put his homeboy up on game. They knew it just wasn't by coincidence them and J-Blaze, that lunatic, out-for-self ass, was just summoned to the boss's hood headquarters. Something was about to go down. And after being slow grilled about the guy who had originally put them on, namely, Li'l Ronnie, it was easy to see he was going to have to pay for what had popped off at Detroit Live. Time and time again everyone had been warned about set tripping in public. Yet when Li'l Ronnie got drunk and high off pills, he broke every rule his uncle had put in place.

The one guy dialed Li'l Ronnie's number, with the intention to tell him what they thought was poised to happen at the hands of Ethan, and his homeboy picked up, laughing. Li'l Ronnie smiled and joked before he got the news that his financial gain celebration was completely ruined.

"I'm not sure, dawg, but your uncle seemed like he was straight pissed. He had all of us standing up like we was about to get fucked up for even knowing your crazy ass! He had that look in his eye."

"Oh yeah?" Li'l Ronnie schemed as his boy spoke, giving him a much-needed heads-up.

"Yeah, fam and that fool J-Blaze still in there, chopping it up with your peoples. Ain't no telling what his grimy ass in there saying."

Li'l Ronnie hung up the phone and decided that just like he brought the noise directly to Black Tone and hit him where it hurt, he'd fuck up his uncle's world too, just like that.

CHAPTER SIXTEEN

After regaining consciousness, Alexis scrambled to get her bearings. Hearing the thunderous noise of arguing voices, she fought to stand on her feet, though she was groggy. Nursing an extremely numb face, with a ripped T-shirt hanging off her shoulder, the young mother quietly stumbled from the rear of the store. With no lights on in the store, Alexis soon noticed Hassan and whoever the men were who had raped her. They now had several more candles lighting up the back area, near the door. As she scrunched down behind the potato chip racks, her fury intensified as she listened to the terrible things that were being said not only about African Americans as a whole, but also about her as an individual, thanks to Hassan. Weak, feeling dizzy again, she knew she had to get on the other side of the door with her brother if she wanted to live. It was apparent whose side her "baby daddy" was on, so from this point forward, Hassan was a non-factor to her survival.

Look at them eating food, drinking pop, and smoking hookah like they just ain't violate me.

Leaving a trail of dark blood with every step she meticulously fought to take, Alexis was determined to make it out of the store alive, but not before making the disrespectful assholes pay for what they did.

Ain't no sense in calling the police, because even if they were working, these rapist bastards' family would pay their way out of it, or they'd just leave the country and go back to where they came from.

Alexis crept toward the shotgun that was propped over in the corner of the store. With Hassan and the two goons preoccupied at the door, arguing with Dre, Alexis searched the dim candlelit area and finally saw Mikey sitting on a milk crate with his face buried in his hands, rocking back and forth. Hearing what Hassan said about her and their baby was the last straw as she eagerly emerged out of the shadows, catching all four of them all off guard.

"I'm a nigga, huh? Is that right? Just another dumb nigga bitch you getting pussy from! It could be any nigga baby, huh? A toss-up?"

As the three spun around in shock and Mikey raised his head, they were met with Alexis standing tall, aiming the barrel of the gun at them.

"Alexis!" Hassan's eyes grew wide, and he wondered where she'd come from and why she had a gun pointed in his direction.

"Open that motherfucking door," she demanded, daring any of them to move. "Right fucking now! I'm not bullshitting!"

Hassan took one step toward her and immediately knew his "baby mama" wasn't playing when she recklessly let loose, striking one of her assailants in the stomach and the other in the chest area. Shocked that she'd actually fired the gun, he started to sweat, fearing for his own safety. He couldn't grasp what was going on. Completely confused by seeing things go from zero to ten just like that, not knowing what to think, Hassan felt his heart race.

Watching both his cousins, who were now on the floor, begging for mercy, he started to sweat as Alexis got closer. When she was finally all the way out of the shadows, he quickly noticed the bruises on her swollen face and her torn shirt.

"Alexis, bae, what happened to you? What happened to your face?" Truly unaware of what had taken place, an innocent to the attack on his girl, Hassan tried taking a step closer and was met with the sound of another shotgun blast. This time the bullet hit Mikey in the neck. "Ask your grimy-ass brother who stood there, watching them motherfuckers rape me." Her arms shook as she held the heavy gun, and her voice cracked as she spoke. "He ain't even help me. I know him and your father never liked me, but to let them motherfuckers violate me like they did, fuck that!"

Instinctively rushing to his brother's side, Hassan was beet red, and his face was full of tears. "Rape? Huh? I don't know what you talking about, I swear! Why you doing this, Alexis? Why? We gotta get my brother some help!" His hands were full of blood as he tried to cover the gushing wound. "We gotta call an ambulance!"

"Ambulance," Alexis loudly mocked, feeling justified in her revenge and not caring about the consequences, which were sure to follow. "You mean the same ambulance your fake-ass brother called for me? You mean that one?"

"Bae, please. He's dying."

"And?" Her response was callous and cold as she still held the gun high.

"And we gotta get him some help quick, before he bleed out. Please, bae, please." Hassan then started praying in Arabic while holding his older sibling, further infuriating Alexis.

"You know what, Hassan? Fuck him and fuck you, too, for sitting up here talking shit about me and letting them thugs rape me like I ain't nothing but garbage!" The earsplitting sound of several shotgun blasts didn't prevent Dre from continuing to bang on the door, trying to come to his sister's aid.

As he continued to knock, Alexis was busy revealing to Hassan that she'd heard everything he'd said about her and their love child. "Did you not hear me say they raped me? Look at me face! Don't you care about that?"

"Yeah, I do," he yelled back across the room. "I swear for Allah I do, but my brother needs help right now, Alexis! Are you crazy or something! You acting like an animal! What's wrong with you people today?"

"Wow. An *animal? You people?* Damn, Hassan. I thought you were different from your father and the rest of your prejudiced family." Alexis grinned slightly, not really believing he had had the nerve to say that stereo-typical bullshit directly to her face. "My brother was right about you," she sadly announced while stepping over one of the barely alive twins. "When it comes down to it, Dre wasn't lying. Bottom line, it's us versus y'all!"

"I didn't mean it like that. Alexis, you know I love you and the baby! I wanna marry you one day, be a family! You being black doesn't matter to me. It never did. I swear," Hassan pleaded and begged. "But please, we gotta get Mikey some help quick, before it's too late. You right. Fuck my cousins. But not my brother. Alexis, please."

Numb to what he was saying now, Alexis kept hearing the many ugly things Hassan had said earlier about her and their baby repeat in her ears. She reached her hand over to the silver heavy-duty bolts and slid each one to the side. Using the back of her body, she threw her weight onto the metal door, causing it to fly open. With the late evening daylight beaming in from the alleyway, Alexis now could get a full, clear view of the gunshot damage she'd done to both men who were helplessly sprawled on the floor, still asking for help, and to Mikey, who was now choking on his own blood. Thrown into some sort of shock, she dropped the shotgun to the floor as Dre and his homeboy seized their opportunity to get finally inside.

"Alexis! Alexis." Dre grabbed her by the arm and spun her around. "What the fuck happened to your face? Who was shooting? You?"

Alexis didn't mutter a single, solitary word as tears flowed from her puffy red eyes.

Full of fury, Dre removed his gun from his waistband, then cautiously stepped all the way inside the store's rear entrance. Realizing the two oversize guys lying on the floor, bleeding out and praying to Allah for mercy, must've been the ones with all the mouth talking shit through the locked door and had to have played a major part in why his sister was looking like she was, Dre raised his gun. Without so much as a second thought, he immediately put them both out of their misery. "Fucking terrorist-ass motherfuckers come over here like y'all, running shit!"

Hassan had no emotions to spare for his newly deceased cousins or the claims of rape Alexis had made. His main focus and concern was to get his brother Mikey to the hospital. "Dre, dude, help me. Your sister done shot Mikey too! Help me get him to the car! He's bleeding bad!"

"So fucking what? He leaking," Dre replied coldly, glancing back over his shoulder at a zombielike Alexis. "If my little sister put something hot up in his bitch ass too, it must've been for a reason! Plus, why in the fuck you lie and say she wasn't in here? You might as well say your prayers too, homeboy!"

"I didn't know she was in here. I swear on the Koran, I didn't! This is all a misunderstanding," he desperately explained as Mikey's eyes started rolling in the back of his head. "Please, Dre. Mikey needs help bad."

"Yo, dawg. Take my sister back to the crib," Dre calmly instructed his friend, as if he hadn't just finished the job of murder that Alexis had started. "Then round up the fellas and come back up here!"

"Why you doing this, man? On everything I love, I ain't know! I thought you was my boy! I thought we was family," Hassan said.

"We ain't family, my guy. You was just another dude from around the way that ran up in my sister and might be the father of what you call my nephew." Dre smiled, not giving a fuck. "Oh yeah, that toss-up hood baby!"

"But—"

"But, my black ass! I ain't blind. I seen Alexis's face and her ripped shirt."

"Dre, wait!"

"Naw. Time's up. Y'all come over here, open up all type of damn businesses, don't pay taxes or give back to the community, and treat our women like shit, especially my sister."

"Dre, wait!"

"Peace! See you in hellfire, Hassan!" With those final words as a send-off, Dre shot his nephew's father right between the eyes. As Hassan's lifeless body slumped over Mikey, who'd died only seconds earlier, Dre felt some strange sense of resurgence of his family's honor, knowing once and for good, Alexis and Hassan could no longer be together.

Don't worry about nothing, li'l sis! I'ma collect your child support from this store! You ain't have no business with that Arab, anyhow!

After dragging the bodies to the side, Dre opened the back door for his crew to come in and run wild. "Yeah, I already done ran all four of they pockets," he told them. With no remorse, he stuffed the newly acquired diamond ring Hassan had intended on giving Alexis into his own pocket, not blinking an eye. "Now let's start getting all this bullshit out this motherfucker and then torch this son of a bitch." He stood proudly, like he was the king of Detroit. "Take y'all's time and get the good shit. We got a damn night, because, after all, ain't no damn police coming!"

CHAPTER SEVENTEEN

Seeing dark, thick smoke pollute the air, Black Tone and Wild Child got closer to the house. They couldn't quite tell where the fire was from the vantage point they were at, but they knew for sure it was in the general vicinity of Tone's house. Not knowing what to expect, Wild Child had attempted to call his mother several times and had received no answer. The fact that they couldn't get through to her since her initial call begging for help for Granny made them panic and break every law there was, such as by speeding, running red lights, and turning down one-way streets.

Though he was known for being extra tough and hard as a rock in the streets, Black Tone's heart was breaking in a million tiny pieces while he prayed that his grandmother was not hurt. Repeatedly, he kept asking himself why he had even left her alone when he did. Especially on a day like today, when anything was poised to jump off. Less than a few blocks away, the smoke in the air got thicker, and Black Tone's worry increased.

What in the entire fuck? Oh, hell naw! He couldn't believe what he was seeing. Amir's family party store was up in flames. Random people were trying to dart in and out of the doors to take their chances against the flames and get whatever they could of value. Normally, Black Tone would have gotten out and checked to see where Mikey and Hassan were, since they were supposed to be posted, but at the time he had absolutely zero fucks to be given about anything that didn't concern finding out what was going on at his own household.

Driving by Alexis's house, he noticed her car parked in front of her house, which was unusual. One, because she always parked her vehicle in the driveway, afraid it might get sideswiped on the street, and two, because Dre was leaning on the hood, arguing with one of his boys. She would never allow her devious-minded brother even to come close to her prized possession.

As he and Black Tone made eye contact, Dre spit on the ground and folded his arms. Wild Child shook his head in disbelief that his older cousin and Dre were still carrying on the beef they had had since they were children growing up on the block. Black Tone didn't have time for any of Dre's petty games. He couldn't entertain anything more than getting down the street to his own home as soon as possible.

Roaring up in front of his house, he swerved in front of his aunt's car. Both he and Wild Child jumped out, on a mission, and bolted up onto the porch. The front door was wide open and unlocked. With guns out, the pair ran into the living room and were met by Wild Child's mother. She was frantic. Her face was full of tears, and she could hardly breathe.

Leaving his cousin to see about his grandmother, Black Tone wasted no time heading down the hallway. Rushing by his bedroom, which looked like it had been ransacked, he stepped over what he quickly realized was his wall-mounted flat-screen, which had been smashed in the middle of the hallway floor. Once he was at his granny's doorway, Black Tone's blood pressure was at an all-time high. His head was pounding, and every vein in his body was budging and on the verge of popping through his skin. He was livid.

Here he discovered his beloved grandmother's bare feet sticking out from behind the metal bed frame, which had been thrown on its side. With the quickness, the gentle giant, when need be, yanked the bed upward and tossed the heavy frame back to the other side of the room as if it were a piece of paper. Once he lifted the mattress, he finally saw his grandmother's entire twisted body scrunched up by the wall. With small whimpers, she was asking for God's mercy.

Black Tone carefully turned her over and saw that her angelic face, which always had a bright smile, was battered and bruised. Part of him wanted to look away, while the other part saw past her pain and knew he had to get her help fast.

In tears, he looked over his shoulder and saw his aunt and Wild Child coming into the room. His aunt explained to Black Tone, just as she'd just done to her son, that when she pulled up and came into the house, she felt like something was wrong. She said she felt some air coming from somewhere and looked in the kitchen and could see that the side door was swinging back and forth. The distraught daughter-in-law then said she ran in the back room and found Granny like this. Still in tears and in panic mode, she expressed how many times she had tried to lift the heavy bed and couldn't. She said once more that the police and the ambulance refused to send help. Lastly, Black Tone's aunt told him she had gone out on the porch and had even tried yelling for his little friend, Alexis's brother, but he had turned his head, ignoring her pleas for help.

Dre and them did this! Them bitches gonna pay! His mind raced, the taste for swift revenge dripped from his lips, and not once did he care that the shoe box containing the money he'd been saving for over a year or so was missing.

"We gotta get Granny some help and fast." After grabbing some sheets and blankets, he lifted her body from the place Li'l Ronnie had cruelly left her. Black Tone placed the one person in his life he could always count on down onto the makeshift pallet. He then wrapped her up like a small baby. Granny was alive and fighting, still praying, as he carried her out to his aunt's car.

After laying his granny down in the rear seat, he instructed his aunt to drive as fast as she possibly could to the nearest hospital outside of powerless Detroit. He told her he would be right behind, on her trail, after he spoke to Wild Child about securing the side door.

"Man, I'm telling you I'm gonna kill that motherfucker and all his cronies. He did that ho-ass shit to Granny. I know he did! That's his ass!" Black Tone declared.

"How you know it was them for sure?" Wild Child quizzed, staring at the other end of the block. "I mean, would they just be all standing down there, posted like they ain't do shit? I mean, it don't make sense. Ain't no fools that damn fucked up in the head."

Black Tone climbed up in his truck and slammed the door shut. Leaning out the window, he gave his cousin a grim look. "I know that punk-ass pussy. Dre been not giving a fuck about jack he do or say for a long time now. He ain't have no respect for me or mines or even his own since he was probably born. Naw, he did this shit. Who else would've just randomly came on the block and picked my damn house outta the blue?"

"Yeah, you probably right. And yeah, they gonna pay. But first things first. Go make sure Granny is good. Then we'll go to war!"

"Okay. Bet." Black Tone looked overhead at the thick black smoke from the still burning party store and was even more disgusted at what his neighborhood had become. "All right, cuz. I'm out. And when you get a chance, hit Amir up and tell him about his people's shit on fire. Nine outta ten, I know Mikey or Hassan done called him, but you call too. And, oh yeah, keep what happen to Granny close to the vest for now."

"Okay. Bet, fam. Keep me posted. I'll catch a ride down to the hospital later," Wild Child agreed, then dialed Amir as soon as his cousin pulled away from the curb and turned around.

Black Tone knew he had to hurry and catch up with his aunt, but he could not resist letting Dre know that as soon as he was sure his cherished grandmother was being taken care of, he'd be back and thirsty for revenge. Smashing his foot down on the gas pedal, he flew down the block and slammed down on the brakes when he got in front of Dre's house. Normally, Dre and his crew would have drawn pistols on the next man pulling a gangster stunt like that, but they knew Black Tone didn't want no real smoke.

"Yo, bitch-ass nigga! That was real fucked up what you did! I mean, you think you can just do that slimeball shit and it's gonna be all good? Y'all just gonna stand out here and be in my face, like I won't kill one of you bitches with my bare hands?"

Dre stood there and laughed. He had heard it all. Black Tone was a joke to him. Naturally, he assumed he was down here in front of his house selling wolf tickets, courtesy of Amir, who, he knew, was the oldest of Pops's sons. Dre believed Black Tone had been sent by his slave master to come see about the fire that was still raging. "So let me get this straight. Your ass came home to call yourself checking me about the next person?"

"The next person? Are you fucking serious, mother-fucker?" Black Tone put the truck in park and proceeded to get out. Dre's boys all took a few steps backward, but Dre didn't move one inch. He stood posted, unbothered by the physical threat his longtime neighbor could pose.

"You kick in my side door and abuse my grandmother, and you think I ain't gonna do shit?"

Dre was shocked. He had seen and done plenty of low-down shit in his day, but what Black Tone was talking about was nothing he would place on his résumé. "Hold up, dawg. What the fuck is you say?"

"You heard me, nigga! Y'all waited for me to leave, then kicked the side door down and laid hands on my granny. Then left her on the floor to die!" Even saying the words made Black Tone angrier as he lunged at Dre, who finally moved out of the way.

Hearing all the commotion, Alexis, still in a daze, emerged from behind the closed screen door, with dark sunglasses on that somewhat covered her face. Stepping out onto the front porch, she begged Black Tone and her brother to stop arguing. Black Tone yelled out to Alexis, telling her about the heinous act her brother had committed, before trying to rush Dre once more.

"Anthony, as much dirt as my brother done did in his life, this time he's innocent. Now, I don't know what happened down at your house or to Granny, but Dre ain't have nothing to do with it. He was with me. Helping me. My brother ain't do it."

This was the first time in years he'd heard Alexis take up for Dre. This must have been the day hell was about to freeze over. Before Black Tone could speak, Wild Child came running down the block, calling out his cousin's name. Finally up on the loud, spirited group, he held his cell up in his hand.

"Yo, cuz. I just got off the phone with Amir. And before I could get a chance to tell him about the fire, he put me up on some four-one-one. He told me Ethan called him, taking a serious cop for what he found out his nephew Li'l Ronnie had done to your grandmother!"

"Li'l Ronnie! Are you serious? That ho-ass nigga had the nerve to come over here and put his hands on my people like that! I'ma body that ass! I swear for God!" Black Tone responded.

Dre paused and thought back to the dude he'd seen earlier, and it dawned on him who he was. "Yo, Tone, I think I saw that young nigga creeping around this way this afternoon. Little dawg was locked up with me briefly in the county on some minor drug charge. He straight pussy. He was around here, pushing a small white Benz truck."

Black Tone remembered back to Li'l Ronnie pulling out of the parking lot last night, and he was driving a white truck. His anger grew even more. Out of all the years of him being a bouncer, this was the first time someone had actually brought the shit to his front door. Knowing he had to get going, he was man enough to apologize to Dre for accusing him of such an awful act.

"Man, I'm sorry about that. It's just, I guess, I'm all up in my emotions."

Dre stuck his hand out to shake Black Tone's. "Look, it ain't no thang. Just know we would never violate your shit like that, let alone do some old ho-ass shit to Granny. That ain't in me. Shiddd, boy, that lady used to make me cookies back in the day, even if I was showing out in these streets. Now, you . . . hell yeah, nigga. I'll bust your ass in a blink of an eye, but her never! That's my word!" Black Tone, along with everyone else standing around, laughed at Dre for keeping it a hundred. "And if you want me to help you do some harm to his gay ass for coming in the hood on that tip, let me know. I'm down."

Not bothering to ask Wild Child what Amir had said about the fire or even noticing the bruises on Alexis's face, Black Tone jumped back in his truck and sped off to the hospital.

CHAPTER EIGHTEEN

Receiving the informative call about his uncle, Li'l Ronnie was done playing games with him. He was done being embarrassed and done having it seem like he wasn't next in line to take over the family business, which had been passed down from his father when he got gunned down while protecting Ethan, who had been accused of cheating one night at a dice game. As far as Li'l Ronnie was concerned, his uncle owed him more than just loyalty and respect; he owed him the entire dynasty that had been built on his deceased father's spilled blood. Now he would make his uncle play his game. Now he would lure him into his own web.

"Sable, please do yourself and me a big favor. I'm trying to tell you, don't fight this. Just chill. Let this evening just go down the way I want it to."

"What, boy? Have you gone all the way crazy?"

"Naw, girl. I mean, seriously, there ain't no type of win in this bullshit for you. Just chill. Relax, baby." Li'l Ronnie cracked his knuckles. Rubbing them together, he felt his palms become sweatier as he took the initiative to transform his recent nightmarish life into a beautiful reality. This day and evening were turning out to be everything he had wished for and more. In between getting revenge on Black Tone and having a box full of money, he was good. If ignoring the multitude of insults being directed at him was the price Li'l Ronnie had to pay for the pleasure of the company he was forcefully keeping, then so be it. The lovesick captor was willing to listen to whatever she claimed him to be.

"Chill? Relax? Have you lost your entire mind, you bastard? Let me the hell go." She squirmed feverishly, setting him on fire with her eyes.

"Girl, I can't never let you go. You know that! We gonna go the distance, the whole nine. So you might as well just fall back with all that. As much as I used to like seeing you sweat when we'd be getting in, a guy hate to see you making yourself all tired for nothing." Li'l Ronnie grinned devilishly as he had a brief flashback of the life they used to share back in the day, before his uncle ruined it. "That is, unless you want me to put in some work or something. I know that fool Ethan you been dealing with ain't been putting it down like me. He been jealous of me since I was a kid growing up with his ugly ass. He's always wanted what I have, with his ho ass. It wasn't bad enough he was older than me and getting all the females. He had to want you too."

"I don't give a fuck about y'all's family beef back then, growing up in his household or anywhere else! Just let me the fuck go. I ain't playing around, Li'l Ronnie. And you can stop talking about him, 'cause when Ethan find out you got me, that's your ass, and you already know it!"

Spread-eagle, Sable bucked her partially clothed small body in defiance. Her eyes darted from the door, which was missing a knob, to the blue blanket covering the window and back to her captor as she tried to figure out a way to escape. She felt as if she was running out of energy both mentally and physically. Drained from the entire tailspin roller coaster of horror she'd been going through, her body was starting to break down.

Since the very moment Sable woke up and her feet touched the floor, she had had an awful feeling about the day and hadn't been able to shake it. She had had two cups of herbal tea and had tried to meditate, as one of her many white, suburban hippie friends who also danced had instructed her. Yet she had still felt uneasy. Wanting to get her exercise on, she walked on her treadmill for over thirty minutes or so and still had visions of bullshit occupying her brain.

Not wanting to bother Ethan by having him pick her up and drop her off at work, like he usually did, especially considering the citywide power outage, Sable was dressed and heading out the door to drive herself when she got the call from her ex. Her first notion was to ignore him, as she'd done so many times before, but this time was different. Li'l Ronnie, unlike the other people that'd come and gone in her young life, was a huge concern. She knew he was still hurt and feeling like she'd betrayed him. Sable knew Li'l Ronnie could have been acting out lately because he'd heard Ethan had asked to marry her. She knew the strange mood she was in could only be attributed to one of the things that had hurt him. She had to make it right; karma was showing up and showing its ass.

Wanting to make sure that at least all was good with Li'l Ronnie, Sable slid the green TALK button on her phone over to the side. Within a matter of seconds of them speaking, Li'l Ronnie asked if he could fall through and at least tell her what he wanted face-to-face. Against her better judgment and the warnings from Ethan about her ex man being bitter, she unfortunately allowed the impromptu meeting. Now here they were. Here *she* was, fucked up, tied up, and at her lunatic ex's mercy.

As the flimsy headboard knocked back against the wall, Li'l Ronnie derived more and more enjoyment. He was not bothered by the idle threats she was spewing about Ethan. No number of consequences was great enough to deter him. Sable was not just any girl, and as he began to slowly stroke her jawline, his manhood twitched. She was more than the average female who displayed a pretty smile, with each tooth perfectly lined up and full lips. Being blessed with shoulder-length hair and a sassy swag to her attitude was definitely a plus. That deep, rich brown skin tone, despite the few blemishes, only added to her beauty. Sable was everything and more than Li'l Ronnie had ever dreamed about, ever wanted, and ever needed to have in his life.

"You know how gorgeous you are to me? You know how much I dreamed about this day since you started acting like I didn't matter, since you started fucking my uncle? Come on now. You're my soul mate. You know that bullshit, baby. Hell, the entire city knows it and knows how we used to get down." He stood to his feet and paced back and forth, still rubbing his hands and proclaiming his feelings for Sable.

"What?" She grimaced, seething with anger and defiance.

"Yeah, Sable, I don't know why you been out in them streets, bugging, treating me like I don't matter no more. You belong to me, like I belong to you. Fuck that old man! Talking about he wanna marry you!"

"Fucking stop touching me, you moron." Her voice echoed off the wall as her heart raced at twice its normal pace.

"Come on, Sable. It's me, Li'l Ronnie, you with now, not Ethan. You ain't gotta front for the streets no more! Think about it for real, though. We're made for each girl, on some old 'red light, green light, Simon says, tag, you it' type of shit. You feel me? Bonnie and Clyde, Kanye and Kim, naw naw Jay and Bey, that's us, freaking hood royalty. That's how we started off making that paper being in love. That's how it was always meant to be, and that's how we gonna end this thing we got going on—in love and on top!"

"Trust me, Li'l Ronnie, we ain't got nothing going on no more. You fucked that up by getting locked up! You. Not me! You! And you know why? Because you's a weak-ass pussy and always have been one! I swear, I hate your dumb ass and hate you even more right about now for this stunt you done pulled. Matter of fact, fuck you and all that 'way back when' bullshit! That life been dead to me! I tried to rock out with you, but you ain't never want shit. No real hustle unless your uncle gave you one, no true ambition!"

Li'l Ronnie was almost six feet tall. Recently, he had shaved his head completely bald but had kept the full beard he started growing some months back. Out of character, he'd started reading books geared toward natural supplements and the effects they had on one's body. Popping pills and drinking way too much, he'd transformed into a person she could honestly say she hardly knew anymore. Now here he stood at the foot of the four- poster bed, listening to Sable berate him.

Irrational, Li'l Ronnie looked at Sable with the eyes of a man in love. It mattered to him none what she said as he smiled. He knew "his girl" didn't mean what she was saying. How could she? Despite her words of discourage-ment and rage for what he was doing to her, Li'l Ronnie remained in his calm state of mind. He refused to waver. His spirit and soul wouldn't let him. Nothing could knock him off his square of revenge. At this point, he'd be content just to look at his resentful, bitter queen for the rest of his life and pray that after a while, in due time, he'd once more be her king and she'd forget about Ethan. In his mind, no sooner than he murdered his uncle, she'd be begging him to be by her side. Li'l Ronnie's adrenaline jumped as he played his fantasy over in his head and leaned in closer to Sable, this time tracing the outline of her lips.

"Get your damn hands off me! I'm not playing around with you, boy, fucking nothing-ass punk! I swear to God, this shit ain't gonna just go down the way you think it is."

"Oh yeah? Is that right?"

"Yeah, I swear, it ain't, you fucking asshole. It ain't," she said angrily, turning her head to the far right and attempting to avoid further physical contact. Not wanting to subject herself even to seeing Li'l Ronnie's face, let alone experiencing the rough feel of his weatherworn fingertips on her skin, she cringed. Wanting to throw up in her mouth as he sat down on the edge of the bed, she took a deep breath.

The dancer turned part-time drug hustler at the strip club wanted to break free. However, the restraints Li'l Ronnie had wrapped around each of her wrists were much too tight. It felt like the circulation in her ankles had been totally cut off. Her feet, like her hands, were numb. Sable hated her former monkey hustle partner in crime, who had learned so many ways to tie knots in summer camp when they were ten, maybe eleven. But he had, and now he was putting his expert skill in tying fisherman and square knots to work. Sable just wanted to go home. In the time that she'd been there, she'd searched the room for any weapon she could possible grab when she broke free. Regretfully, a determined Sable had struggled for hours on end already and had made the reinforced rope that bound her grow tighter with each twisting movement.

Standing to his feet, Li'l Ronnie felt a sense of entitlement when it came to this female, who was technically no longer his, but his uncle's. He wanted to beat on his chest and shout out his victory in making Sable his woman again, whether it was true or not.

She might not love me now, but she will again real soon! Arrogantly, he walked over to a bookshelf on the far side of the dimly lit room. With his back turned to Sable, he removed several items off the shelf and set them on the table. Making sure he had everything required for his street love potion, Li'l Ronnie took a seat. Removing a lighter from his front pocket, he lit the vanilla-scented candle that served as a centerpiece. Placing a bottle cap right side up and a cotton ball alongside it, next to a syringe, he was almost ready to make magic pop off for his renegade lady love. Cutting his eyes back over to Sable, he knew it wouldn't be long before she stopped resisting the inevitable and loved him once more.

Li'l Ronnie reached over and took one of several small Baggies out of his jacket pocket. He lifted it up and held the edge tightly with pinched fingers while tapping the sides to bring the addictive mixture down to the bottom. Seeing that it had evened out, he ripped the top of the Baggie off. He poured a small bit of water into the bottle cap and felt anxious, as if he was about to feel the ultimate rush, not the virgin veins of Sable. Soon the spoon was heated over the burning candle, bringing the sometimes lethal combination together, to where it needed to be. As he allowed the cotton ball to serve its purpose of filtering out the unneeded bullshit in the barely stepped-on product, Li'l Ronnie's smile grew wider. After sticking the needle into the center of the cotton ball, he filled the syringe with Ethan's product. Finally ready to put things back in order, Li'l Ronnie stood to his feet.

As he approached Sable, sweat was pouring down her face from fighting a losing battle to get free. She'd been watching him like a hawk as he prepared a blast, which she prayed to God would be for him. The closer he got, the more she continued to buck and rattle the entire bed frame. Her wrists and ankles were now bleeding as the twisting rope had gnawed through her skin. Li'l Ronnie got closer, and Sable grew more terrified with each passing second. Her heart felt as if it was going to jump out of her chest. She couldn't breathe. She couldn't think or see straight.

"Li'l Ronnie, get the fuck away from me with that bullshit! Are you fucking crazy or what? Get the fuck back, nigga! I ain't playing. Get the fuck on." Sable knew what his intentions were and was going berserk. In all her years of living, she had not once smoked a cigarette, smoked weed, or even been drunk. Now this asshole who claimed he used to love her so much and still did wanted to shoot some dope into her, like she was some common junkie off the street. Sable couldn't fathom the thought of being high on any shit but counting her money. Not her. Not now. Not ever.

"Look, look, listen. Hold up, boy! Wait! Chill! Wait," she begged, hoping to reason with him, convince him to put the needle down so they could talk. "Why you doing this, huh? Why? You said you love me so damn much. This how you gonna do me, huh? Like this? Damn, baby! Hold the fuck up!"

Li'l Ronnie paused. He watched "his girl" slowly abandon her attempts to break free. Sympathetically, he listened to her pleas and questions as to why it had come down to this. Caught in his feelings as well, he wanted nothing more than for them just to kiss and make up and let things go back to the way they were before Sable decided to be "a bad bitch out in these streets" and leave him behind in the dirt, like he was nothing but a piece of shit. However, Li'l Ronnie knew there was no changing Sable's mind-set without a little bit of help. Never once giving up on the dream, he'd done and said just about everything he could think of underneath the sun, stars, and moon to get Sable to just love him again—but, tragically, no dice. So just to make his uncle hurt, he would now use her as bait.

As he looked around the small, filthy, out of the way house he'd rented from a crackhead for a few days, he grinned. He was killing two birds with one stone. He was making Ethan suffer, and he was back spending one-on-one time with his precious Sable.

"Me and you are made for each other. We done been through hell and back. I was there when you ain't have shit. I put up with all your garbage and still loved you." He reached for the small amount of rope that was left after tying her up. Carefully, he set the filled syringe on the edge of the nightstand.

As Sable continued to fight, Li'l Ronnie grabbed her arm forcefully and wrapped the rope tightly around it. After he tied her arm, his beloved multiple veins started to emerge. Having his choice, he tuned out her panic-filled screams.

"Look, be still. Just relax, before you mess around and get this needle broke off in your arm. You'll have a blister growing full of this shit and a damn sore. So stop fighting me."

Sable's eyes seemed to pop out of her face. She was going into shock. She couldn't stop him. She was trapped. "Please don't," were the last two words she said as Li'l Ronnie stuck the needle through the first layer of her skin and finally filled her vein with the unstepped-on poison she'd sold grams and grams, for which she'd gotten paid. As Sable's bloodshot eyes rolled in the back of her head, her body tensed up, then started to tremble. Her arm started to bleed as he eased his love potion out and grinned with satisfaction. She'd never felt no shit like this before. The room started to spin as she had been made to break the first law of the game. *Don't get high on your own supply.* As Sable drifted off to a place in her mind she'd never been before, Li'l Ronnie stood up and waited. After taking pictures with his cell phone of Sable sprawled out in the bed, he started texting them to Ethan.

It was now pitch black outside, and Ethan was constantly getting reports from all his lieutenants on how the various dope spots they were in charge of were going. His first mind was just to shut all of them down for the night and start back slinging at the crack of dawn. However, the product they had was already stepped on twice and had to be sold before he fell. Ethan had stretched the rest of his last shipment as much as possible, anticipating the re-up that should have taken place earlier. But now, thanks to Li'l Ronnie, he was almost at point zero. After speaking to Amir two separate times in the middle of the afternoon, he felt like he was making a little progress in securing his new bag, in spite of the confusion. But after the last embarrassing and remorseful conversation he was forced to have, Ethan knew that deaded their union.

Leaning back on the couch in the dark, he tried to gather his thoughts and see who he could call to get his stash off craps. The other few dealers he was somewhat cool with would have no problem asking why Amir had taken him off his line, and then either he'd be forced to fess up and tell them or they'd check with Amir and find out on their own. Either way it went, he was fucked. Push come to shove, he'd have to take a flight down to Miami and secure a new avenue. Lost in his thoughts, he closed his eyes and nodded off for no more than a few brief minutes before his cell notification alerted him.

Oh, hell naw! What this nigga want?

Ethan was disgusted that J-Blaze hadn't caught up with his nephew and done what he was asked to do in the name of crew loyalty. Here Li'l Ronnie had the nerve to be sending him a text message after all the dirt he'd done.

After tapping the icon on his phone, he read the first of three back-to-back texts out loud. "Catch me. I got you."

Ethan didn't understand the first secret squirrel message, so he went on to the next. Upon opening the second text, he almost dropped his cell to the floor. His eyes burned and filled with blood. His entire body stiffened with resentment for Li'l Ronnie. In disbelief, he stared at a picture of Sable, his woman, half naked and tied to some bed. In the next picture his nephew so proudly sent, he showcased the empty Baggie that had clear heroin residue on it and a needle mark in Sable's arm.

Enraged, Ethan tried over and over again to call Li'l Ronnie's cell but was sent straight to voice mail. He left messages and tried texting back but received no response. The old-school player knew the boy had crossed the line. He knew he was playing the game with him, making him suffer by not knowing Sable's whereabouts or fate, so the only thing Ethan could do was wait it out and hope J-Blaze found him or, hell, even Black Tone at this point.

CHAPTER NINETEEN

Amir was receiving back-to-back calls from his father. Pops kept complaining that he couldn't get in touch with Mikey or Hassan. The twins had not been picking up their calls, either, and Pops said he was worried. True enough, Amir found that to be strange, but he knew if something was really wrong, one of the four of them would have called. Not too long ago he had had a call from Wild Child, and he hadn't mention nothing much going on up at the store, and he was in the neighborhood, at Black Tone's house. After he had informed him about the disturbing call from Ethan, he knew his two main security staff would be tied up with family business. Even though he wanted them there with him, he understood. Although Amir did his own thing for the most part, he still loved his family and would hate for someone to violate them, as Black Tone's grandmother had been.

Taking it upon himself, Amir started to call and text his younger siblings, but he got no response. Reasoning that their cell phone batteries must have all gone dead from them being on Facebook or listening to music, Amir took it for what it was for the time being. Cell still in hand, he tried calling Black Tone just to check in and see how his grandmother was doing, but he got voice mail. "Damn. Is everybody shit going to voice mail?"

After going to the local news Web site on his phone, Amir watched countless reports of firsthand accounts of crimes being perpetrated within the city limits. They ranged from everything from petty larceny, strong arm robbery, burglary, and car theft to arson, hit-and-runs, and murder. Shaking his head over how bad things had gotten throughout the day, he poured himself a drink as he watched videos from the Channel Seven News helicopter that showed some of the homes and commercial businesses that had been or still were on fire. After seeing five, maybe six mouth-dropping dwellings that had to be left to burn down to the ground, Amir stopped sipping and dropped his glass to the floor.

He paused the last video he was watching and pushed the PLAY AGAIN arrow on the TV remote. Raising his eyebrow, he repeated the process three more times, making sure the reporter had said what he thought he had said. Amir had to watch it twice more to ensure he was seeing the eagle-eye view of what he thought he was seeing. "Oh my God," he shouted out as he leaped to his feet, grabbed his keys and rushed toward the club doors.

Black Tone went out into the parking lot of the suburban hospital. He had not been able to get a signal inside, and so as soon as his reception improved, a multitude of notification alerts started to chime. He searched through the text messages. The most important person he wanted to return a call to was Alexis. Still emotionally drained from seeing his grandmother in the abused state she was in, he need to talk to a friend. Someone he not only trusted but loved as well. After three rings, Alexis finally picked up, and he smiled.

"Hey now. What's popping?"

"Hey, Anthony. How is Granny? Is she good?" Her voice was soft, but he could easily tell she'd been crying.

"Yeah, she's better now. They have her stabilized. But what's wrong with you? You didn't seem yourself on the porch. And what was all that about Dre helping you? Helping you with what?"

Alexis was bombarded with questions. While she had been wishing she could talk to him and cry on his shoulder since the very moment she walked into the party store and sat down, hearing Black Tone's always soothing, deep voice had her feeling overwhelmed. Now she had her chance, but she was hesitant and remorseful after what she and Dre had done. Of course, those awful twins had got what they had coming to them, but Mikey and her son's father, Hassan . . . Alexis was torn up inside over what had popped off, and she was scared to death that she would soon be going to jail for murder.

Hassan might have been talking a lot of smack about her, but like he'd claimed, maybe he had just been showing out or trying to fit in. Maybe he hadn't known what terrible thing his cousins had done to her. And she already knew Mikey was too weak and incapable to stand up to his wife. So the chances of him standing up to two monsters, not one, were slim..

"I need to talk to you, Anthony. I need to see you in person. Talk to you face-to-face."

"Alexis, what's wrong? What happened?" he asked, watching the overflow of Detroit hospital patients crowd the parking lot and the emergency room. "You can tell me. You know I'm not gonna judge you, no matter what."

Suffering from pain all across her face and in between her legs, she knew she needed to seek medical attention from the brutal attack and rape, but she couldn't bring herself to leave the safety of her bedroom. "I . . . I . . . I know," she stammered. "It's just that what we did, what *I* did . . ."

"*We?* Who is 'we'? You mean Dre? Alexis, tell me what happened." Black Tone was confused as he walked around the perimeter of the entire parking lot.

Before she could answer any more of her best friend's questions, she heard a light tap on her closed bedroom door. "Hold on, Anthony." She was sobbing as she spoke. "Yes, come in."

Dre pushed open the door and barely poked his head inside. A constant headache to his sibling, he knew that he had not been allowed to cross the threshold of his sister's bedroom for years. And even though they'd just committed murder together, he still knew that rule stood.

"Hey. I hate to bother you. And trust I ain't trying to get off into your business, but don't you think you should go to the doctor or some shit like that? I mean, ain't no telling what them nasty-ass Arabs got. I know you don't be really giving a shit what I think, but this time . . . Well, you know."

She still had Anthony on hold. Her eyes were almost swollen shut from the beating she'd taken and from her crying, not to mention the fact that her legs were almost too weak to stand on. Out of options, she asked Dre if he would do her a favor. His answer was, "Yes. Of course." Considering he had just killed over her and had torched a liquor store, whatever else she needed for him to do would be a piece of cake.

"Hey, Anthony. What hospital are you at? I'm gonna come to you," she said into the phone.

Amir locked up Detroit Live as securely as he could. With just two men left on duty from Zero Fucks Given, he advised the skeleton crew to keep a careful eye on the perimeter of the building. Not in the best mind-set, he hopped in his car and sped off into the darkness of the city. He navigated the best he could through the potholed streets, but his expensive sports car rattled with every bump, ditch, or rock he could not avoid hitting. What would usually take him fourteen minutes in travel time turned into an almost thirty-minute ride through the crime-infested city. Anything that the chief of police had warned of had already taken place. The town that Amir and his family had spent years doing business in was in complete shambles.

By the devastating way things looked to him in the high-beam headlights that illuminated his path, he could easily tell that by daybreak Detroit would mirror a war-torn third-world country. The bankrupt city would be last in line for good odds of being able to make a comeback. Having the news radio station on low, Amir was praying to Allah that what he'd seen on his phone was a mistake. Maybe his eyes had played tricks on him. It was possible that the video he'd watched repeatedly had been shot in some other location, one that resembled the area around Pops's long-standing store. He tried to call Mikey first, then Hassan. After calling the twins as well, Amir feared the worst and no longer bought the dead battery story he'd convince himself of back at the club.

Turning off of Davison onto Linwood, Amir swerved seven or more times, attempting to avoid crashing head-on into the abandoned vehicles that filled the road. The cars had probably run out of gas or been in accidents, and the drivers couldn't get a tow truck to remove them. Needless to say, besides the drivable cars and the people darting out from here and there, the only thing that gave off any kind of light was the multitude of uncontrolled fires burning every few miles or so. Off in the distance he saw a familiar landmark and knew the store was coming up. Although he could not see down that far, he was relieved that he didn't see a blaze in that general direction. Slamming down on the brakes so as not to hit a small child and his mother, who was carrying what appeared to be laundry baskets full of miscellaneous items, Amir glanced up at the street sign and knew he was only three short blocks away.

Pulling the car over in front of what used to be Pops's store, Amir kept his high-beam headlights on. He couldn't believe it. His worst fear had come true. He had not been mistaken. The gigantic fire on the video was indeed burning here. It was at this location.

"Oh my God! Oh my fucking God! Naw! It can't be." He tried getting closer, but in the structure that remained, small scorching hot flames were still shooting up. The blackened wood cracked and smoked, giving off the smell of charred bits of tar. In denial, he looked over toward the back area of the property and saw what looked like both his brothers' vehicles. Amir was confused. He wondered why they hadn't been in touch with either him or Pops. Maybe they'd left their cells inside when escaping from the fire. That had to be it. He couldn't fathom any other reason for them not letting their family know what had taken place. Maybe they were just ashamed that they couldn't stop the abeeds from burning the store down.

Taking his own cell phone out of his pocket, Amir stepped over debris and headed toward the alley. Not one bit scared of the ruthlessness people had been displaying since nightfall, he bravely ventured toward what was once the rear exit of the building. He then called Pops, hoping to hear that Mikey and Hassan had shown up at his uncle's store and revealed to them the tragic news of the fire.

"Hey, Pops. What's going on?" He tried his best to remain calm and not alarm his old man.

"Amir, have you heard from the boys? Did they call you? Why are they not picking up the phone? Why?" Pops had question after question about his sons not being in touch, but Amir had no answers to give his frantic father.

"I'm headed over there now to check on them. Just sit tight and give me a little bit," he lied to ease the old man's worry. After agreeing to call the second he got over to the store, Amir hung up. Still not willing to think the impossible was possible, he walked over to the chain-link fence the cars were parked behind. Standing as close to the surely hot metal gate as he could, Amir could see that the lock was still on it.

"Oh my God." His voice started to crack as he started to give up all hope of his brothers being alive. Not knowing what to do next, he started to pace back and forth in the alley, tears forming in his eyes, and a lump in his throat. The lingering smoke made him feel light-headed.

I gotta sit down. I have to figure this shit out. What am I gonna tell Pops? Oh my God. This is gonna kill my mother. Oh my God!

Amir walked back down the seemingly empty alley and headed to his car. Before he could put his hand on the door handle, he heard a voice call out his name from the darkness. His first instinct told him to pull his gun out of his hip holster and let off a few rounds. Thank goodness he remained calm, as he quickly found out it was the neighborhood guy Tommy, who always helped out at the store, doing this or that when need be.

"Hey, Amir. Can I talk to you?" He walked closer to the oldest of Pops's sons, the strong smell of cheap gin on his breath.

"Oh, hey, Tommy. What's the deal? Did you see what happened to the store? And, most importantly, do you know where Mikey and Hassan went off to? Did one of their friends pick them up after the fire started?"

Tommy didn't say a word. He just looked over at the one place where he'd made a couple of dollars and shook his head. It was like he was in denial also as he finally struggled to speak. "Ummm, Amir. I ain't see nobody come get them boys. Or them other two of your kinfolk, either."

"Okay, Tommy. Then what you saying? Do you know where they went or not? Is they with that girl that got a so-called baby with Hassan or her bad news brother?" he asked, praying the answer was yes while knowing deep down inside it was no. "You have to tell me, Tommy! Say something! Are they with her! Huh? Are they?"

Tommy hesitated. His mind started to play the what-if game with the information he was holding on to. He didn't want to say what needed to be said next. He fought with himself on what to do next. Sick to his stomach, he wanted another strong drink to block out what he'd seen take place. Tommy knew the right thing to do was to tell Amir everything that had jumped off, well, at least what he had seen and heard from the outside of the building. He hoped if the tables were turned, Amir would do the same for him. But he knew in reality that would never happen. Yet before he confessed, Tommy realized that long after Amir had gone back to his elaborate condo miles away from the burnt-out store, he'd be left in the hood, labeled not only a drunk but a snitch as well.

"Look, I'm sorry, Amir. I can't get involved in all of this," he slurred, then swiftly walked away, rubbing his hand on the side of his unshaven face.

"What in the hell you mean you don't wanna get involved in this? What exactly the fuck is this? And after all my damn family has done to help you, and you think you don't owe us?" Amir snatched him back by his shoulder and shoved his gun deep into the inebriated man's ribs and slow walked him back in the alley. "Now, stop bullshitting around with me, Tommy! Where the fuck are my brothers at?"

Tommy was terrified. He felt damned if he did tell and damned if he didn't. Wanting to throw up, he grew dizzy as he breathed in the smoke from the smoldering ruins of the store. He knew death was in the air. He felt like he could taste it for certain as he parted his cracked lips to speak. "There." He nodded his head in the direction of the burnt-out rear storeroom.

Amir let his grip on the man's shoulder go. He didn't need him to tell him more, insinuate, or draw a road map of what he was saying. Wanting to break down in the alley and ask Allah why, he stood as strong as he could, then made his way back to his car. Sitting down, he reclined the seat and then covered his face with both hands. Allowing the tears to pour out of his eyes, he felt his sorrow turn to rage as he started to bang on the steering wheel, followed by the dashboard. Stopping just shy of causing the air bags to deploy, Amir snatched up his cell phone. Scrolling down his extensive list of contacts, he came to the number of the fire marshal's right-hand man. Calling the second in command, Amir closed his eyes and waited for the guy to answer. Once, twice, three times it rang, and still no response.

Just as he was about to go another route, his cell rang. "Hey, guy. I need some help. I need a huge favor," he said right after taking the call.

Amir went on to explain that there had been a fire at his father's party store on the West Side and that he thought his two brothers and his cousins had been trapped inside. Sadly, he told the man on the other end of the line that he knew that they were likely dead, but he couldn't see because of the darkness, not to mention the fact that remains of the property were still burning and smoking. In spite of the grief and other emotions he was feeling, he knew he was about to ask the man the virtually impossible on a night like this in the city of Detroit. For Pops's, as well as his uncle's, sake, he posed his question.

Of course, he knew what the answer would be. The response was that not one fireman employed by the city would be able to come out and even stand in front of the location in an official capacity. He advised Amir to reach out to either private security or other family members and at least try to stand guard over the area until daybreak. This way if it was true that his four relatives had been trapped in the televised blaze and were now deceased, the scene would not be disturbed or compromised by the countless looters, opportunists and other monsters of the night that this fateful day had allowed to run wild.

Amir hung up the phone. Confused and desperate, he had to make a quick decision if he hoped truly to get to the bottom of what had taken place with Mikey, Hassan, and his cousins. The older sibling needed to know what or who had prevented them from getting out alive, from escaping a fire that was suspicious in nature. There was only one person whom he trusted to have his back when it came down to it. Black Tone. Amir knew Black Tone was dealing with his own set of problems, with his grandmother having been beaten by Ethan's nephew, but he selfishly made the call to him just the same.

CHAPTER TWENTY

Black Tone stood in front of the hospital emergency room entrance. Alexis had texted him saying she was no more than five minutes away and for him to meet her there. He wondered what was so very important that she was coming way over there to speak to him face-to-face. It was puzzling, to say the least. The entire day, or at least since the power had gone out in the city, had been full of mishaps and the unthinkable happening. It was like he was watching some bad low-budget movie and not actually living it in reality.

After years and years of Alexis doing her best to avoid any contact with Dre besides hello and good-bye—if forced since they lived in the same house—tonight was different. Tonight was strange. She had come outside not to cheer him on when he was about to mangle her brother's rotten, devious ass for all the trouble and mayhem he'd caused, but to defend Dre. Black Tone had found it strange while the whole scene played out, but he had had too much on his mind regarding his grandmother's well-being to give it much thought.

"What the fuck?" Black Tone mumbled under his breath as Alexis's car came into view. He rubbed his tired eyes. He felt he must be seeing things. The strange day had just become stranger. Alexis had indeed come to the hospital, just as she'd said she would. However, she wasn't alone. While she was riding shotgun, Dre was behind the steering wheel.

None of this bullshit makes sense. What the hell is going on with these two all of a sudden?

When the vehicle came to a complete stop, Black Tone reached over and pulled up the door handle. As Alexis took her seat belt off and then lifted herself up, he saw she had on a pair of sunglasses. Immediately, he noticed that her face was swollen on one side and her lip appeared to be busted. Raising his eyebrow, Black Tone got heated. He had just calmed down some from seeing his granny's face battered and bruised, and now he had to deal with this. Both of the most important women in his life were hurt, and he hadn't been there to protect them.

"Alexis, what the fuck happened to your face? Who did this? Who? Tell me," he demanded, blocking her from moving any farther from the passenger seat.

Alexis was ashamed of what she'd been through at the hands of her small son's cousins. When she came within arm's length of Black Tone, she broke all the way down, knowing he would comfort her. After she removed her sunglasses so he could better see her face, Black Tone's body locked up. Leaning back out of the car, he stood straight up and grabbed the sides of his head with both hands. Applying pressure to his scalp, he closed his eyes as tight as he possibly could. Tilting his head backward, he slowly opened up his eyes and looked at the bright, scattered stars that filled the sky. After silently questioning God as to why all these things had happened to him today, he looked over at Dre, who had gotten out of the car.

"Yo, man, come over here. Let me holler at you on the real about some shit." Dre nodded his head toward the rear of the car. "We need to kick it before I leave my sister with you."

Black Tone sympathetically looked once more in the car, at Alexis. His best friend had stopped crying, had her arms folded and snuggly pressed against her chest, and was rocking back and forth. Not knowing what to do or say, Black Tone did as Dre had asked. Standing near one of the taillights, he demanded that Dre tell him what the hell had happened to Alexis. Not in the mood to mince words, Dre began to run down the whole story. Not scared of anything or anybody's judgments or any consequences, and definitely not remorseful about what he felt had to be done, Alexis's older brother didn't leave out a single thing. He knew Black Tone was especially close with Amir and his family and practically ran Detroit Live for him, but so fucking what? This was Alexis we were talking about.

"Yeah, dawg, I got a nine-one-one text from my sister this evening, before dark," Dre revealed.

"Yeah, she texted me too," Black Tone interjected.

"Well, it said she was up at the store. So at first I ain't think nothing about it. You know how she be when she get going on a nigga. I thought maybe she was just cussing Hassan ho ass out for not buying the baby some new shoes or something."

Black Tone nodded his head in agreement. He knew Alexis was known for having a short fuse when she felt she was being wronged, and he wondered if she was the one that set the store on fire, perhaps by accident.

"But then something came over me. I dunno what the hell it was. It was just a damn crazy feeling, so I stopped what I was doing and headed that way." Dre paused in telling the story. "Matter of fact, that's when I saw that dick-sucker nigga pushing that white truck. I almost ran his ho ass off the road."

"Yeah, that nigga. He as good as dead, but go on, guy. Finish." Black Tone frowned from even thinking about Li'l Ronnie still alive out in the streets, as if he had gotten away with something as horrible as beating up on an old woman, not to mention stealing his money.

Dre went on. "So yeah, when I got up to the store, I already knew they was closed for the day. I was up there earlier, kicking it with Hassan, when they was locking it down. I seen Alexis's car parked around the back, so me and my boys pulled back there. I had knocked on the door more than a few good times when some random ho-ass sand nigga came yelling through the door, trying to go for bad. Man, I swear that motherfucker was going like he couldn't get got."

Black Tone knew that had to have been one of the bigmouthed twins who always caused trouble and were the known black sheep of Amir's family.

"Well, finally, after that fool kept running off at the mouth, Hassan came to the door, talking that bullshit. I asked him to let me talk to my sister, and both them clowns kept saying she wasn't inside. I mean, what the fuck they was lying for? Shit. She had just texted me she was there, so I wasn't just dreaming that bullshit, ya feel me?"

"Right, right," Black Tone mumbled as he looked through the rear window of the car to see if Alexis had stopped rocking back and forth. She hadn't. He then returned his full attention to Dre. This was the most interaction the two of them had had since Dre used to jump on both him and Alexis as kids just for fun.

"I kept banging on that bitch and told them I was gonna run my car up in that motherfucker if they ain't send my little sister out. I kept calling her cell, and it kept going to voice mail. So a nigga like me was seconds away from getting back in the ride and going straight movie gangsta on them and that store. Just then I heard gunshots!" Dre finished giving Black Tone a blow-by-blow account of exactly what had popped off from the time Alexis cracked the rear store door and let him inside until the minute she came out on their front porch to take up for him when he was accused of bringing harm to Granny.

Black Tone was enraged. What Dre had told him made his soul ache. He couldn't believe it. He had encountered the twins before and knew they were capable of rape and just about anything else. But Mikey and Hassan, Amir's little brothers . . . He was stunned. Black Tone knew Mikey was a coward. The entire world knew that. Yet he just couldn't wrap his head around the fact that Hassan would allow those two idiots to violate Alexis. Black Tone was fully aware that Hassan had not told his ailing mother about the biracial relationship he was in or about his small son. But the rest of his immediate family knew about Alexis. They might not have accepted her as kin and would taunt Hassan for his choices, but they still would never go that far, especially Mikey. It didn't make any sense, none of it.

Dre and Black Tone spoke a little bit longer to get a deeper understanding of what had to happen next in order to make sure that both he and Alexis could walk away clean and free after having committed murder and arson. For the time being, it was decided that Alexis, after getting treated at the hospital, would stay with Black Tone. And Dre, who was built for this type of thing, would go back to the neighborhood and stand tall, like he had done no wrong and knew nothing about the crimes, which they all three felt were justified. Normally, it was just Alexis and Black Tone who ran together and was thick as thieves. But this time around Dre, their frequent enemy, was strangely and finally a part of their secret club. The table for two had just grown to a booth. If they stuck together, maybe they could make the lie seem like the truth.

Of course, Black Tone was far from being a fool. He knew that when Amir found out that not one, but both of his brothers were dead, having been shot and burned to death, there would be hell to pay. He'd want revenge on those responsible for the deed, no matter what their reason was for doing it, and honestly, Black Tone couldn't blame him.

"This shit is messed up, but we gonna make it do what it do." Black Tone angrily slammed a closed fist down on the corner of the trunk, creating a gigantic dent. Startled by the sound, Alexis was shaken out of her trance and called out for her most recent protector, Dre. After she asked Dre to please help her out of the car, because her legs were weak, Black Tone took over and picked Alexis up in his arms. Then he told Dre that he could go home and that he would keep him posted. He then softly kissed Alexis on her forehead and disappeared behind the hospital doors.

In between avoiding calls from Pops and just outright lying to him, Amir was growing weary of standing guard himself. He was like a fish out of water. Most of the people that were up to no good this time of the night were thinking about trying to rob him as well. He'd tried to call everyone he knew who could possibly come and help him. But all his close friends either had their own businesses to guard over on this terror-filled night or had flat out refused to take a chance and come into the city. He was running out of options.

Black Tone had finally texted back, explaining that there was no way he could leave his grandmother's side, even if there had been a fire and Mikey and Hassan were missing. Amir's next thought was to pull the remaining two guys off of safeguarding the club and have them come help him, but Amir knew that he had not only thousands upon thousands of dollars' worth of liquor, food, and electronic equipment but also a stash of heroin locked up in one of the club's utility closets. He couldn't afford to risk that potential loss.

Thinking about the dope that was stashed at Detroit Live, Amir came up with an idea. He knew that Black Tone wouldn't like it, but just like the other man's loyalties were with his grandmother, Amir's had to be with his family. After getting back inside his car so that he could hear, he texted Ethan. Just like every other self-respecting drug dealer, Amir assumed he'd be up checking his traps, especially on a night like tonight. In a mere matter of minutes, just as Amir had prayed, his text was answered. Seconds later, his cell rang.

"Hey, Ethan. Thanks for getting back to me so soon."

Ethan was shocked to hear from Amir. Naturally, after what Li'l Ronnie had done to his right-hand man, Black Tone, he figured all contact with them as a whole was over. "No problem, Amir. But I ain't gonna front. I mean, I'm surprised to hear from you. And I want you to know that damn nephew of mine is gonna pay the ultimate price. Not only has he overstepped the rules of the game with the old woman, but he has crossed me out also. For both those offenses, his blood will run on these streets."

Amir was, of course, glad to hear that the disrespectful youngin' would pay, but he had more things on his plate to swallow than that. Not wanting any more slow stroking of each other's egos, Amir cut straight to the chase. "Look, Ethan, here's the deal. I need you to do me a favor. And I need it done with the quickness. No delay."

"If I can, I will," Ethan replied, hoping he could redeem himself and make amends.

"Ethan, man, some fucking assholes set my father's store on fire. I don't wanna go into details, but I need some manpower to come over here and kinda stand guard until daybreak. I got all my people tied up on other bullshit. So what you say? Can you make that happen for me or what?"

If nothing else, Ethan had a small army of East Side soldiers standing in line, begging to be put to work on anything for him. Quick to respond, he asked Amir for the address to the store and asked how many guys he needed to show up. Amir replied that he needed at least three, to be on the safe side, but Ethan informed him he would be sending five, and they would be there shortly.

Before ending the conversation, Amir told Ethan that all that bullshit his nephew had done at the club and to Black Tone's grandmother would be squashed in return for what he was doing.

"I swear to God, I appreciate you, man. Up until that fool showed out, we been doing good business, and I wanna keep it that way," Ethan said. He was relived he was back on the ticket and hung up from speaking to Amir with a smile on his face. Now, if he only heard from J-Blaze or if only his girl Sable came walking through his front door, his life would be back on track.

Amir got back out of the car and holstered his gun, just in case. He was glad that Ethan had agreed to what he needed and that reinforcements were on their way. Of course, he had deliberately failed to tell Ethan that he feared four of his family members were dead, buried under the collapsed and still scorching hot beams of the building, the very place he wanted the men to guard over. But that really wasn't Ethan's business or concern, at least not now. Amir already knew Black Tone wasn't going to be happy about the choice Amir had to make in joining forces with Ethan to help protect the store, but in the real world, blood was always going to be thicker than water, and Mikey, Hassan, and even the twins were blood.

CHAPTER TWENTY-ONE

Sable briefly opened her eyes. As she drifted in and out of her first heroin trance, she didn't know where she was at. None of the walls that surrounded her or the bed she was lying in seemed recognizable. It felt like there was a lump in her throat, and she had cotton mouth. Trying not to be dizzy and to get her bearings, Sable closed her eyes once more. Fighting off an anxiety attack, she struggled to breathe as her mind somewhat started to return to normal.

"I see you awake now, huh, my queen?" Li'l Ronnie smiled as he leaned over to kiss Ethan's woman on the cheek. "You hungry? You want one of these BLT sandwiches I got? They still hot!"

It was then that Sable came back to her senses. It was then that it dawned on her what had taken place and where she was at. This fucking idiot who had the nerve to kiss her, like he was some innocent guy she was in love with and not the son of a bitch, sinister piece of shit that he truly was, had filled her veins full of dope. Now Li'l Ronnie was acting like it was all good. Like it was gonna be all smiles and handshakes.

"You nothing-ass nigga! How could you do that grimy shit you did?" She looked over at her arm, which was bruised from the needle entry and her fighting for the needle not to go in. "I promise you when I get free from here, you is as good as dead."

Li'l Ronnie found her threats cute and nothing more. Besides the breakfast sandwiches he'd eaten, he had also popped a few pills and swallowed them down with a double shot of Seagram's Gin. It would be daybreak in a few short hours, and he wanted to make sure he was ready and in rare form to keep fucking up his uncle's mind with pictures of Sable. While she was knocked out cold behind the amount of dope he had pushed into her veins, Li'l Ronnie had untied her arms and feet, had staged all sorts of poses, and had taken pictures. It would make any dude crazy to see his woman do such things with the next man. After tying her back up, he'd left to go get some food and laugh at all the fake calls of concern J-Blaze was hitting him off with.

Li'l Ronnie might have been wild and out of his mind from drinking and whatnot most of the time, but he wasn't a dummy. He knew J-Blaze was a "do anything" type of hustler who was always on the come up. And since his other boy had said J-Blaze had had a one on one with Ethan, the rest was apparent. It didn't take a rocket scientist to see the play J-Blaze was trying to make. That boy had sent him five different messages throughout the night, claiming he would meet him at this location or another. If J-Blaze wanted to play the game, then so be it. *Run all night!*

"Let me tell you something about my uncle. He never loved you like I did and still do. He was cheating on you all the time with different women, especially when we'd go out of town. He said you was just a piece of ass to him, something to do when he was bored." Li'l Ronnie was trying his best not only to turn Sable out on drugs but also to turn her against Ethan. He was still very much in love with her but was bitter over how they'd both fucked over his feelings.

Sable refused to look at him. The things he was saying about her man might have been true, but as long as she was eating good, driving good, and had that good dope to sell to all her white friends at the strip club, she didn't care what Ethan did with his dick. She'd learned a long time ago from an old ho in the game that a bitch would grow old before her time from trying to patrol a man's dick. Men were put on this earth to fuck anything that would run, hop, or skip.

After taking a few more pictures of Sable, this time with Black Tone's money scattered all around, Li'l Ronnie sent all the pictures to Ethan. You ain't the only one getting money! he wrote in the text that followed.

Minutes later he got a reply from his uncle, and it was simple: 187.

Li'l Ronnie laughed out loud as he filled a syringe full of Sable's next uncut fix.

Dre and his boys were camped out on the living-room floor, something they always did. It was almost dawn, and although their free-for-all crime spree had been interrupted because of the situation with Alexis, they still had plenty of stolen items to keep and sell. Having no power or city services for twenty-four hours was the best thing that could've happened to their otherwise flat pockets. Dre was the first to get up. He grabbed the remote, then checked to see if the television would come on. It didn't. He then checked his pockets and the dining-room table before discovering he was out of Newports.

His first mind told him to shoot up to the gas station, but he knew they were probably still shut down, with no power. After throwing on his Jordans, he went outside on the porch. Checking out both ends of the block, he could easily still smell the fire he'd set at the liquor store. The scent was surely mixed with that of a few other random fires that had been burning strong since last night. Hearing the sound of a helicopter flying lower than usual, Dre could only imagine what the city looked like from the pilot's seat.

Dre took Alexis's keys out of his pocket, jumped in her car, and slowly backed it out of the driveway. Never up at this time of morning, he heard the birds beginning to chirp and saw the creatures of the night go into hiding, where they would remain until nightfall came once more. Not caring one bit about being directly responsible for blazing the skin off four men, Dre brazenly drove up the block. Pausing at the corner, he took note of some young guys who were not familiar faces in the hood. As they kept their eyes on Dre, he returned the favor by watching them as well. With what used to be his favorite liquor store now burned to the ground, it was easy to see both what used to be the front entrance and the rear exit at the same time. It was also easy to see more mysterious faces posted in the alleyway.

Still mean mugging the unknown visitor in the car, one of the guys threw up an East Side hand sign at Dre. Holding down his neighborhood since back in the day, Dre's first instinct was to go home, get his chopper, and spray all they asses. He had no problem laying their bodies down on top of Mikey, Hassan, and them two other dead motherfuckers who was still resting in the rubble. But he'd made a pact with Black Tone just to fall back and peep what would pop off when the power came back on.

East Side faces throwing 'em up in a West Side hood. It's fucking shameless!

For his little sister's good and his own, he drove off in search of some cigarettes, letting the youngsters live, for now.

Listening to radio reports as he drove, Dre imagined all the money that had been out in the streets the night before. He had to weave in and out of the yellow lines on the street: he had no choice if he didn't want to hit either abandoned vehicles that had crashed into one another in the darkness of the night or the last of the scavengers darting out in the streets, carrying armloads of property that belonged to those who had got caught slipping during the power outage. Some items Dre saw them struggling to get home or to a place to sell were useless to him. However, in true Dre fashion, anything that he felt was of real value, or that he felt he or his team could benefit from having, he went after. And so the always roguish hustler pulled over; jumped out of his vehicle, gun in hand; and robbed the thieves who had just robbed the next man.

"Shit be like that sometimes, nigga! Now take the L and move on before I start feeling some sort of way and nut up." The few people who wanted to take issue with having their stolen goods strong-armed from them changed their minds when the barrel of Dre's gun was shoved in their faces. Even though it was early morning in Detroit, there was still no law. So the "anything goes" rule was still in full effect.

With the sun fighting to rise, Dre crossed over into Highland Park. Even though that city was just as broke as Detroit, at least they had electricity still pumping. Being so close to Detroit, Highland Park's restaurants, gas stations, and other businesses were jumping, even at this early time. With a trunk and a backseat now filled with ill-gotten gains, Dre pulled up in the parking lot of a Coney Island and parked in a spot where he would be sure Alexis's car was in clear eye shot from the restaurant's window. After ordering his food, he took a seat in a booth near the door. Dre did not have an inch of remorse about Hassan's and the others' untimely deaths at his hands, and his appetite was intact. Staring up at the television, which played the local news, he couldn't fathom what the reporter was saying. It was like she was talking about a war that had taken place in Iraqi or Syria, not Motown.

"Good morning, all. It's the morning of July thirty-first. I'm here reporting from the heart of the city of Detroit. I don't know what I can say. For once in my long career of covering stories from here and there, I'm almost speechless. The things that we've encountered just from setting up within the last thirty minutes or so are shocking, to say the least. We've had people coming up to us and asking for simple things, like water, and a few needing diapers for their baby because they lack transportation and the stores within their walking distance are closed until further notice. And speaking of transportation, there are absolutely no buses running in the city. The company halted services at noon yesterday, like every other business normally operating in Detroit, citing it was much too dangerous for their drivers."

She took a deep breath and had her cameraman pan the immediate area. "As you can see, there are several fires still burning around us, and we have no idea when they started and, to be honest, no idea when the fire department will be able to respond. There have been hundreds of nine-one-one distress calls reported to have come in, about everything from looting, arson, and strong arm robbery to hit-and-runs, shootings and, sadly, murders. There are rumors that victims have been relying on neighbors, family members, or privately owned companies to be transported to hospitals if they don't have vehicles themselves.

"The president is rumored to be sending in the National Guard shortly. The only thing I can say at this point is for the citizens of Detroit, the state of Michigan, and the United States to pray the power is restored soon to what once was a great and proud gem in automotive history. Officials are saying it may take place mid-afternoon. Like I said, let's pray!"

Dre knew he and his crew had definitely contributed to the long list of mayhem that had taken place overnight, and shrugged his shoulders, not caring. All he knew was they had to eat one way or another, and if preying on folks that were slipping was the only way to accomplish that, then so be it. After finishing his breakfast, Dre then stopped by the gas station and bought two packs of Newports.

Driving back to the hood, he wondered how Alexis was doing. He wanted to call her, but he knew she was in good hands with Black Tone. That guy might not have been Dre's favorite person in the world, but they did share one common interest—his little sister and his baby nephew. After turning on the block, he slowed down once more at the corner, peeping Pops and some other older man getting out of the cargo van they used to pick up stock. Amir was nowhere to be seen, but Dre assumed he wasn't far. When he got back to the house and parked, Dre went inside and woke his homeboys up, telling them to tool up, as shit could be about to get real.

CHAPTER TWENTY-TWO

Black Tone was ecstatic that his grandmother was doing better. After all the tests that were run and the X-rays, it was discovered that she had no broken bones or internal injuries, only a badly bruised face and extreme soreness. Her constant prayers, which had enraged Li'l Ronnie, must have worked. God had covered her, just as she'd asked. Going back and forth from Granny's bedside to Alexis, Black Tone was worn out.

Hearing from the nurses that Granny had been given a mild sedative and would be asleep for some time to come, Black Tone went back to see Alexis. She had been tested and treated for her wounds and given a rape kit. She'd pretended she didn't know her attackers, and her name had been placed on a long list of Detroit residents who had come in for treatment due to accidents, crimes, and other things related to having no power. Thank goodness Black Tone's best friend had snapped out of what she was going through the night before.

It was almost daylight, and Alexis was no longer feeling sorry for herself. She had turned her sorrow into anger once more. Although she loved Hassan and he was the father of her son, she had had no choice at the time and knew it. Given the way he had spoken about her when he thought she wasn't there, the way he had treated her when he found out his cousins had brutally violated her, she had seen no other way if Dre saw fit to kill him. Hassan's true feelings about dating her and about their child, or so she thought, had been shown at her expense.

"So they gave you your discharge papers, huh?" Black Tone bent down and handed Alexis her shoes.

Still not wanting him to look directly at her lumped-up face and busted lip, Alexis slightly turned her head before replying. "Yes. They said I need to follow up with my own doctor as soon as possible."

Black Tone and Alexis had been through just about everything one could imagine throughout the years. He knew that not only was she physically hurt, but she was embarrassed, humiliated, and crushed all rolled into one. He could not forget everything Dre had told him about what had popped off when he first arrived at the rear of the store and then got inside, but Alexis had never given him a detailed, blow-by-blow account. Knowing she was keeping all her emotions bottled up, Black Tone helped her down from the bed. After informing her that Granny would be fine, they headed toward the exit. Alexis was still very weak. Even though she was given pain medication, the trauma that she had received between her legs and on her thighs, courtesy of the twins, had her unable to stand for long.

"Listen, you sit here and rest up. I'm going to get the truck." Black Tone took her forearm and guided her to the bench.

While he sprinted off, Alexis took her cell out of her bag and held it up. Seconds later she found that she now had reception. Suddenly notifications of missed calls and texts started going off. She ignored them all. The first thing she wanted to do was call and check on her son. Besides her brother, he was the only blood she had. She wanted to tell her people she was on her way over there to pick him up, so they should have her baby ready, but she didn't. She wanted just to go hug him and tell him how sorry she was that his daddy was no more than a lying, cowardly, prejudiced piece of shit whom his uncle Dre had to kill, but of course, she couldn't.

Poor Alexis had no real way of knowing Hassan's true feelings for her and their baby and the events that had really taken place the evening before. No way in hell was Dre going to tell her that he took what was going to be her diamond engagement ring from Hassan's pocket as he lay bleeding to death. Just as Hassan had gone to his Maker believing Alexis didn't love him anymore, she would one day go to hers believing the same of him.

Black Tone pulled up to the curb. He got out and ran over to help Alexis up. As they slowly made their way to his vehicle, he paused and turned to face her. Alexis didn't have the opportunity to look away so he couldn't see how ugly the beating had her looking. Yet he didn't care how damaged she felt her face looked. Ever since they'd been kids playing on the block, he'd been in love with her. Everything he'd done in the past to protect her was out of love, and everything he was willing to do in the future was also based on that same devotion and love. He'd lay his life and freedom down for Alexis, and he wanted her to know.

"Listen up. I know me and you been hanging out here and there for years. And I done stood by and watched different dudes, one after the other, trying to push up on you. Some was all right, some was just assholes, but I ain't never said shit about it. I just let you be. You know, let you do you." Black Tone was caught up in his feelings and had to keep going before he lost his courage. "Even when you had little man, I was posted right by your side, even getting to work late to take you to doctor's appointments so you wouldn't be alone. Now, I ain't mad at you being with Hassan. Never was. But he's gone. And I swear on everything I know, my timing is fucked up, but just like Granny could've died yesterday, so could've you." He braced himself, not knowing how his best friend forever would react to what he was going to say. "And I don't want another day to go by without you knowing I love you."

Alexis wasn't shocked at what he'd just said. Over the years they'd told each other how much their love was real. She tried hard to smile, but it only hurt her sore jawline. Instead, she reached her arm up and held his arm.

"Boy, you know I got love for you."

Black Tone quickly realized she didn't understand what he was saying, so he had to make it clearer. "No, Alexis, I don't just have love for you. I'm in love with you."

Now this sudden revelation. It was like everyone around them was going in slow motion. Alexis didn't know what to think or what to say. She was speechless. It wasn't that she had never had her own set of extra-special feelings for him, because she had. But he knew all her innermost thoughts, the terrible secrets and the dirty lies she'd told over time. Black Tone had seen her at her worst, so she had only assumed he would never really want to wife a female like her. Besides, she had just been raped, had just shot a man, had lost her son's daddy, and had committed arson.

Taking her silence as a sign of rejection, Black Tone apologized. He then helped her up into the truck. He was a real man. He was her true friend. And even if she wasn't feeling him like he was feeling her, it was still all good. He'd always have her back, no matter what. That was who he was.

"Okay, look, I don't think you should go back home right now. Let me take you somewhere where you can chill out at and relax. Somewhere that you can get your mind right until I get back at you," he said. "I don't know if you talked to your brother or not, but I need to go see what's happening on the block firsthand. Plus, I need to see what Amir is talking about and what bag he trying to come out of. I mean, fucked up as them monsters was for that bullshit, them was his people. I need to go do some homework on the entire thing before you or little man come back around the way."

Alexis still didn't speak. She didn't say a word, just nodded and put on her sunglasses.

Eleven minutes later, Black Tone pulled up at a hotel. Leaving his truck running in the registration area, he jumped out. After going inside and handling his business, he returned with a receipt and two card-shaped room keys. He gave Alexis both keys, along with the paperwork. He wanted her to know it wasn't his intention to try to take advantage of the situation. His heart was pure.

"I paid for the room for three days. The swelling in your face should go down by then. Plus, I think, depending on how shit goes back in the hood, we should move you to another spot before the staff out here starts to get to familiar with you. Just in case things don't go as planned." Black Tone dug in his pocket and took out some of the money he'd gotten from Amir down at the club. Even though Li'l Ronnie had hit him hard in the pockets by stealing his main cash stash, he still had other revenue put up here and there. He wasn't broke by a long shot. "Here take this money and order room service or whatever else you want. I'll come back later today and bring you some personal shit you females like, or maybe we can run to Wal-Mart or something."

Alexis took the cash and put it in her bag. She then got out of the truck on her own and shut the door. She still didn't say a word, not even "Thank you." After looking at the card to find out the room number, she disappeared inside the double glass entryway.

Now alone in the truck, Black Tone started to return all the missed calls and texts he was just now receiving because of the awful reception inside the hospital walls.

Trying to take his mind off the fact he was going to hunt Li'l Ronnie down and kill him with his bare hands, he placed a call to Amir. After being sent to voice mail twice, Amir finally returned his call. By then Black Tone was only minutes away from being back in the hood.

"Hey, Amir. What's up? Where you at? I'm in the streets," he said anxiously, trying to peep game.

"Hey. I just left Home Depot." Amir's voice was solemn and cracked with each word he spoke. "Meet me over at Pops's if you can."

Black Tone agreed easily, knowing the shit was about to hit the fan. But whatever was about to jump off, right or wrong, he was gonna ride with Alexis until the wheels fell off, just as he'd promised when they were kids.

CHAPTER TWENTY-THREE

Amir had avoided his father's calls all evening and night. As daybreak was quickly approaching, he knew he could not keep lying to the person who had taught him to be the man he was. He had no choice whatsoever but to go over to his uncle's store and speak to Pops. Amir felt he owed it to him to deliver the awful news about what he now knew was true. When he finally showed up at his uncle's store, he sat outside in his car for ten minutes, trying to gather the courage to go break two men's hearts. Somehow Amir got it together and informed the patriarch of each family about the tragic fire and what he thought was their son's fate. His father turned pale as a ghost and had to sit down before he fell down. Amir watched all the joy and pride Pops really felt deep down inside for Mikey and Hassan leave his body. His face was blank, as was his uncle's. Amir called a few other family members before he left and had them come by the store and escort the two elders back to what had become a temporary tomb for their loved ones.

Amir headed over to his father's burnt-out store. When the rear area of the store was cool enough, Amir put on one of several pairs of fire-resistant gloves he'd purchased from Home Depot and grabbed some contractor-size garbage bags, which he'd also gotten from Home Depot. Not telling any of Ethan's East Side soldiers that were on loan to guard the property what he was looking for, he carefully stepped over the huge cinder blocks that had made up part of the reinforced wall. As Ethan's guys all looked on, trying to figure out what the owner of Detroit Live could possibly want to retrieve in the charred rubble, with its melted metal racks and fallen beams, one lit a blunt. Another pulled out a pint of Rémy and passed it around. It didn't matter much to them what time of the morning it was. They had been out here all night, babysitting a smoldering burnt-out party store that would never rise again.

Wishing he had on better shoes or boots with thicker soles, Amir took his time navigating through the debris that was once his father's pride and joy. After no more than five minutes of poking around with a steel pipe he'd taken from the alley behind an abandoned house, the distraught oldest son stopped. Glancing up and outside the building, he saw the young men passing a blunt back and forth and laughing about something. It had been a long night for him. He was exhausted and mentally drained. This was a nightmare, and he'd been living it alone for hours. Paranoid and in his feelings, Amir felt it was he who was the source of their amusement.

"What the fuck y'all niggas laughing at? What's so fucking funny? Huh? What? Somebody tell me?"

At first Ethan's guys didn't say a word. They were trained and knew that they were here doing their boss a favor. On the regular, none of them rocked out on the West Side, anyhow. It was a Detroit thing that most people who didn't live there wouldn't understand. Although they stopped laughing and tried to figure out Amir's sudden problem with them, he got loose lipped again and called them niggas.

"Hey, watch your damn mouth," one of the guys advised.

"Yeah, we ain't with that nigga shit," said another.

"Yeah, nigga. Watch your damn mouth," a third guy yelled out, not realizing he'd called Amir the same name he didn't want to be addressed as.

Amir didn't have time to argue with them and their attitudes, although he felt justified. He had to deal with the worst thing ever imaginable. Turning his head, he got back to the gruesome task at hand. After a few more seconds of working his way to what was once the storeroom, he started to get goose bumps.

Amir's hand shook as he moved smaller items in the storeroom with the aid of the steel pipe. He was terrified of what he would find, but he knew for his father's sake, as well as his own, he had to continue. He had to know if his younger brothers had been somehow trapped inside. After leaning the pipe against what used to be a bin used to store returnable bottles, Amir bent down. Using both hands, protected by his gloves, he lifted up one of the smaller beams. He wanted to yell. He wanted to cry. He wanted to ask Allah why. Most of all, he wanted to throw up. This was the one time he was right but didn't want to be.

Here he was, looking at the most gruesome sight he'd ever seen in person. Here lay one of his cousins. He knew this could not have been his sibling, because the blackened, almost skeleton-like remains were too big. The face and arms were a dull red in some small spots where the skin had burned off the bones. The rest of the body looked as if it had been dipped in hot tar and had melted to the floor. His clothes were almost nonexistent, and what was left of them could not be differentiated from what used to be skin.

As the beam grew heavier, Amir wanted to drop it back down, he but didn't want it to strike whichever one of his cousins this was. Instead, he used all the strength he had to shove the beam to the far side of the room, praying it didn't land on another body. Knowing his father and uncle would be arriving soon, Amir wanted to locate all four bodies to ease their grief. He knew there would be no police, ambulance, or other agencies that could help them, so as the oldest son, Amir felt that showing some respect and reverence to his kin was his sole responsibility.

Looking back over his shoulder, he sucked up his present feeling of contempt for the young guys and asked a few of them to grab a pair of the gloves he'd left in the bag by the wall and come help him. Of course, after his arrogant comments, none of Ethan's guy's moved an inch toward the bag. Amir asked again. This time when they laughed, he had no question in his mind that it was directed at him.

"Look, I need some help over here. Can a few of y'all just please grab some gloves and come help me?" Amir swallowed his pride for Pops's sake.

"And get my new gym shoes dirty? Hell, naw. I just got these Jordans," the biggest of them all responded.

"Yeah, he right. We niggas can't get our shoes or clothes fucked up by messing around with you." His boy gave him a fist pound as he sipped on the last of the Rémy.

Amir was no fool. He had found out a long time ago the one rule of the streets. *Money talks, and bullshit walks.* "Okay, I tell you what. If I can get some help, I'm paying a thousand dollars, plus replacing them shoes." The offer of cash had their attention. "And if you don't think I'm good for it and don't know exactly who the fuck I am out in these streets, east and west, call Ethan. But trust when you do call him to ask about me, I'll bet that thousand you'll be over here helping for free."

One guy, then another thought about what he was saying and knew it was true. If Ethan had them come clear across town to stand around some dumb-ass building that had been on fire all night, Amir was right. Just like that, that thousand dollars seemed like a million. After following just about the same route through the debris as Amir had, the guys who had opted to come had almost the same response as Amir—shock.

"Oh, hell naw! What the fuck you want us to do with this bullshit? These is burned-up bodies! I ain't picking up no dead, burned-up motherfucker."

With all of them refusing to help lift both his deceased cousins, who were laid out close to one another, Amir knew that trying to get them to help pry Mikey and Hassan apart would be like asking them to kill their own firstborn. He was glad he had found his brothers' bodies. And glad they were together. Amir couldn't figure out what exactly had happened to make them all be this close to the rear door of the storeroom and yet unable to escape. The huge steel door appeared to be unlocked, further confusing him.

After practically begging them for help, Amir upped the ante, offering five thousand dollars to whichever one or two of them helped. Needless to say, they were fighting with each other to help remove all four bodies from the ruins. After they placed them on the trash bags in the alley, Amir hurried to his trunk and grabbed the beige-colored painter's tarp he'd also purchased during his early morning trip to Home Depot. He had them assist him in wrapping each body completely, so no parts were showing, not even their faces.

Amir was out of breath. He felt as if his soul was damaged. Both his brothers were gone, and he didn't know why. One of Ethan's soldiers who had wrapped either Mikey or Hassan swore the body had a huge hole right through the front of the skull. If that was true, then it was easy to figure out why they couldn't escape from the flames. Seeing through the almost wall-less structure that Pops and some more of his family had shown up, Amir knew better than to uncover either of the four bodies. It was best that they remembered them the way they were, and not as what the fire had made them become.

When Pops came around to the alleyway and almost fell to his knees in grief, Amir broke down as well. Out of nowhere Black Tone bent the corner. Seeing that his friend and Pops were hysterical, he could only stare down at the four dead bodies that lined the side of the store and wonder how he was going to protect Alexis if and when the truth ever got out.

"Oh, hey, Tone. I see you finally made it." Though Amir was devastated as he mourned the loss of his brothers, he still found the time to add sarcasm to his tone, as if his troubles were more important than others.

Black Tone sucked it up, knowing he had to remain calm. He was definitely sad that Hassan and Mikey had died, but considering the circumstances that led up to their untimely demise, it was hard to shed a tear. Yes, he was going to support Amir, knowing he and Pops had to be going through hell right now with their loved ones laid out in the back alley of their party store, but Black Tone's number one mission was to try to see exactly where Amir's mind was as far as how the fire initially started, to ascertain whether he had any suspicions or had heard anything. Most importantly, Black Tone wanted to know if Amir or any of these other strange faces standing back there with them had noticed anything wrong with the bodies. He knew if any of the four had sustained half the gunplay Dre had said went on inside the storeroom, there would have to be visible holes in their bodies, burned or not.

"Yeah, I'm finally here. I was posted with my grand-mother all night. She was doing really bad at first."

Amir didn't respond. His attention was focused on the four wrapped painter's tarps. Nothing anyone else said mattered, not even Pops, who was praying out loud, in denial. Black Tone took it upon himself to fall back just a bit and let the entire scene play itself out. Keeping an eye on the guys he didn't know, he started to wonder what he'd really missed while he was posted up with his grandmother and out of the loop.

Something seemed strange about the way they were glaring at him. Black Tone tried to remember if he'd maybe thrown them out of the club before or even denied them entrance because of what they had on. However, he'd come in contact with so many people and glanced up briefly at so many faces, it was hard to tell what exactly their fascination with him was. But whatever it was, his gun was on his hip—locked, loaded, and ready to make an example out of anyone who felt some sort of a way about this, that, or the third thing. He'd find out for sure who they were; he was just giving Amir time to cope with the ugly reality he was dealing with.

After a short while of just standing around, allowing Amir to come to grips with the fact that Mikey, Hassan, and his cousins were gone and were not coming back no matter how hard Pops and his uncle prayed, Black Tone decided to move forward. He told Amir they had to move the bodies.

Amir knew that under normal circumstances, it wasn't a great idea to disturb a body, let alone remove one from a crime scene, but this was different. This morning was like none other. Even if he did choose to wait for the fire trucks, the police, an ambulance, or the county morgue, there would be no telling how long they'd be out in the alley. The sun had come completely up, and it could only cause the four burned bodies wrapped in thick bur-lap-type cloth to decompose even more, if at all possible.

Black Tone was ecstatic that they had somehow man-aged to get the bodies outside and onto the ground. They had compromised and tainted any evidence that Alexis and Dre could have possibly left behind. If the scorching hot flames had failed to eliminate indications of who did what and when, Amir and whoever these guys were with the gloves lying at their feet had. There was so much going on within the city limits, the blame game could go on forever and a day. Black Tone exhaled. This situation seemed like it might work out. If it did, that would be one less worry on his plate. Li'l Ronnie, however, was a horse of an entirely different color. That worry would never work itself out until he had choked the life out of him.

Pops was growing weaker by the moment, not only physically, but in his faith as well. Clutching his prayer beads, he closed his eyes. Amir saw his father's spirit deteriorate as the elderly but still proud man fought to stand on his feet. This horrific sight of death behind what had once been his thriving business was more than any parent could bear to withstand. Wasting no more time trying to figure out who to call that might owe him a favor or two, Amir stepped up, as well as he should. He asked one of his family members who were standing off to the side to go drive the cargo van back around to the alley where they had all congregated.

Black Tone stood in the alleyway, directing the man while he was attempting to back in. While his back was turned, he suddenly heard a lot of commotion. Instinctively, he grabbed his gun off his hip. On the other side of the alley stood Dre and some of his cohorts.

Well, I'll be damned. Didn't I tell this crazy fool to just sit tight?

Not knowing what Dre's next move was going to be, or why he even had shown back up at the scene of the crime, Black Tone paused.

"What's up with all that East Side weak-ass bullshit now?" Dre shouted out, throwing up his Ls for Linwood. "N.F.L. all day around this motherfucker, ya heard!"

Black Tone being confused did not last for long, as all of the random young guys he'd never seen in the neighborhood or running with Amir returned words.

"East Side until the day we die, nigga! You Linwood pussies don't want it! We over on the East Side are making that real money and slow fucking y'all hoes! It's Eagle Hawk Bag our way!" one of them yelled.

Eagle Hawk Bag? What the fuck? Black Tone held his gun down at his side and let the two crews link up.

The fighting words from both sides caused them all to whip out their guns. Showing no signs of fear, each group walked closer. When they were within arm's reach, one took a swing at the other, and the battle was on. No guns were fired; it was just fist-to-fist combat. Seconds into the slugfest, Pops was knocked to the ground by mistake and cut the side of his hand while trying to break his fall. Disrespectfully, all four of the dead bodies were trampled on, as if they were bags of garbage. Amir yelled out, demanded that they stop and for Dre to get the fuck on, but no one listened. Having let Black Tone and others handle his dirty work for so long, the self-proclaimed heroine kingpin had forgotten there were no time-outs in the streets; it was just "nonstop until you drop."

Bloodied and bruised, the two cliques finally separated. Vowing revenge and gunplay when they met again, Dre and his boys left the alley the same way they had come in, talking cash shit.

"Why you didn't do shit? How you let them wild animals come back here and disrespect my family like this?" Amir looked up at Black Tone, throwing question after question in his face.

"Hold tight, Amir. Who are these guys? Why they yelling, 'East Side,' and throwing up Ethan's dope brand name like that? Who the fuck are they?"

In the midst of all that was going on, Amir had almost forgotten about the deal he'd made with Ethan. The deal that he knew was going to infuriate his right-hand man, Black Tone. Not wanting even more trouble and controversy to pop off, he tried to break down to his boy what he had done and the reason why.

"Listen, Tone, I needed to do something. Last night people were coming and poking around like they wanted to go digging through the store. I tried calling you, but you said you were busy."

"Busy?" Black Tone fired back, heated over Amir's poor choice of words. "What the fuck you mean, busy? My damn grandmother was hurt, laying up in a hospital bed, fighting for her life, and you saying I was busy. Is you crazy or what?"

"Naw, I ain't crazy, but I had to protect my family. Like I said, I called you first, but then I had to call in and get some extra eyes and boots on the ground."

"Yeah, so? And? What that got to do with why these little motherfuckers shouting Eagle Hawk Bag?"

Amir tried to slow walk Black Tone away from everyone who was ear hustling, his own family included. "Listen, I asked Ethan to do me a favor and send me some of his soldiers who was not afraid to post up on this side of town."

Black Tone was starting to get the picture. He didn't need it spelled out. His boy Amir had betrayed him, knowing they had an agreement about dealing with Ethan until Li'l Ronnie was made to pay for what he'd done to Granny.

"So it's like that, huh? Well, guess what? That ho-ass nigga Li'l Ronnie still gonna die for that shit he did. That's my word! Fuck Ethan! Fuck Eagle Hawk Bag and fuck all these niggas you got over here on a dummy mission."

Amir knew deep down inside he was wrong for the backroom deal he'd cut, but he told Black Tone that with him family always had to come first. Black Tone grinned, knowing that when and if the time ever came to stand tall, Alexis was his family, and she would come first as well.

CHAPTER TWENTY-FOUR

Amir had made sure the bodies of his loved ones were respectfully laid out in Detroit Live's walk-in freezer, which was still ice cold. He was trying to keep them as cool as possible. He was torn on what to do next. Pops wanted to follow Muslim tradition and bury his sons as soon as possible, so as not to prolong further the disrespect for their remains. Amir, however, wanted some sort of autopsy performed on all four, or at least a proper criminal investigation. He realized he'd already messed up by removing the bodies not only from the rubble, but also from the entire scene by taking them way across town. He wanted legal justice for what he believed was no accident. Just as one of Ethan's soldiers had mentioned, Amir had also seen what he thought were bullet holes in one of the bodies when he looked under the tarp as they unloaded the cargo van in which the bodies were transported.

Black Tone stood silently by, letting Amir run different scenarios by him. Some sounded like he was grasping at straws, while others were surprisingly close to what had truly transpired. Yet considering how Amir had played him about his rekindled alliance with Ethan, even if Black Tone felt the need to put him out of his misery over what had taken place during Mikey's and Hassan's final moments on earth, it was a no go. Black Tone was insulted that not once since he'd arrived had Amir even bothered to ask anything about Granny or his stolen money. Amir was out for himself, and now so was Black Tone. Black Tone had decided back in the alley, as he showed mercy and helped load the corpses, that he would keep his friends close and his enemies even closer. After Amir did what he did, he was indeed Black Tone's foe, no questions asked, needed or answered.

"Hey, I know you cool with the girl Alexis. The one that claiming she got a baby by my little brother. Where she at? Why she ain't been around since this shit happen? Any other time she all on his dick, trying to come up," Amir said.

Doing everything in his power to remain calm, Black Tone tried his best to play the game and not drop his cards, like Dre had earlier. "Whoa. Slow down, Amir. First of all, that is Hassan's son. Have you seen the baby? He looks just like your brother spit him out. And secondly, she's not even in town."

"She's not?" Amir raised his eyebrow, knowing he'd run into another dead end in trying to put together the pieces to the evening before.

"Naw. She's down in Miami with some of her friends," Black Tone lied, hoping to throw him off Alexis's trail. "I was gonna call and tell her what happened, but that ain't the type of thing you wanna tell a person over the phone."

"Yeah, I guess you right. But you know what else I wonder? I wonder why that crazy-ass brother of hers, Dre, showed up in the alley with them knuckleheads he run with."

Black Tone looked at Amir as if he had three or four heads. He couldn't believe he would be so dumb to even ask him that. "Dawg, are you fucking serious? What the hell did you think was going to happen when you brought some East Side niggas over to where they lay they head at?"

"Yeah, I guess so. But still that bullshit Dre did was fucked up. Them idiots knocked Pops down and disrespected my brothers."

"Yo, hold the fuck up. I mean, I ain't taking sides, but why you keep saying Dre name like he was out there in that alley, banging by himself? Fuck Ethan's people that was out of pocket and they zip code. They wanted to go so hard, then so be it. That's on you. That was your call to bring them Eagle Hawk Bag fools into the mix."

Amir sat back. Something about the attitude Black Tone had didn't seem right. He knew Black Tone was pissed about the situation with Ethan's nephew, but Amir felt like he was taking it too far, and he let him know. "Wow. So after all this time of us doing business, I didn't know you were with all the territory gangbanging mess. I thought you was bigger than that local bullshit. And besides, truth be told, we is Eagle Hawk Bag too. Where you think they dope coming from?"

"I am bigger than that, but that walking dead man Li'l Ronnie straight violated. That bitch came into my crib and put his hands on my grandmother! That shit ain't never gonna be all good with me. Never. And for the record, I thought Eagle Hawk was taking a time-out?"

"Okay, Tone. I feel you about the boy. But he made a mistake. And we do a lot of good business with his uncle, so . . ."

Black Tone stood to his feet and towered over Amir. "So what in the fuck you saying, Amir? Be real clear with it, motherfucker!"

"All I'm saying is maybe you should let all that wanting to kill his nephew go. It's bad for business. What's done is done, and you can't turn back the hands of time."

It was as if you could hear a pin drop inside the club. Black Tone did everything in his power not to reach down and choke Amir. After all the shit he'd been saying about how family came first with him and how family loyalty was everything, here he stood, having the nerve to tell him to fall back and forget that a nigga fucked over Granny like she meant nothing.

"Bitch, fuck business! Your ass over here going on and on about that nigga Dre knocked Pops over in the alley and cut his precious hand on them dead, burned-up motherfuckers back there in the freezer. You got me all the way fucked up around here! You ain't once asked if my grandmother is okay, if she needed anything, or how I'm carrying it! Instead, you want me to roll over and play dead and be a good ole obedient Negro because Li'l Ronnie's uncle does good business with us. Fuck all that! Now, turn back the hands of time on that!"

"Damn, Tone." Amir tried his best to protest but was stopped by the threat of Black Tone laying hands on him.

"Naw, dawg. I'm out. You go ahead and rock with Ethan. I'm gonna go check on my real family, and you stay here with yours." Black Tone callously pointed back toward the walk-in freezer turned temporary morgue before storming out.

Amir had never seen this side of Black Tone. Deep down inside, he accepted the fact that Li'l Ronnie had to die for principle's sake, but something about the way his partner in crime had gone so hard didn't seem right. It was as if he was hiding something. Not trusting anyone until he found out what exactly had happened to Mikey and Hassan, the oldest remaining son of Pops made a call. He had to cover all his bases.

While driving on the freeway, Black Tone, along with the rest of the city, finally got the good news they had been waiting on. In less than twenty minutes the restoration of power would commence. He took the back roads as he drove toward the neighborhood, which was a change for him. Preoccupied with the major disagreement he and Amir had just had, Black Tone knew it would be only a matter of time before they parted ways. They each had a different mind-set on how the business that Amir had been the face of since linking up should now be run.

He'd taken a nice-size hit when Li'l Ronnie had discovered his shoe box. Although he was not destitute, he knew he wanted and needed to make that cash back up. After getting out of the truck, he walked around to the side door. Wild Child had put his high school wood shop skills to work and had the door barricaded with an extra-thick sheet of plywood. Content with the side entrance, Black Tone then walked around the rest of the perimeter of the house to ensure that there had been no more break-ins or possible breaches.

At this point he had no idea where Li'l Ronnie was, and he knew he was going to get no help whatsoever from Amir. He was on his own in the hunt for the monster that had attacked his grandmother, and he would leave no stone unturned to find him. Going up on the porch, he noticed Dre and the fellas sitting on the stairs of his and Alexis's house. Black Tone nodded, showing Dre the same respect they had always shown to each other over the years. Once inside, Black Tone angrily walked down the hallway. As he stepped over the smashed flat-screen that partially blocked his bedroom doorway, his taste for revenge intensified. The damage that Li'l Ronnie had done to his private domain was nothing major, nothing that couldn't be fixed or replaced. It was the point and principle that Ethan's wayward nephew felt he could get away with violating someone else's space that really got to him.

After picking a few bottles of cologne up off the floor, ones that hadn't been smashed, Black Tone went into his granny's room and started to clean up the best he could before he became enraged. Looking in the oval-shaped mirror attached to her dresser, he rubbed his hands together, knowing that he was going to end up in jail or dead soon. It was going to be Li'l Ronnie living on this earth or him. Black Tone knew they both could no longer coexist, not after the pain, fear, and disrespect Li'l Ronnie had brought into his grandmother's life.

Knowing nothing would make him feel better than seeing his granny's face, he locked the house back up and headed back out. As he drove down the street, he stopped in front of where Alexis's car was parked and signaled for Dre to come to the truck.

"Your sister is good. I don't know if she called you or not, but she gonna stay out the hood for a little while, until I make sure shit is all good."

Dre agreed as far as Alexis was concerned, but he wanted to know what was up with his boy bringing them East Sides their way. "Yo, dawg. I know you told me to keep a low profile, but if you start letting one of them bitch niggas come over this way and stunt, soon it's gonna be two, then three."

Amir had been right earlier in what he said. Normally, Black Tone didn't go for all that east-west shit. Everyone was welcome to party and have a good time at Detroit Live as long as they knew how to behave. And any real player that came correct in the city could cop some of that good product he and Amir were pushing. But this time and this day were different. Black Tone was riding with Dre and his decision to bang out all the way. If he wasn't trying to keep his fronts up for Alexis's sake, he probably would have put his boots to a few East Side heads his damn self.

"Don't worry. I got you on that. I'm sure it won't pop off again. Besides, y'all was cracking heads." Black

Tone laughed and gave Dre a fist pound. "And as for the situation up there, he lost right about now. He grasping at straws but gonna keep coming up empty if I play his ass right."

Dre spoke a little bit more about the info he'd found out about Li'l Ronnie, who had been locked up with him. To Black Tone, finding out that the dude who had been his sworn nemesis for years now had his back, like he was forced to have his, was strange, to say the least. But whatever the case or circumstances that now had them on the same team, he was good with it as long as Li'l Ronnie paid for his sins. As he pulled off and turned off the block, he heard the cheers from people in the neighborhood when they learned they had power once more. By the time he had crossed over out of Detroit, the radio was reporting that the city and its infrastructure were back in operation at 68 percent and growing.

When Black Tone reached the hospital, he dialed Alexis's number before he stepped inside and lost his reception, but she didn't answer. He assumed she must have been asleep from all the pain medication she was given, and he texted her where he was at and what time he'd be leaving the hospital and heading her way.

CHAPTER TWENTY-FIVE

"Something ain't right. I can't put my finger on it, so I need you to just stay close and tell me the blow-by-blow play he makes. I can't use anybody from this way, because he'll peep that out way to easy," Amir said into his phone.

"No problem. Which hospital?"

Amir hung up and tried not to think twice about his decision. He knew what he was doing was foul, but he felt like he had no other choice. Tone was his manz. And yeah, he'd always held the club down and his end of their illegal ventures. He was a stand-up guy in Amir's eyes. Well, up until now, he thought that much was true. Black Tone was putting personal matters over business, and to Amir, they didn't mix. But Amir was much too blind to see that he had done the same by even bringing Ethan's guys over to the store to do his bidding. Amir knew Black Tone lived in that hood, and if there was any trouble behind Amir's selfish, desperate decision, Black Tone would be the one to suffer the fallout. He didn't care. He wanted what he wanted when he wanted it. Part of Amir wanted to be wrong about Black Tone, but his gut told him he was not. His homeboy was hiding something.

J-Blaze rolled a blunt and sat back in the car Ethan had let him use. The old-school player had told him that no amount of money was too much and that he didn't care who got hurt in the process. At first Ethan's anger was maybe an eight or a nine for what Li'l Ronnie had done to the old woman and the rift he'd caused between the connect. But now it was much deeper than money and drugs to Ethan. Suddenly this had become extremely personal. Li'l Ronnie had taken Sable. He had kidnapped her sometime during the late evening and had been holding her hostage. Ethan was fucked up in the head behind his woman being held against her will by her ex-boyfriend, his nephew. Having no filter, Li'l Ronnie had sent J-Blaze the same pictures he'd sent to his uncle, and he had made sure to let his uncle know that.

Li'l Ronnie had lost it completely. He was threatening to go live on Facebook and expose the entire organization, naming names and the whole nine. Ethan and anyone else who was working an Eagle Hawk Bag should have been worried. If it was ever discovered that someone on the team had betrayed the family and hadn't fessed up that they knew where Li'l Ronnie was holed up at, they would have to die as well for assisting in his bullshit. Not only was Li'l Ronnie a coward for beating up the old lady; he was now a potential rat with a bounty on his head.

J-Blaze was on the grind for that come-up bread. He had done his homework. As he lit the potent medical trees he'd copped from his peoples, he decided that all the running from here and there that Li'l Ronnie had put him through during the night had finally paid off. He had just left the last place Li'l Ronnie had him go. Li'l Ronnie had claimed he was going to meet up with him there just to talk. Of course, it was a dummy mission, like the others had been earlier.

Yet it was as if the hustle Gods were shining down on J-Blaze. He'd been driving around in the general area his former friend had told him to meet him at and had had to pull over to take a leak. After ducking behind the gas station wall, he'd been surprised when he peered around the corner while zipping his pants back up. He'd seen Li'l Ronnie leave through the door, jump back in his Benz truck, which he was still driving in, too dumb to hide. J-Blaze had allowed him to pull off and had followed him from afar in the plain, average vehicle, which no one would ever look at twice. Now here he was, posted a few doors down, ready to put in work and make the bounty money his.

J-Blaze stayed slumped down in the driver's seat so as not to draw any attention to himself. Keeping a careful eye on the front door of the run-down house, he placed a call to Ethan and told him to get his bread ready to cash out. "I'm seconds away from running up in this bitch, blazing this chopper on his ass."

Ethan cautioned him not go inside that fast, because he didn't want Sable harmed. J-Blaze was disappointed to hear that, but he would do as he was told. In his mind Sable was no more than a used-up tramp who had traded one young, weak-ass slimeball Negro for the next, only an older model. At first Ethan had wanted his blood brought back alive and was gonna make him start back at the bottom of the food chain for jacking off the plug of plugs. But now he wanted Li'l Ronnie dead behind some pussy that he had stretched out in the first place. Ethan wanted the address, saying he wanted to be there when his sister's son took his last breath. J-Blaze thought that was a tad bit harsh and uncalled for, but once again he did as he was told and texted his boss the info after they hung up.

J-Blaze had just pressed SEND, as luck would have it, when the front door opened. Li'l Ronnie wasn't done running. He came out of the house and stood on the porch a few minutes, then jumped in his truck. Faced with the choice of following Li'l Ronnie and catching him slipping out in the street or getting inside the house somehow and waiting for him to return, J-Blaze let him pull off.

He hoped he had made the right decision and had not let his "for sure" money out of his sight. After making sure the taillights had turned the corner off the block, J-Blaze jumped out of his ride.

Making as little noise as possible, he crept around the small-framed house and peeked in any window he could. Not seeing anything but a table, a couch, and a few blue plastic milk cartons on the floor, J-Blaze could tell the house was empty, for the most part. The rear bedroom windows had newspaper covering them, and he wondered if that was where Li'l Ronnie was holding Sable.

Not knowing how much time he had before Li'l Ronnie returned, J-Blaze raised his gym shoe off the ground and kicked in the flimsy back door. Once inside the house, he aimed his gun in every possible direction, as if he was the police executing a search warrant for a mass murderer. After discovering that all the front rooms of the shotgun dwelling were vacant, he then eased open the first bedroom door. There was nothing in there but what appeared to be old bags of clothes. Just as he was about to open the second bedroom door, he saw a flash from a pair of headlights pulling into the driveway. Assuming his friend had returned faster than he'd thought he would, J-Blaze hid in the corner behind the old piss-stained couch and waited for his meal ticket to come back inside.

Unaware of what was on the other side of the door to the rented crackhead house, Li'l Ronnie stepped across the threshold, holding a bag in his arms. After closing the door, he headed straight toward the bedroom J-Blaze had not had the opportunity to check out yet. Before Li'l Ronnie's hand could touch the knob, J-Blaze was on him.

"Hold up, fool. I'll take that." J-Blaze eased his hand around the front of his boy's waistband and removed his gun.

Li'l Ronnie was shocked. He couldn't understand how he had been found. He had turned off his GPS. He had been careful not to meet anywhere near this house. Nevertheless, J-Blaze had peeped out where he was held up at. It was over now. The only thing left to do now was to negotiate his life and his freedom. Not wanting to waste time, Li'l Ronnie went right to it as they walked into the room where Sable was tied to the bed, high as hell and speaking in tongues, as if she was possessed by the devil himself. J-Blazed looked over at her like she was filth. He had no sympathy for the conniving bitch, because she was part of the reason they were all here and things had gotten so twisted in Ethan and his nephew's relationship.

Li'l Ronnie started to beg, hoping to change his would-be killer's mind. "Listen up. You ain't gotta do this. I know my uncle offered you money, but it ain't no thang, J. I got the bread on the floor too. Go check out that shoe box over there on the table. I know you want what's inside. We can split it right down the middle."

J-Blaze kept his gun held high and aimed at Li'l Ronnie's head. He gave a slight nod in the direction of the table, and Li'l Ronnie got the hint that he was to go open the shoe box. Doing as he had been told indirectly, he flipped open the top to the shoe box. Only a few hundred-dollar bills were missing from what was once Black Tone's stash, and Li'l Ronnie threw out the idea of them dividing the funds equally and J-Blaze just telling his uncle that he couldn't be found.

"Naw, nigga. Sorry. Too late for all that. Your punk-ass uncle already on his way. And as for that money, come on now, fool. What the fuck I look like, splitting some money with a dead man? You can't spend that shit in hell."

Li'l Ronnie continued to beg until the moment J-Blaze slow walked him to the front of the house to unlock the door for Ethan, who had come alone and unarmed. Ethan didn't even want to speak to or look at his blood until he made sure his young pussy was okay. Freeing her from bondage, Ethan had tears forming in his eyes as Sable continued to behave strangely. It was as if she was deranged. After letting her weak body fall back on the bed, Ethan then focused on his nephew.

"I should kill you myself for all the dumb shit you've done. First, you get drunk and embarrass me by getting your ass kicked. Then you almost fuck up the connect by beating up some damn old lady that was already half dead when you went inside the house in the first place." He looked over at Sable and finally let his tears drop. "Then you follow up all that wild bullshit by taking my woman, my lady, and trying to turn her out!"

Li'l Ronnie knew this was it for him. He felt he'd been fucked over by his uncle long enough, and if he didn't say what he wanted to say now, he'd go to his grave regretting it. Now crying as well, Li'l Ronnie started telling his uncle everything he could think of that had been bothering him since birth. For J-Blaze, being forced to hear story after story was like being slowly tortured. The more things the nephew mentioned that he thought the uncle should be held accountable for, the more things in return the uncle brought up to blame the nephew.

J-Blaze had been up all night and easily grew tired of both of the grown-ass men with shared DNA acting like straight bitches. Li'l Ronnie was on the verge of being a rat, so in J-Blaze's eyes he had to go. Ethan was so emotionally weak, turned out, and twisted by his nephew's secondhand ho Sable, J-Blaze felt the old player couldn't effectively control his own life anymore, let alone lead an army of young, hungry soldiers trying to come up out in the Detroit streets.

"You know what? Both of y'all straight pussy." J-Blaze curled his top lip upward, ready to put in work.

"What the fuck you just say?" Ethan turned to face J-Blaze, ready to warn him to watch his mouth, but he was met with a single bullet, which entered right underneath his left eye and exited through the rear of his head. With fragments of his skull mixed with blood splattered on the wall behind where he stood, Ethan dropped to the floor. Within seconds Eagle Hawk Bag was no more.

Li'l Ronnie's jaw seemed to be stuck in the open position. While part of him was overjoyed that his uncle, who he felt had messed him over for so many years, was dead, he couldn't believe the only father figure he knew was gone. Finally, he swallowed the lump in his throat and spoke. "Damn, dawg. Good looking out. I knew you wasn't gonna let him just kill me. Damn good looking. We can still split that bread and try to link back up with the plug."

J-Blaze was amused. He couldn't believe how dumb Li'l Ronnie was to think he'd ever do business with a weak-ass rat like him. "Dig this, lame. Me and you could never really rock out together. Yeah, you hooked me up with your uncle, but I ain't jack shit like you or him. I was born to be a boss, not some do boy. So naw, we can't split my money over there in the shoe box, and naw, we can't link back up with the plug. What part of you a dead man didn't you understand?"

Before Li'l Ronnie could repent for his sins or J-Blaze could send him on his way straight to hell, they both heard Sable—half out of her mind, her arms folded, rocking back and forth as she sat on the edge of the bed—repeating the same bible verse Granny had said before being tossed out of the bed and thrown against the wall.

"Yea, though I walk through the valley of the shadow of death, I will fear no evil; for thou art with me, thy rod and thy staff they comfort me."

Li'l Ronnie turned to look at his ex-woman, whom he still was in love with, one more time. He never had a chance to turn back, as J-Blaze let one round go ripping through the lovesick wanksta's temple and sent another barreling through his neck. Like his uncle, Li'l Ronnie folded and fell to the floor. Not wanting to leave any live witnesses, J-Blaze went over to the table and filled two needles with lethal dosages of heroin straight from that Eagle Hawk brand. The opportunistic female was already so out of it, she didn't feel the two pricks in her arm and didn't fight death when it crept up on her. After running through Ethan's pockets, J-Blaze snatched up the shoe box with Black Tone's money in it and Li'l Ronnie's gun. With a huge smile plastered on his face, he left the dilapidated house and shut the door behind him. Once back in the car, he received a text message that made him smile even harder.

CHAPTER TWENTY-SIX

Black Tone left the hospital in good spirits. His granny was doing 100 percent better and was even preaching to him to leave that late-night job at the club alone. She was back to telling him that he needed to find himself a nice girl and settle down somewhere. Granny was back in full effect, and he couldn't wait to share the news with his best friend, Alexis. Driving to the hotel, he tried calling her cell again. This time she answered.

"Hey, girl. How you feeling?" he asked, glad to hear her voice.

"I'm much better. I just got out of the tub after soaking awhile, but now I need some clothes and stuff."

"Don't worry. I told you I got you." Black Tone didn't care that she didn't want him in the same way he wanted her. She was still Alexis. She was still his best friend for life. "I just left from seeing Granny, so I'm on my way. Meet me down in the lobby in, like, ten minutes, and we'll go pick up some things to hold you over a few more days, until I figure all this shit out."

Alexis agreed, and they ended their conversation. She hadn't stopped thinking about what Anthony had told her, but she couldn't just turn off the love she had for Hassan, dirty as he had turned out to be.

"He left the hospital and picked some female up at a hotel far from the hood."

"Oh yeah? A female, huh?" Amir quizzed, knowing something was going on with Black Tone, his supposed business partner and friend. "What she look like? Describe her."

"I dunno. She just look like some bad-ass female from around the way, with dark sunglasses on. She did look like she got a nice fat ass on her when she walked out the lobby, though."

Amir told him to trail Black Tone and the female from afar and, when they stopped somewhere, to try to get a picture. After a short ride to Wal-Mart, he parked two aisles over and followed them inside. Trying to remain as inconspicuous as possible, he finally got his chance and snapped a picture. After texting the picture to Amir, he walked around, waiting for a response. Almost immediately he got one. He then texted Amir the address to the hotel and told him he'd meet him back there, just as Amir had asked.

Once back at the hotel, Alexis asked Anthony if he would come up to the room and keep her company. Of course, he obliged, wanting to make sure she was mentally good, considering all the drama she'd been through. As they sat and talked, he informed her that Granny was doing so much better that they wanted to let her go to physical therapy first, then home. He knew he was pushing the envelope, but Black Tone let Alexis know that by the time his grandmother was due to be released, he would have found them another house to live in, somewhere maybe out near the hotel they were at. He felt that with Li'l Ronnie coming to his house so recklessly, there was no telling how many other bastards would try the bullshit. Even though he knew his grandmother would be upset to relocate from the place she'd called

home for years, she had no choice but to roll with what
he decided.

Black Tone didn't have any problem leaving the
neighborhood, but the idea of leaving Alexis on
the block, possibly in harm's way, he couldn't stand.
He knew she was trained to be a CNA and could help
out with Granny. Holding her hands, he told Alexis he'd
make sure to buy a house big enough for her and her son
to come and live in with them for as long as she wanted
to. Before Alexis could respond to her best friend's offer,
there was a knock at the door. Assuming it was room service with the food she'd ordered, Alexis opened the door
without asking who it was.

"So how was your trip to Miami?" Amir asked after
barging his way inside the room.

"What? Huh?" Alexis was stunned, at a loss for words.

Black Tone stood to his feet immediately as one of the
East Side guys from the alley stepped inside the room
after Amir. Trained to go, he pulled out his gun before
the uninvited guests had the chance to do the same. "Yo,
Amir, what in the fuck you doing here? What you call
yourself doing? And why you got this guy with you?"

Amir knew he'd caught Black Tone off guard and in
several lies. He smirked as he sat down in the chair like
it was his room, then leaned back and asked Alexis once
more how Miami was. Leaving one of Ethan's lapdogs
looking stupid standing up, Black Tone went over to the
East Side guy with his gun on both of them.

"Okay, li'l dawg. You holding or what?" Black Tone
was not in the mood for games, and definitely not in the
mood to have to shoot someone at such a nice hotel. As
he patted him down, the guy shook his head.

"Look, I swear, big fella, I ain't got shit. And I ain't
come here for all this. All he told me to do was follow you
from the hospital and told me where you was at. I swear,
I'm good."

With that being said, Big Tone released the grip he had on the guy's clothes and told him to go into the bathroom and shut the fucking door. He couldn't risk him leaving the hotel room because there was no telling what other deceptive trips Amir had up his sleeve.

"So you had me followed, huh? Like some female that be cheating on your ass."

Amir had a judgmental expression on his face that Black Tone wanted to knock off.

"In a way, you are cheating on me. I thought you said this bitch was outta town somewhere and didn't know what happened to my brother," Amir replied.

"Look, Amir, you on some other shit now."

"Naw, Tone. It looks like you are. I swear, my father said all you niggas is alike when it comes down to it, and he was right."

Black Tone had had just about enough of that bullshit Amir was talking. He'd let it go on long enough. "Look, asshole. You a piece a shit, just like that family of yours. While you sitting here, running off at the mouth, throwing around accusations, let me keep shit real with you."

"Yeah, Black Tone." Amir said his name real slow, trying to be funny. "Keep shit real with me and tell me what this gutter trash got to do with my family being dead. I know she got something to do with it, 'cause why else would you be hiding her out with your disloyal ass!"

"Disloyal? Are you kidding me? You got one of Ethan's soldiers trailing me, and then you had the nerve to bring him up here. You like, 'Fuck your grandmother and fuck what that fool did to her.' Your family ain't no better than mine. Believe that."

Alexis was done. She was tired of the entire back-and-forth shouting match that was taking place between both men. She was the true victim, not Amir's rotten cousins or Mikey's cowardly ass or even her once beloved Hassan.

She was done being quiet and ran down what happened, not leaving out one despicable, disgusting detail. By the time Alexis, with a face full of tears, was finished, Black Tone wanted to rush down to Detroit Live, pull all the burned bodies out of the walk-in freezer, and kill them all over again, especially the cousins.

Black Tone paced the floor, angry that all of what Alexis had described had happened to her. Amir showed no emotion. He seemed to have no remorse or sympathy for the female his family members had treated like filth. Finally, he spoke.

"So let me get this straight. My brothers and cousins are dead because this tramp gave up the pussy in the wine cooler, like she been doing, and then all of a sudden found religion? This black nigga bitch that swing upside down, naked, from a pole and probably take four different dicks a night, anyway, wanted to act brand new when it got a little rough?"

Black Tone didn't let him speak to or about Alexis any longer. He had told her back in the day that he was always gonna look out for her, and today was no different. After yanking Amir up from his chair, he started choking him until he was close to passing out. If it wasn't for Alexis begging Black Tone to stop, Amir would have been dead on the spot. He removed his hands from around Amir's throat and let his body fall to the floor.

"Get your bitch ass out this room while you still can," Black Tone ordered when there was a knock at the door yet again. Assuming that it was hotel security and that they would be asked to keep it down, Black Tone opened the door. "Yeah? Who the fuck is you, and what the fuck you want?"

The bathroom door opened a crack, and the fool that Amir had brought with him slowly emerged. "That's my boy J-Blaze. I called him."

"Are you fucking serious?" Big Tone was ready to kill, and it showed. With Amir still on the floor, holding his neck, J-Blaze quickly promise he'd be brief. He, like his boy, got patted down. He was asked what was in his book bag before Black Tone snatched it out of his hand, about to search it as well, and then J-Blaze informed him it was something that belonged to him. To Black Tone's surprise, it was his shoe box, with the money still inside. "Hey, where in the fuck did you get this from? Don't tell me you run with that bitch Li'l Ronnie too. 'Cause if you do . . ."

"Fuck Li'l Ronnie. He dead. I killed him and took that shit," J-Blaze proudly announced, grinning.

"That nigga dead? Seriously?" A smile then graced Black Tone's face. He had wanted to have the pleasure of killing Li'l Ronnie himself, but as long as he was dead, that was all that mattered.

"Yeah, I killed his bitch ass right after I killed Ethan. They was both weak, so they had to go."

Amir couldn't believe what he'd heard. Neither could Black Tone.

"Why you call him, and why you come? I'm confused. Don't y'all both work for Ethan?" Black Tone questioned as Alexis looked on from the far corner of the room.

"Well, I called my boy J-Blaze because this ho ass Amir talks too much shit. He did back in that alley, and he did while I was just in that bathroom."

J-Blaze then spoke up. "And me and him, we don't work for Ethan. We work for the bag, no matter who got it. And to me, just like Ethan was a weak-ass pussy and had to go, it's about Amir's turn to retire too!"

Black Tone looked down at Amir and spit on him. "You two may be right. Matter of fact, why don't y'all escort him out. . . . And what you say your name was?"

"J-Blaze."

"Well, J-Blaze, why don't you work some of your retirement magic on this fake kingpin? Then both of y'all come holler at me tomorrow about running the East Side. I heard they over there looking for some fresh blood. Y'all down or what?"

As the infamous pair slow walked Amir out of the hotel room, Amir turned around, as if to say, "Please don't let this happen." "Tone, I thought we was family," he struggled to say, still trying to breathe.

Black Tone looked over at Alexis, who shook her head. He laughed at Amir and told him, "Naw, dude. We was never family. You was just a guy I was getting money with in the game. And if you ever get a chance to play it again in the afterlife, bet on *black*!"

CHAPTER ONE

Years up in that motherfucker; straight wasted. Caged up like some wild animal that's used to roaming the streets. Alienated from my people like a nigga had the plague or something. I swear, I hope the garbage-mouthed rats that sold me out rot in hell. You don't turn your back on a real one like me; we a dying breed, and that's on everything. Yup, hell, yeah, them bastards tried to hold me up. And yeah, they slowed me down, that ain't no lie. But fuck outta here. I'm back on the block in full swing on some O. G. shit. On top of my game where a guy supposed to be. Now if that ain't God blessing my hustle, then I don't know what the hell you call it. Stackz was tipsy, feeling good as he turned up the sounds in his truck. For him, everything was lovely. He'd done his time in the penitentiary, and now it was time to live like a king; stress free. *Yeah, tonight was a good-ass night for me! Matter of fact, the entire day was off the chain. The streets was acting right with my money, and them dusty females at the club was acting like they never seen a dude as polished as me. Shit can't get no better. Now all I need to do is get my stomach off craps, and I'ma be all the way a hundred.*

Stunt profiling in the butter-soft leather seats of his truck, all was well with Stackz as he reminisced. Blasting the rhythmic sounds of jazz, the music flowed out of the custom-installed speakers. Each beat of the multiple instruments seemed to be felt deep in his muscular built bones. Content with life, his fingertips tapped on the side of the steering wheel. Off into his own world, the semiwasted young-style gangster with an old-school mentality wanted and needed something hot to put on his empty stomach. After throwing back several double shots of 1738 at Club A.F.S.C., short for another fucking strip club, he was about spent.

Fighting the beginning numbness of a slight headache, he felt the rumbling movements of his ribs trying to touch his spine. Realizing he couldn't fight the need for food to soak up some of the liquor in his system any longer, he knew he had to get right. Stackz finally turned the radio's volume down to focus. Slowing down, he hit his blinker and busted a quick U-turn. Knowing relief from hunger was only minutes away, he pulled up to a local favorite late-night spot. They served breakfast twenty-four-seven which always came in handy when the pancake and scrambled eggs with cheese munchies kicked in. Stackz and his close-knit crew were semiregulars at the greasy spoon. They often stumbled in there to get their grub on after clubbing or getting wasted. But this time was different. Stackz wasn't crewed up with his team of menacing cohorts. He was rolling solo.

Looking through the huge neon-lit window, he immediately took notice that the "hood" restaurant was unusually empty for that time of night; a perfect setting for the impossible to be made possible. Any and everything was subject to jump off after 2:00 a.m. in Detroit, and no one, not even the toughest gangster, was exempt from getting got if caught slipping. Being cautious, Stackz had second thoughts of even stopping at the hole-in-the-wall, yet his stomach growling once more made up his mind for him. Stackz wasn't scared of the crime-plagued city at all. Matter of fact, he felt the city oughta be scared of him. He'd just come home after serving time in prison and was still on parole. But that wasn't going to hinder him from being the man he was on the streets or handling business on a daily basis; legal or not. And on that note, Stackz reached over to the passenger seat, grabbing his pistol. After putting one up top, he placed it on his lap.

Fuck that ho, a motherfucker don't wanna act a fool tonight bullshit; a nigga straight hungry as hell. Chili fries with cheese is just what a brother need to get me back right, Stackz thought as he pulled to the side of the building.

Stackz put his vehicle in park. With no worries, he jumped out of the triple-black Jeep Commander, gun in hand. Like a hawk hunting for prey, his eyes searched the general area, being mindful of his surroundings. Tipsy not drunk, the trained street soldier was on high alert and on point. Pausing momentarily, he tucked the rubber-gripped .45-caliber thumper in his waistband, adjusting it. He was a hood sniper when it came to automatics, so the fact he had his "li'l act right" with him, he was all good. Pulling his shirt down in an attempt to conceal the illegal peacemaker, Stackz reassured his still-disgruntled stomach that satisfaction was shortly on the way.

Shutting the truck door, he hit the lock button on his keychain. Checking the lot once more, he headed toward the restaurant entrance. As he made his way past the window, Stackz took notice of the people inside; three guys who appeared to be silly and harmless and two young females. Listening to their laughter from the outside, he assumed they were here on the same buzzed mission he was: needing a greasy fix.

With confidence, Stackz pushed the glass door wide open, stepping inside. It was whatever. On some Martin Luther King shit, tonight, he was fearing no man. As if on cue, all the laughter he'd overheard while walking up abruptly ceased. It was as if Jesus had jumped off the cross or Tupac's ghost had appeared for a final farewell concert; all eyes were on him. After a few brief seconds of uncomfortable silence, the three initially-per-ceived-to-be-harmless dudes took on the form of pure thirstiness. Although Stackz felt he was outnumbered when it came down to it, he knew he was good with the hardware and would put in work, if need be. Maybe it was the 1738 flowing through his bloodstream making him paranoid—and maybe not. But whatever the case, Stackz immediately felt like the trio of guys possibly had some bullshit brewing and put his game face on.

Making eye contact with both of the girls, Stackz had the ability to quickly study people's body language and act accordingly. It was a gift that his grandmother passed down to him; one he often used to his advantage. The lighter skinned one with all the weave appeared to be wild. Smacking on her gum, sucking her teeth, and talking loud, she was everything that Stackz didn't like in a woman. He might have been locked up for some years, but he knew she was out of order. Her clothes were too tight and definitely too revealing for his taste. Whoever she was, Stackz could tell she was trying too hard. Not wanting to stare at the group of people too much longer, he quickly glanced at the other female. Immediately with ease, he read something in the caramel-complexioned female's mannerisms that said she wasn't down with the clown antics her group was into. Stackz made a mental note that although she was cute in the face and had potential, she was dumb as hell for hanging with dudes that appeared to be bottom-feeders.

"Hello, there, can I help you?" the girl behind the security glass asked, pen in hand as he approached the counter.

"Umm, yeah, dear, let me get some chili fries with bacon, Swiss, and American cheese, along with fresh chopped onions," he calmly responded, still being aware of the eerie silence since he'd come inside the building.

"Will that complete your order?" she leaned closer to the bulletproof glass, getting a whiff of Stackz's cologne that had somehow floated through to the other side.

"Yeah, sweetheart. That's it," Stackz replied, taking his money out of his pocket. While waiting for the total, he stared down at her name tag which read Tangy. He thought he knew her but couldn't call it for sure. Although he and his boys were semilate-night regulars, the virtually unskilled cashiers working the graveyard shift changed like clockwork. Waiting for the female who seemed somewhat familiar to give him his total, it suddenly hit Stackz where he remembered her from. She was T. L. people; his young soldier who he'd raised from a youth. He ran with a lot of chicks, but this girl's cat-shaped eyes were what he remembered.

Tangy had run with Stackz's protégé a few summers back and easily knew who he was. As soon as he had walked through the door, her heart raced. Tangy hoped her hair was on point and wished she'd worn her good push-up bra. She always had a secret crush on Stackz, like most females from around the way, even if they were banging one of his boys. Stackz always dressed nice, stayed driving good, and most importantly, was rumored to have a big piece of meat between his legs he knew how to work. She wanted nothing more but for him to sit in the dining-room area and eat his food, but with the three stooges and their girls still tucked away in the corner of the restaurant acting a fool, Tangy knew that would never happen. She was disgusted, constantly giving them the side eye as she rang up Stackz's order.

No rookie to the streets, Stackz peeped her unease and body language. He felt like something was up and knew right then and there he should get ready.

"That will be $5.37, please, Stackz," she quietly announced, seductively licking her lips.

Like Stackz thought he knew who she was, the fact she called him by his street name confirmed he was right. Tangy did, in fact, used to run with T. L. Nevertheless, Stackz was used to females openly flirting with him so he paid her no mind, especially at this moment. Without hesitation, he pealed a twenty-dollar bill off his medium-size knot and slid it to her, insisting she kept the change. Just then, Stackz overheard the biggest of the three guys posted in the far corner try to go hard.

"Who in the fuck this pretty-ass nigga think he is! All fly guy and shit with his red Pelle on and rocking them overpriced Robin's Jeans. He must not know where the hell he's at. He gonna mess around and get all the shit ran, plus that truck he drove up in."

Stackz clearly wasn't moved by his hating punk-ass comment. He knew just where he was; in the heart of the city; the city that he got hella money in. Stackz had already killed the nigga with all the mouth and his homeboys eight different ways in his mind before he could blink twice. *Got me a few to go, I see. Any sign of fuckery and they people ain't gon' be able to sell enough fish dinners or raise enough money in a GoFundMe account to bury they asses quick enough.*

"Stackz, you heard that right?" Tangy asked on the sly.

"Yeah, baby girl," he grinned, winking his eye. "I know where I am; just where the fuck I wanna be." Casually, he turned, looking over his shoulder at the trio, especially the one with the big mouthpiece. "Listen up, you ho-ass nigga; this ain't what you want. This right here ain't what you looking for tonight; none of y'all. So fall back with them bitches and relax. Don't tempt me to show out."

Overly intoxicated, the three drunk wannabe thugs huddled together, obviously getting their courage up to attack. With ill intentions of going for bad, each kept looking over in Stackz's direction, hoping their intended target was just talking that ballsy shit to convince himself he wasn't about to get got.

Stackz had already sized the dudes up when he first stepped inside the restaurant and knew if and when the time came, he'd lay all they asses down; the two groupie skanks also, if need be. In Detroit, females were known for having "gangster moments" too. So fuck all that "I'm innocent and was just with him because" bullshit. In Stackz's eyes, everybody could bleed blood if they jumped into the murderous street arena; hoes included. Holding his own, like the O. G. he was, Stackz stood by the counter. With his phone in one hand and the other ready to whip out his .45 and go to work, he was hyped.

"Dang, why y'all always stay on some unnecessary crap?" one female remarked loud enough so Stackz would hopefully hear. What she was really doing was dry snitching on the always drunk, belligerent clowns she was sitting with. She'd been around them long enough from time to time to know they were seriously out of their league where this guy was concerned. The way he stood and carried himself, Ava knew dude was right; trouble with him was definitely not what they wanted. "Look, Leela, I'm ready to go right fucking now. Fuck this dumb shit! Y'all tripping!"

"Naw, Ava, slow down—chill; we good. You always acting like you too good to hang out with me and my friends," Leela smartly replied with a look of disdain.

"Yeah, and creeps like these right here is the reason why I don't fuck with your ass on the regular." She stood to her feet, leering over at the plotting haters with disgust.

"Creeps, huh?" Mickey had been called worse in his life so he let that little insult roll off his back like water but took offense to her trying to cause a scene. "Yo, Leela, shut your sister the fuck up," he urged in a hushed tone as to not be heard by their soon-to-be victim. "Calm her uppity-acting ass down; all loud and shit. She gon' spook dude before we even get a chance to run his pockets."

"Oh hell to the naw," Ava loudly clapped back at Mickey, not caring who heard her. "I'm out of this motherfucker for sure! I ain't into catching no cases or bodies for the next dummy; especially your thirsty-trapping ass. Y'all do y'all!"

"Dang, sis, hold up for a few," Leela cut her eyes. Reaching over in an attempt to grab her little sister by the arm as she tried heading toward the door, she knew things were about to get out of hand.

"Yeah, hater, listen to Mickey and your sister. We on to something big right now, so chill! You can break out when we done and not before."

"Fuck your bum ass," Ava instantaneously snapped on Devin, the biggest in size of his wannabe tough crew; the one with all the mouth Stackz had overheard. "You might run Leela's simpleminded self 'cause y'all fucking around, but you ain't running nothing this way. You can bet that much." Still protesting her readiness to leave and the fact she wanted no part of whatever they were on, she pulled away from her older sibling's grip.

Devin grew heated. He hated to be contradicted, and hated even more for Ava to talk down on him and his boys. She had a bad habit of behaving like her shit didn't stank and she wasn't born, raised, and still posted in the same part of the city as he was. He didn't want her hanging with them anyhow tonight, but in between Leela wanting female company and Mickey always hoping he could one day get on, here Ava was; going against the grain, as usual. "Look, girl, I swear on everything I love, I'm straight bulldogging and skull tapping that ass if your people blow this lick for me with that bad luck mouth of hers."

Leela wasn't gonna front and act as if Devin's wrath meant nothing. Those ass kickings she received at her man's hands leisurely were taking a toll on her body. With that in mind, she once again pleaded with Ava to stop bugging. Leela tried reasoning with her that it was just about to be another simple strong-arm robbery that was about to take place.

So she believed.

Stackz was no fool by a long shot. He knew his own pedigree in the grimy streets he ran in. Real gangsters move in silence. So he didn't say one word, because if it came down to it, he didn't mind being the suspect in the interrogation room on the next season of *The First 48 Hours*. Unbeknownst to the three drunken thugs, Stackz had firsthand experience with cold-blooded murder and had no problem whatsoever sending them on their way.

"Here you go. You have a good night and be safe out here," side eyeing the thirsty trio yet again, Tangy gave Stackz a brown paper bag containing his chili-cheese fries.

Sensing some sudden movements from behind, Stackz was fast and on his 360 spin. Having already grabbed his food with the left hand, he swiftly reached behind his back with the right. Whipping out his .45 upping it as he turned around, it was on. Game time. Meeting the big man Devin's mouth with the pistol, he stopped him dead in his tracks as he brought it crashing down into his dental. The steel barrel shattered a few of Devin's teeth and busted his lip. Stackz was now in his zone. He'd stepped over into the dark side. With a menacing look on his face that read *I'm about to catch a case on that ass,* his heart raced.

"Arrggh." Blood ran out of Devin's mouth, dripping all over his once winter-white shirt. Feeling as if he was done before he even got started, Devin held both hands up in the air like the Mike Brown protester with his eyes closed. Bracing himself for the worst that was evident to come, the other would-be robbers jumped up ready to come to his aid.

Stackz was stern in his demeanor and words, dropping his much-needed bag of fries to the ground. He wasn't with no games, and he made sure everyone understood that much, shoving the gun's barrel in Devin's mouth as hot piss flowed down the wankster's pants leg. "Yup, come on with it, and I'm gonna send this here fat nigga to the upper room first. Then I got sixteen more 'li'l friends' to make sure you lames catch up with this big pissy bitch before he reach Jesus' front door. So what in the fuck it's gonna be, fellas? We rocking out or what, 'cause my food getting cold?"

Rank and Mickey straight-away stopped. They stood perfectly still, taking in all Stackz had just said. It was as if they were frozen in time. They both considered their fate if they took another step, as well as Devin's. Confused and concerned, they turned to each other, not knowing what move to make next. Stackz was not in the mood to play around as his stomach was still growling. Ready to put an end to this entire failed attempt of them playing at being gangsters, he helped them decide. Snatching his burner out of Devin's bloody mouth, he pointed it at the defeated voiceless duo. Motioning his peacemaker toward the booth where the females were still posted, Rank and Mickey quickly got the idea and politely sat back down.

"Oh my God," Leela gasped on the verge of tears, seeing her meal ticket getting his ass handed to him.

"Okay, back to you, fat boy." Stackz turned his attention back to Devin, "Mister, I'm the winner of the ho-ass nigga of the night contest." Not done with showing these fools that if you play with fire you *will* get burnt, Stackz gripped up tightly on his gun. With brutal force and an overwhelming taste for violence, he smacked Devin across the top of his head with the butt of the pistol. An echo rang throughout the walls of the restaurant. Cracking Devin's skull, blood started to leak from an instant deep gash. He was dizzy. The room was starting to spin as smells of bacon, cheeseburgers, and chicken finger aromas filled his flaring nostrils. Stackz had proven his point just as he claimed he would. Tangling with him wasn't what Devin or his crew of cowardly misfits wanted. "Now, okay, motherfucker, you see what it really is and what's really good. So we done here tonight, or you wanna go a second round?"

Devin tried to stand strong but couldn't maintain his balance. His knees buckled as his heavy frame dropped to the ceramic floor. Speechless, Mickey and Rank were in shock. They had never seen their peoples so humiliated by the next manz. It was like Devin was nothing to Stackz but a small child being punished for speaking out of turn.

With their mouths wide open in disbelief and horror, Ava and Leela held each other tight. The different-as-night-and-day sisters stayed at each other's throats, but at this point, they were as one. What started off as a late-night run to the restaurant to grab a bite to eat and hang out had turned to them being terrified to move an inch. Motionless, afraid for their lives, the girls did what most females would do in that situation.

Cry.

Praying they would make it out of there alive, Ava searched Stackz's eyes for any small glimmer of mercy he was willing to grant them. In between hoping she and Leela would see daylight, Ava was secretly elated Devin and them had finally met their match. They had a bad habit of thinking the world owed them something so Mickey and Rank getting ordered to go sit in the corner like some punk bitches was priceless. And as for Devin's big-mouthed fat ass sprawled across the floor, mouth busted, drenched in his own piss, that was nothing short of Christmas, her birthday, and tax refund time all rolled into one. Ava wanted to do cartwheels across the restaurant and break out in a cheer celebrating Stackz, but the fact he was holding a gun on her and her sister thwarted that thought. As crazy as it seemed, Ava was turned on in a sexual way. She was mesmerized seeing this fine-ass mystery man in total beast mode. Her pussy ached and tingled with every word he spoke and movement he made; even when his rage was directed at her.

"Okay, you two silly, sour-faced broads, bust the fuck up; get the hell on before I change my mind," Stackz irately ordered, giving them the opportunity to leave unharmed.

The fact they had come with the plastic thugs meant nothing. This was not one of those all for one, one for all moments. This game would be played solo, if need be. Terrified Devin's fate could easily become theirs if they got too close to the man didn't stop them from taking Stackz up on his offer before he did actually change his mind. Hauling ass toward the door, Leela was surprisingly first in line. Rushing by Stackz, who was towering over a bloodied mouth and head Devin, Leela's body trembled with fear. Lying on the floor holding his open wound, Devin tried to slow down the loss of blood. While he begged for his life to be spared, Leela never once made eye contact with her so-called man. Instead, almost knocking Ava to the ground to get by, she pushed the double exit doors wide open. Fleeing into the parking lot, Leela disappeared into the darkness of the late night not looking back, with Ava trailing closely behind.

CHAPTER TWO

Tangy was all in. Stackz had just become her hero. Watching him regulate not one, but three thugs at the same time, he'd definitely be her new man crush Monday on Facebook. Just as Ava was feeling some sort of weird sexual tension seeing Stackz boss up, so was Tangy. Working the graveyard shift in the hood, Tangy had seen just about every type of crazy shit pop off and heard the unimaginable. But tonight was the icing on the cake of them all. The dude she'd been crushing on since the first time she'd seen him was full-blown flexing and making that shit seem easy. T. L.'s mentor was holding court on the wannabe thugs that'd been trash-talking and intimidating customers all night. The guy Stackz had laid out on the floor had called Tangy out her name repeatedly. He also had his girl threaten to beat her ass not more than twenty minutes prior. So in Tangy's eyes, it was like *fuck him*. He needed some act right in his pathetic life.

The foreign cook felt the exact same as Tangy. He didn't want any trouble so he kept his head down, working on peeling potatoes. To him, it was just another normal late night at work. Since he didn't have his green card yet, he wanted no one from any of the two sides to even look at him as if he was interested. Barely speaking English, he was there to cook food and go home to his wife and four small children. He saw nothing; knew nothing; and cared about nothing.

"All I wanted was some damn chili fries. Maybe swing by a freak bitch crib to get some pussy and head and call it a night. But, naw, y'all thirsty niggas wouldn't let that shit go down like that. That shit was too much like right. Y'all wanted to see what it was like to go toe to toe with a dude of my caliber. Y'all was looking for this heat, so now you got."

"Whoa, hold on, bro," Devin spoke out as the room continued to spin from the blow on the head he'd suffered.

"Naw, shut the fuck up! Ain't no 'hold on' or 'time-out.' This shit is all the way live, and it's gonna stay that way. And for the record, I ain't your bro," Stackz announced, enraged what a simple stop at the local late-night food spot had turned into.

Devin did as he was told. He knew he had no win with Stackz at the moment. Dropping his head with his hands up, as to say okay, whatever you say, he prayed he could get to his gun. He looked over at his homeboys with a look of shame on his face. He wished Mickey and Rank would've backed him up when he originally made his move on their intended victim. Maybe then, things would have flowed differently. The tables would definitely be turned. Stackz would be half dead on the black-and-white dirty tiled floor, begging for his life instead of him.

Realizing it was time to bring this situation to an end, Stackz had to break out. A born thinker, especially in chaotic bullshit such as this, he formulated his next move. With only one way out of the restaurant, he knew what he had to do. Staring down at Devin, he let him know that for every action, there was going to be a reaction; some reactions worse than others. With those words of hood wisdom being bestowed upon Devin, Stackz then kicked him directly in the face. Just to make sure he got his point across, he then callously stomped the side of Devin's already traumatized head. The crispy fresh wheat Tims he'd copped earlier in the day now had bright red splatters of blood not only on the toe area, but the sides as well. Taking in account the door was at least ten or so feet away, Stackz slowly inched his way to the exit. Keeping his eyes focused on Rank, Mickey, and Devin, he wasn't sure if the thus far cowardly trio had guns on them or not. Raised in the streets of Detroit, he cautiously treated the situation as if they did.

Just as Stackz was nearing the front door, Tangy came from behind the bulletproof glass. Stepping over Devin like the piece of nothing nigga he was, she smiled, handing Stackz another bag. "Here you go, bae, some fresh chili fries on the house."

Stackz happily accepted the fresh hot food, almost forgetting the reason he'd stopped in the first place. "Good looking out, girl," he winked, backing up slowly toward the doors. Watching his would-be attackers like a vicious pit bull ready to pounce in a dogfight, his finger stayed on the trigger. Finally arriving at the exit, Stackz placed his back against the door. Using his weight, he pushed it wide open. Gun in his right hand, food in his left, in a quick movement, he tucked the brown paper bag food under his arm. With that now free hand, Stackz reached down in his pocket. Pulling out his keys, he pushed unlock on the multibutton pad. In one click, the driver's door of his Jeep Commander popped up. Safely in the parking lot, the victorious warrior momentarily stood at the side of his truck. Looking back into the Coney Island, he saw a lot of movement.

Making sure they were well out of harm's way, Mickey and Rank ran over to their boy's side. Lying on the floor both severely beaten and bloody, Devin moaned out in pain. Bending down, they aided him to get on his feet.

"Dawg, come on, get up! Get up! Let's go get on his ass before he dip." Mickey was now brave hearted in words, gripping the big man's elbow as he stood. "I'm gon' kill that pretty-ass nigga. Look what he did to you."

Almost in tears, Devin desperately fought to catch his breath. Suffering from high blood pressure, the overweight ruffian was already two or three cheeseburgers away from a heart attack or stroke. Stackz's rough house blows to his face and side of the head had him still dazed even after the fact. Being helped over to a nearby booth against the wall, Devin sat down, looking as if he was moments away from passing out. Barely having control of himself to sit upright, he told them to go handle Stackz as he slumped over on his side.

Mickey and Rank stood tall. They didn't have a choice if they wanted to save face and have any sort of dignity left. Finally revealing their weapons from underneath their shirts, each ran outside. With guns drawn, the pair sought Stackz out to deliver a little bit of payback for his disrespectful treatment of Devin. Revenge would soon be delivered in a deadly fashion. Easily finding him at his vehicle, Rank knew they had to act fast seeing Stackz already had one foot inside his whip with the rest of his body soon to follow. Raising both pistols, the calmness of the late-night, early-morning air was interrupted as shots rapidly rang out.

Round after round was recklessly let loose. One, two, three. Eight, ten, twelve. It seemed like the hail of gunfire would never let up.

"Fuck, naw," Stackz mumbled as bullets whizzed past him, rocking his Jeep.

Posted side by side, Mickey and Rank were going all-out commando-style. Close up enough to see the fruits of their ill intentioned labor, the menaces' courage increased, seeing the bullets rip through the truck's rear door and shatter the thick, tinted glass hatch.

"What up, doe, now?" Mickey shouted, directly hitting the driver's side mirror.

Rank then chimed in, promising the ultimate revenge while doing his own equal amount of damage to the washed and triple-waxed Commander, "Whack pussy-ass

nigga, yous as good as dead! Dead as a motherfucker!"
Squeezing the trigger of his .45-caliber automatic, Rank
held his firearm sideways like you see hooligans do in a
bad, low-budget hood movie.

Stackz was heated; beyond pissed. Never mind the fact
bullets were zipping around his body barely missing him.
Of course, he was mad they were shooting at him; that
goes without saying. But he was even more so enraged
because his ride, his baby, was being abused, taking in
huge gaping holes left and right. Simple Street-olgy 101;
the worst thing a player in the game can do is shoot up a
nigga'z ride. Especially if he had money invested in it.

Stackz wasted no time snapping into defense mode.
His fury reached a hundred in no time flat. Automatically
diving all the way in the truck, he ducked down, taking
cover. Tossing the damn bad luck food in the brown
paper bag aimlessly inside the truck, he listened to the
ear-popping sounds of round after round being let off.
Crouched over, Stackz reached into the driver-side door
compartment where a normal person would often keep
meaningless bullshit. Thank God, Stackz's DNA dictated
that he was far from normal. Retrieving an extra clip he
kept fully loaded, ready, just in case for situations like
this, he was ready to go to war.

Climbing over to the passenger seat, he quickly put
the clip in the back pocket of his jeans. Pulling the
handle out, he swung open the door. Staying low, he
positioned himself behind the car door. Stackz peeked
with caution from behind his makeshift barrier. He knew
from firsthand experience, the longer he stayed in one
position, he'd be more likely to be a sitting duck, and one,
if not both, of the amateur marksmen may get lucky. As
the bullets continued to rock his truck from side to side,
gaping holes started to appear in the door he was behind.

These young boys want it . . . Well, they 'bout to feel me.
1, 2, 3, he counted to himself, then brazenly made a mad
dash toward the rear of the vehicle, gun blazing. Once

making it there, he started to return fire more deliberately aimed at Mickey and Rank. With the first volley of shots, he aimed high at their faces. Stackz's motto was if you kill the head, the body will surely follow. In a matter of a few brief seconds, Stackz introduced them to what it was like to do battle with a real-life gangster.

Mickey's courageously tough-guy stand was abruptly cut short. His upper body jerked back. Instantaneously, his shoulder cap exploded on impact from the .45-caliber slug Stackz sent his way. "I'm hit! I'm hit! I'm fucking shot," he agonized before being struck once more. This time, the force of the bullet spun him completely around. As he dropped to his knees and fell to the pavement, Mickey held his shoulder. Bleeding profusely from the two wounds, he crawled behind a huge green metal trash Dumpster located in the rear of the restaurant. Almost in shock, Mickey started to pray, begging God to spare his life.

Having no focus or discipline, Rank was blindly shooting at Stackz, hoping to hit his mark. The more rounds he let loose, the more he realized it was as if Stackz were superhuman. None of his bullets struck the polished player, even though he'd emptied his clip. Taking cover behind a car also parked in the lot, Rank was terrified, feeling some wetness in his head. Reaching his hand up, he brought it down to his face. Rank wanted to pass out. It was blood. Like his cohort Mickey, he'd been hit as well. Hearing footsteps, he braced himself, knowing death was near. Fortunately, he heard his boy Devin's voice yell out.

"Yo, nigga, you think you just gonna do me like that up in that motherfucker, and shit gonna be all sweet? Naw, dawg, shit ain't going down like that. You gonna pay, homeboy." Gun in hand, Devin stumbled out of the restaurant door in search of Stackz. As blood from his open head wound dripped down onto his face, he went on with his impromptu rant, vowing retribution. "Yo, Mickey, Rank; where y'all asses at? Posse up, niggas! Let's bury this bright-skin faggot!"

Turning his head for a split second to the right, Devin caught a quick glimpse of a terrified Mickey lying slumped over behind the Dumpster. Unfortunately, for bad-boy-to-the-end Devin, it was the last thing he'd ever see. One of Stackz's bullets ripped through Devin's neck. The next slug tore through his left ear, exiting the right side of his face. Devin's brains showered the already filthy glass of the window's restaurant. His body collapsed onto the pavement. His pistol fell out of his once-closed hand and slid across the asphalt.

An eerie silence filled the air. Stackz had counted the rounds each shooter probably had and realized unless they had an extra clip like him, they were out of ammo; hit; tapped out. Stackz hoped they had seen what just took place with their appeared-to-be leader and scattered out of Dodge. On parole, the eager-to-stay-free Stackz had no intentions whatsoever to wait and find out if his calculations were correct. He wasn't a fool. He knew it wouldn't be long before the Detroit police either crept up on the fresh murder scene or were dispatched there. Either/or, it was time for him to do what he was trying to do before aggressively interrupted by Devin, Mickey, and Rank; go home. If the two survivors turned out to be rats and told the cops what they knew or bossed up to be loyal to the game and wanted street justice remained to be seen in the days to follow. Stackz would have to deal with either play they made next.

He took in mind everything that had just popped off in slow motion. He didn't panic before, during, or now. This wasn't his first shoot-out with wannabe assholes who mistakenly believed they were about that life and the way he lived, Stackz surely knew it wasn't his last. Running through in his head the list of things he had to do next, he took a deep breath. *#1 Get away from the scene as soon as possible. #2 Get rid of the murder tool after making sure his prints were clean. #3 Call T. L. or Gee for damage control,* and lastly, but most importantly, *#4 find out who these three clowns are and who their people are.* If their folk were in the game, or even dreamed about being in the game, they might have the notion of getting revenge. And if they did feel ballsy, then the body count would have to go up; no questions asked.

Searching the now-seemingly deserted parking lot with his eyes, Stackz wanted nothing more than to go over and spit in Devin's face but had watched enough episodes of *CSI* while locked up to know his DNA on the deceased would be like signing his own arrest warrant. Climbing up in his bullet-riddled truck, he prayed it would start. Once again, blessed by the hustle gods, it did. Gun still in one hand, he threw the metal warrior in reverse. Backing out of the lot like a normal person that'd just picked up their carryout, Stackz played his departure cool, seeing how his rear window was shot out.

Driving maybe a good few miles or so, he stumbled up on an abandoned gas station. Full of trash and other debris scattered about here and there, he pulled around to the back. Checking his surroundings for the possibility of late-night crackheads in search of their next blow or greed-driven scrappers who might be lurking, Stackz turned off his headlights. Without fear, he then got out of the truck with his favorite throwaway in tow. Once more, he looked around to see if anyone was out and about. Seeing it was all clear, Stackz wiped the gun clean with not only a dirty rag but some Windex and tire cleaner as well.

As quietly as possible, he lifted the lid of the rusty industrial-size Dumpster. The big blue commercial monster was full beyond capacity with probably just about every discarded unwanted item from nearby residents and other businesses that didn't want to bother with proper disposal. Trying his best to not inhale the awful stench that leaped into his nostrils, Stackz spit twice. The way it smelled, a dead body might already be in it, so any other random person would definitely think twice about Dumpster diving and lucking up on discovering his gun. Stackz said his final good-byes to the pistol he'd been carrying since his release from prison and tossed it inside its new home. Using a stick, he then covered it up the best he could with the other rubbish. Casually, Stackz walked back to his whip as if he'd not just minutes earlier committed a murder and disposed of the weapon used to commit that felony. Starting the engine, he drove off.

Stackz did what was next on his list of things to do if he hoped to get away with murder: get ready to call T. L., his always-on-point cleanup man. Extremely loyal and trustworthy, Stackz knew he could count on his young dog. He was a soldier in the true sense of the word. Stackz been feeding and grooming T. L. since he was nine years old and his mama was out there getting high, addicted to crack, heroin, and popping pills. T. L. saw a lot growing up and had been through shit no kid should have to. Stackz and his little brother had stepped up and practically raised T. L. Stackz and Gee used to trap out of his mama's crib. When they saw the conditions he was subjected to, the two of them took him into their own home, treating him like a son, making sure he went to the best school, buying him everything a normal kid should have, and should have kept him doing right, but the streets were embedded in T. L.'s DNA. Having everything still couldn't quench the thirst for the street life out of him. So they kept "their son" close to them every day, teaching him so he'd learn how to think like a gangster and move like a boss.

They could count on him to get whatever task at hand done; quickly and efficiently. Still haunted by his mother throwing him away like garbage, T. L. was resentful at times and a known hothead when need be. However, he looked upon Stackz and Gee like the father figures he never had; he was their family. And he was willing to do anything to protect his kin; blood or not.

Now, T. L. was loved by many and feared by the shady-ass seedy side of Detroit just like Stackz wanted and needed a true hood warrior to be. T. L. could put in work and clean up the dirt he or Gee couldn't touch.

With one hand on the steering wheel, the other hand held his cell. Pushing the button on the side, he used the voice command to call T. L. In a matter of seconds, it connected the lines. The phone began to ring as Stackz caught a night air chill from the draft of not having a rear window. Looking over at his radio, Stackz saw the clock on the face read a little bit after three forty-five. Yet, it didn't matter how early or late it was. T. L. was on call twenty-four-seven always ready for action; good to go. For him, if it meant going to full-blown war at daybreak, he'd be as wide awake as if it was four in the evening.

On the second ring, T. L. answered. "Big bro, what up doe with you?"

"Yo, fam, what it do? I need you on deck ASAP on some real type of no-way-back-from-the-darkness business." Stackz seethed, still angry the three clowns had forced his hand into murder, even though it was self-defense.

T. L. was at his crib laid up with one of his many FFs, short for fuck friends. He grabbed the remote control to the flat-screen television and pressed mute. Having heard Stackz say "no way back from the darkness," T. L. sat straight up. He knew that was code name for someone had just got sent on their way. Intensely listening to his mentor run the evening down almost blow by blow, the eager-to-please goon got heated. Remembering he wasn't alone, he got out of bed with ole girl, not really knowing who she knew or could've been related to. She could be playing like she was asleep while ear hustling on the sly.

T. L. understood Detroit was the smallest big city ever, and if a nigga was trying to hide his black ass after doing dirt, unless you were as careful as him, Stackz, and Gee, that feat would be damn near impossible. Gathering his clothes, he got dressed while still listening to Stackz's game plan. "Yeah go ahead, bro. I'm on you. I'm throwing my shit on now and half out the door on my way." T. L. left the sleeping female in his bed, knowing she knew better than to touch a damn thing in his crib and risk getting her head knocked clear off her body.

"Okay, dig this here. I need you to shoot over to the spot where we always grab the food from."

"The spot with the food?" T. L. questioned, wanting to get the facts right.

"Yeah, the spot over from around the way," Stackz reaffirmed as he slowed down at a red light. "You know, where we hit up at when we come from the club. I had to turn up on these fucking clowns. I guess they was bugging and was sleep on a nigga thinking I was some sort of come up."

"Word?" T. L. quizzed, grabbing his car keys off the table.

"Yeah, your homegirl a cashier now up in that motherfucker. Taking orders and shit."

"Who you talking about?"

"You know, what's her name? The honey with them funny cat eyes. The one you used to run with from the East Side. I saw her name tag, but that shit done slipped my mind."

From the description Stackz was giving, T. L. easily now knew who he meant. "Oh yeah, Tangy."

"Yeah, yeah, that's her," Stackz replied, nodding his head. "She saw the whole play go down; her and the damn cook."

"Word?"

"Yeah, my dude. So you already know I need that surveillances footage. I can't risk making the news on some murder shit. You know I get banged on any more felonies, my ass is straight cooked."

"Naw, naw, say no more, bro-bro. I got this! I'm on it right now! I'm on my way out the door and en route as we speak." T. L. jumped in his car as his adrenalin pumped. "The way the police move in Detroit, I can beat them there and swoop up that tape."

Stackz knew he could count on his young dawg to handle things. "Good looking out."

"Come on now, fam, it ain't no thang. You know how we do. So I'll hit you back when I'm good with it."

"The way she was playing it with me, I think she up for helping us out. She seem street as hell."

T. L. laughed, knowing Stackz had hit the nail on the head. Tangy was street as hell; a little *too* street for him. That's why he stopped messing with her. She wanted to mean mug and skull drag every other female he knew. "She definitely about her coins, so I got a couple racks on me to ensure I don't hear 'I can't,' 'no,' or 'I'm scared' shit fly outta her mouth. You feel me? Money talks and potential cases get bought."

Stackz had one reply equally as clever and true as T. L.'s statement. "You already know real ones buy what they want, what they need, and what they please. Right about now, I needs that surveillance footage."

CHAPTER THREE

Ava couldn't believe what had just taken place. She was pissed, not only at her sister for dragging her out of the house tonight to hang with Devin and his whack-minded cohorts, but herself for being so stupid to agree to come. She knew Leela's MO when it came to being in the middle of drama. It was like she craved that bullshit and found a way to find it, even if it wasn't looking for her. Now just like that, here they were on foot, in sandals, no less, running down a no-streetlight-deserted block, trying to make it to their mother's house.

"What the fuck be wrong with you?" Ava barked, glancing back over her shoulder while keeping it moving.

"Huh?"

"I said what in the fuck is wrong with you? Why you always down with this dumb shit? I can't believe you sometimes."

"What? Huh?" Leela once more replied, trying to keep up with her obviously angry sibling.

Ava wasn't having her older sister play the dumb role; not now; not tonight. "Listen, don't *huh* me, bitch! You know good and damn well what the fuck I'm talking about. You seen how that oversized sloppy animal you be running around with tried to attack that dude. Him, Mickey, and Rank always tripping."

"Okay and . . ."

Ava was infuriated with her big sister as well as almost out of breath but still kept it a hundred. "Okay, and he was minding his own business trying to place his order and *bam!* I guess that was too much like right to Devin and them, huh? Both of y'all dumb asses deserve each other. I swear to God I'm done with you!"

"Whoa, why you care so much about some random-ass buster? You must've been feeling ole boy or something, even though he called himself going on us." Leela dialed Devin's number but got no response.

"Leela, please stop being so damn stupid all the time. I ain't feeling nothing except for doing the right thing before karma comes around calling. You think that shit a joke, but it ain't. Karma will mess the fuck around and skip over your dumb ass and latch ahold of your kids."

"Yeah, whatever; man, fuck karma," Leela arrogantly giggled while running by a yard full of thick overgrown bushes, cell still in hand. "Karma don't want shit messing around with me or my badass, good-begging kids!"

Ava was outdone that her sister, a mother herself, had such little regard for doing the right thing when need be. She hoped her nieces and nephew would not turn out like the rest of the bloodline in their shady family tree: ruthless, rotten, and worthless. "Look, girl. Like I said, I'm over you and your no-good friends. The next time you wanna ask me to hang with Devin, Mickey, and Rank, don't—because the answer is going to be naw. Matter of fact, *hell naw!*"

Leela wanted to stop dead in her tracks and curse her little sister out for going so hard, but the darkness of the night changed her mind. She wisely decided to just keep it moving and deal with Ava and her opinions when they reached their destination. Hopefully, their mother would not be drunk and passed out and they could get in. Two blocks later and creeping through the vacant lot, the sisters were soon in the backyard of their childhood home. Seeing the blue light from the television peek through the tattered shades of the back bedroom, Ava exhaled as Leela reached up, tapping on the window. After what seemed like a lifetime, they finally heard a voice mumbling. Seconds later, they were met with their mother's bloodshot eyes peering at theirs.

"Why you two ungrateful bitches over here bothering me, waking me up? Y'all got y'all own damn house," she slurred as the flimsy door flung open. "Well, at least, Ava wannabe uppity ass do!"

"We know, Mom, but it was an emergency," Leela blurted out as she brushed past her mother's shoulder, barging inside. "Where my kids at? What they been doing?"

"Emergency, my ass! Ava, why you ain't just used the damn spare key I gave your butt!" Standing in the doorway, Leela's mother was almost snatched out of her drunken state of mind hearing her oldest child act so dense. "And as for you! Listen, you silly tramp. You know good and damn well them babies is sleep this time of morning, just like you and old wannabe white over there should be. But, naw, y'all disrespectful asses all up over here in my shit knocking on back windows and asking dumb shit."

Once both girls were inside the dimly lit dwelling, their mother finally stopped running off at the mouth and stumbled back to her bed to continue to sleep off the half pint of cheap wine she'd gulped down before passing out. As if on cue, the sibling arguing resumed.

Ava wasn't against her sister; she just had officially grown tired of backing up all her stupid plays. She was done with agreeing with the chaos she brought, not only into her own life but into the lives of everyone she'd come in contact with; not excluding her own children. Leela had a bad habit of not wanting to pay her rent wherever she lived, ultimately resulting in her and her babies getting put out, leaving Ava and their barely functioning alcoholic mother to step in and pick up the slack. This time was no different than the others; the kids were staying with their grandmother, while Ava was allowing Leela to temporarily stay in the converted dwelling home she'd bought in a county auction late last summer. But the unfit mother that lived to keep up bullshit and bring unwanted drama to her sister's home had just about worn out her welcome.

"Leela, please just tell me why you insist on hanging with those dirtballs? They always off into some devious shit; especially Devin. If he wouldn't been trying to start shit with that man . . ."

Examining the broken strap on her sandals, Leela casually glanced up, shaking her head like her sister was speaking in some sort of foreign language. "I'm sorry, but are you still talking to me? I already done told you forget that nigga you so worried about! Was you not just there in that motherfucker when he was pointing a gun at our black asses, calling us sour! You see how he had Devin; talking to him like he was crazy!"

Ava shook her head. Leela was everything she was not. Even though their mother claimed they had the same father, Ava wasn't so sure if that was the truth. Leela had to be the spawn of Satan. No matter what the younger sister said or tried, Leela was not in the business of listening. Instead, she continued to boast and brag about Devin and the many times he'd blessed her with money from his small-time hustles and capers. The fact that Devin and his boys oftentimes fucked over innocent people to get that "come up" Leela seemed to think was as great as, if not better than, winning the Powerball, meant nothing.

"Have you lost your damn mind? You sitting over here talking about Devin like he some sort of person that needs an award or something. That boy ain't nothing but a small-time, nickel-and-dime hustling thug. Him and Mickey and Rank out here always trying to go for bad."

"And . . ."

"And that's why that dude got him and them at gunpoint. Shit, matter of fact, they probably halfway to jail by now, so . . ."

Leela paused protesting Ava's statement as she whipped back out her cell to once again call. "Girl, you sound like a fool. Devin is that real deal. Trust me, I done seen him turn the tables and walk the fuck away from shit way worse than that. He gonna bless me big time off the pockets of that pretty boy nigga you seemed so worried about."

Yeah, we'll see. Ava sat back gathering her thoughts while watching her naïve sister live in a fantasy.

ORDER FORM
URBAN BOOKS, LLC
97 N. 18th Street
Wyandanch, NY 11798

Name (please print):_____

Address: _____

City/State: _____

Zip: _____

QTY	TITLES	PRICE

Shipping and handling-add $3.50 for 1st book, then $1.75 for each additional book.

Please send a check payable to:

Urban Books, LLC

Please allow 4–6 weeks for delivery